H

Adventures by Sea and Land of the Count DeGanay

Or, the Devotion and fidelity of Woman. An episode of the colonization of Canada

SALZWASSER
VERLAG

H. Emile Chevalier

Adventures by Sea and Land of the Count DeGanay

Or, the Devotion and fidelity of Woman. An episode of the colonization of Canada

Reprint of the original, first published in 1863.

1st Edition 2022 | ISBN: 978-3-37500-778-2

Verlag (Publisher): Salzwasser Verlag GmbH, Zeilweg 44, 60439 Frankfurt, Deutschland
Vertretungsberechtigt (Authorized to represent): E. Roepke, Zeilweg 44, 60439 Frankfurt, Deutschland
Druck (Print): Books on Demand GmbH, In de Tarpen 42, 22848 Norderstedt, Deutschland

ADVENTURES BY SEA AND LAND

OF THE

COUNT DeGANAY;

OR, THE

Devotion and Fidelity of Woman.

AN EPISODE OF THE COLONIZATION OF CANADA.

RANSLATED FROM THE FRENCH OF

H. EMILE CHEVALIER.

NEW-YORK

1863.

INTRODUCTION.

To M. H. X. Garneau,

Quebec, Lower Canada.

Monsieur,—In the second chapter of your excellent History of Canada, "one of the best productions of the human mind," after having recounted the jealousies which the nephews of James Cartier had to encounter on the shores of the St. Lawrence, you say:

"In order to avoid being exposed any longer to those attacks, they solicited from the crown the renewal of the privileges, which had been accorded to their uncle, namely, the exclusive right of trading with the savages, and to work the mines which they had discovered. In consideration of the services of the great navigator, letters-patent were granted to them in 1588. But as soon as the affair was known, the merchants of St. Malo petitioned the privy council to have those privileges revoked, and they succeeded in doing so; but without profiting much by it themselves; for from 1598, the year of the establishment of peace, the Marquis de la Roche, of the province of Brittany, caused himself to be confirmed by the king in the office of Lieutenant-General of Canada, of Acadia and the adjacent countries, which Henry III. had already granted to him, but which the troubles of the kingdom had prevented him from enjoying, with powers which had the same extent as those of Roberval, and which annihilated the liberty accorded to the merchants of St. Malo. He was authorized to select in the ports of France such ships, masters, and sailors as he might require; to raise troops, to make war, and to build cities within the limits of his viceroyalty; to promulgate laws in the same, and cause them to be executed; to make grants of lands to noblemen, as fiefs, lordships, baronies, counties, etc.; in short, to regulate the commerce left now under his absolute control. Thus clothed with an authority as complete as despotic, he sailed for the New World with sixty men. No merchant dared to raise his voice against the monopoly of this nobleman, as had been done against the nephews of Cartier; his rank imposed silence on them; but other causes were destined to ruin his projects.

"The Marquis de la Roche, fearing the desertion of his people, composed of malefactors and believing that place more convenient until he had found on the main-land a territory more suitable to his design, landed them at the Isle of Sable at the entrance of the Gulf of St. Lawrence. This island, in the form of a crescent, narrow, arid, and of wild aspect, produced neither trees nor fruits—nothing but a little grass and moss around a lake, situated in the centre. After having placed his colonists in this desolate place, surrounded by sand-banks, indented by the sea, La Roche passed into Acadia. On returning, he was surprised by a furious tempest, which in ten days chased him to the shores of France, where he had no sooner set foot than he found himself enveloped in a multitude of difficulties, in the midst of which the Duke de Mercœur, who commanded in Brittany, detained him for some time, as a prisoner. It was not until the end of five years that he had an opportunity of relating to the king, who happened to be at Rouen, what had befallen him in his voyage. The king, touched with the fate of the unfortunate men abandoned in the Isle of Sable, ordered that the pilot who had left them there should immediately proceed in search of them. Since left to themselves, these men, accustomed to give full scope to their passions, would no longer recognize any master. Discord had armed them against each other, and several had perished in quarrels, which rendered their miserable situation still more sad. At length, however, misery had subdued these fierce characters, so that they finally assumed habits more peaceable, and better calculated for their preservation. They constructed huts with the debris of a ship wrecked on the rocks of the shore; and they subsisted for some time on the animals which Baron de Lèry had disembarked there some twenty-four years previously, and which had propagated themselves in the island. They domesticated some which furnished them milk. But this resource had begun to fail; and all that remained for them now, as a means of subsistence, was to turn their attention to fasting. When their clothes were worn they replaced them by seal-skins. On their return, Henry IV. wished to see them dressed as they had been found. Their beard and hair, which they had allowed to grow, hung in disorder on their bosoms and shoulders. Their forms had already assumed a hairy and savage appearance, which made them resemble Indians rather than civilized men. The king caused fifty crowns to be distributed to each, and permitted them to return to their families with the privilege of being exempt from all punishment for their former offenses.

"The Marquis de la Roche, who had invested all his fortune in this enterprise, lost it in consequence of misfortunes, which did not cease to oppress him. Ruined, and without any hope of being able to resume a project which he had always so much at heart, grief seized on him, and took him slowly to his grave. The history of the voyages, and misfortunes, of colonists which followed him to the Isle of Sable, form an episode worthy of exercising the pen of a romancer."

There is in your narration the outline of a beautiful historical romance; I am happy to have responded to the appeal which serious literature has made to light literature; would that I could have suitably done it, and been able to secure for this book sufficient success to encourage me to dramatize the most remarkable episodes of the history of Canada!

Accept, Monsieur, with my sentiments of high consideration, the assurance of my sincere friendship,

H. EMILE CHEVALIER.

Paris, *January*, 29 1860.

CONTENTS.

PROLOGUE.

IN BRITTANY.

Part I.

AT SEA.

Part II.

FIVE YEARS AFTER.

ADVENTURES
OF
COUNT DE GANA.

PROLOGUE

IN BRITTANY.

CHAPTER I.

THE BANDITS.

ON a fine morning in the month of May, 1598, two cavaliers started from the city of St. Malo, took the overland route which led to the South, and advanced towards a steep plateau.

These two cavaliers wore a costume half military, half courtly. The elder appeared to be forty-five years.

The other was a young man clad with a taste, at once sobre and *distingué*. Although armed like his companion, he seemed as if returning from a *fete*, or going to some spruce reunion of lords. His physiognomy had an air of feminine intrepidity which characterized the offshoots of the old nobility; his features were delicate, but his eye sparkled with pride; his face was white as marble, but large and full; his nose finely designed, but bold in its cast; his mouth small, but sarcastic; his chin agreeable, but elongated; his body slim, but muscular and vigorously formed. In a word, he was the type of that Frankish race which imposed itself on Gaul, by brute force, after the decay of the Roman Empire.

The first was William, Marquis de la Roche-Gommard; the second, John, Viscount de Ganay. The former was a Breton, the latter a Burgundian.

Both numbered coronets among their ancestors, and although the feudal ice had begun to thaw beneath the sun of royalty, the De la Roches and De Ganays were forced to follow the superannuated traditions of their fathers. Hence it was that John had been sent into Brittany by the Count Germain de Ganay, his father, there to learn his first lessons in the use of arms under the patronage of the Marquis de la Roche, with whom he had formed a friendly intimacy during the wars of the League. After having discharged the duties of a page, John caused himself to be promoted to the rank of grand equerry, and under this title served William de la Roche.

For half an hour the two cavaliers rode on without saying a word. The road they passed was zigzag and rugged, and deeply incased between a double hedge of hawthorns and cherry-trees in blossom. The marquis, grave and thoughtful, abandoned himself to the easy gait of his charger; the viscount, not less thoughtful, looked closely at the horizon, and no doubt would fain have pressed forward the hands of his watch, but a sentiment of deference restrained him from leaving his companion, who followed at a short distance. Suddenly, as they reached a place where the road formed an angle, five cavaliers, fully armed, dashed out before them, and ordered them to halt.

"By the mass, what does this mean?" exclaimed William de la Roche, drawing his sword.

"Surrender, or you are dead men!" commanded one of the cavaliers, whose helmet was surmounted with a black plume.

"By my word," retorted De la Roche; "the invitation is as curious as it is courteous. Who are you, my good man, that you come into our presence without permission? Back, clown! if you don't, I will have you hung high and short, both you and the cowardly bandits who accompany you."

This menace did not intimidate the assailants, for they replied only with a shout of derisive laughter, during which the chief resumed his summons.

"I am of a good family, Marquis de la Roche," said he; "and I declare you my prisoner."

"Wait till you have captured me before you indulge in such bragadocia, chevalier-traitor and felon. Now, I will knock you down, or fire on you, as on a mad dog."

De la Roche, after a sign to De Ganay, rapidly replaced his sword in the scabbard, and raised a pistol in each hand. The young man imitated this movement with no less promptitude.

"Come on! Come on! Sieze the miscreants, my braves!" shouted the chief of the ruffians.

"Coward! Come down and measure yourself with me at arm's length!"

"A hundred crowns of gold for you if you bring me the marquis living," he contented himself by saying to one of his underlings.

"Receive this, at all events, on account," replied De la Roche, pointing one of his pistols at his adversary.

But, although he took deliberate aim, the shot had no effect. The ball rebounded from the cuirass of the chevalier without even indenting it, and the bandits sought to surround our heroes, in order to cut off their retreat. Three more shots were heard almost instantaneously. John had fired with his two pistols, and De la Roche with the one he had left. In the midst of the smoke, produced by the triple explosion, it was impossible to tell the extent of the result. However, a man vacated his stirrups, rolled on the ground, and the issue of the combat was worse than doubtful when a troop of *gens d'armes* debouched from a neighboring underwood.

"Mine, mine!" exclaimed William de la Roche," distinguishing the colors of his flag, and the newcomers immediately put spurs to their horses, but the bandits foreseeing that they would be overwhelmed by numbers, turned their reins and rode off at a gallop.

The marquis selected some men to pursue them, then he alighted to ascertain who was the victim of the attempt on his person. John de Ganay wished to aid him in the investigation, but a glance prevented him. Covered with blood and dust, the wounded man panted heavily under his envelop of iron. He was struck on the right shoulder, the cuirass being defective in that part, and writhed his whole body a prey to horrible tortures. William de la Roche approached him, rested his knee on his breast, unbuckled the ties of his helmet, lifted his cap, and for an instant examined the face of the bandit.

"Who are you?" he asked.

"I want a drink—I'm thirsty—I'm burning; for the love of Heaven, give me something to drink!" replied the unknown, in a choking voice.

By order of William de la Roche, one of the armed men ran to a neighboring spring, took some water in his helmet and brought it to the wounded man, who drank with avidity the refreshing liquor.

"Ah!" said he, "that does me good!"

"But who are you? To whom do you belong?" reiterated the marquis.

The stranger remained silent.

"Speak, or I will perforate you like a miserable heretic;" added De la Roche, with a significant gesture.

"Monseigneur!" said the unfortunate, trembling with freight.

"Will you speak?"

"Well," stammered he in a tone so low that William was obliged to stoop almost to his mouth, in order to hear him, "I am in the pay of the Duke de Mercœur."

"Duke de Mercœur! Ah! I doubted it. It was he who wore the dark plume. Was it not?"

"I don't know."

"My God, you lie, soldier!"

"No, monseigneur; I swear it to you on the bones of my happy patron."

"Do you think you can deceive me by these impostures?"

"I am suffering; oh, I am suffering infernal pains and chastisements!" groaned the soldier, the convulsions of pain suffocating him.

"Let his cuirass be taken off, and let him be put on a horse," ordered De la Roche, jumping into his saddle. We are but a short distance from the manor; there he will be shaved by our barber, and to-morrow he will have to undergo an examination. You will answer for it to me on your neck."

Immediately the little troop commenced its march, headed by the two noblemen.

"The scoundrel!" muttered the marquis between his teeth, "attempting to capture me by an ambuscade! He has no more courage than a wet hen. Why not call me to the field, and then, if he has so many griefs against me, we shall see."—

Turning himself suddenly towards John de Ganay, he added:

"I hope, my friend, you have received no hurt."

"No, sir, thanks to Heaven; the wretches failed to touch me. But do you know the traitor-chevalier whom they obeyed?"

The marquis regarded his interlocutor with severity, and lowered his eyebrows.

"Pardon!" said John, disconcerted by the scrutiny of this cutting look.

"Your curiosity is excusable, viscount," replied De la Roche, changing his tone. "Besides, it is time that I should initiate you into the secrets of the family into which you desire to enter. Do not blush; I know you are attached to my niece, Laura de Kerskoën: and I believe the young lady does not look on you with any unfriendly eye. I feel, therefore, that I ought to confide to you certain affairs, of a very grave nature, before accomplishing a project which will perhaps cost me my life. Will you swear to me that, in case I perish, you will take Laura for your legitimate wife."

"I swear it, on the guard of my sword!" said John de Ganay, solemnly.

"Your oath satisfies me. Learn then, that I have in the Duke de Mercœur, governor of the beautiful province of Brittany, an implacable enemy, who for twenty-five years has done all in his power to sully the escutcheon of De la Roche, and dishonor its chief. I will explain to you the motive of this hatred:—The duke was smitten by my youngest sister, Adelaide de la Roche, the mother of Laura. As he was a man of dissolute and perverse habits, my father refused him the hand of his daughter, whom he married to Count Alfred de Kerskoën. Thenceforward, De Mercœur breathed an enmity, which time only increases. After having circulated odious reports about my sister, he challenged her husband to single combat, and killed him. Then, with his hand, dripping with the blood of my brother-in-law, he dared to renew his propositions to the widow. She repulsed him with horror, and died almost immediately giving birth to Laura. This took place in 1581; I was at the siege of Cambray. On my return to Brittany I received this sad news. Without waiting to change my dress, I proceeded to Rennes, where the duke held his court, and there, before all his fierce barons, I insulted him grossly. Next day we fought on horseback, determined that one or the other should die. He having been dismounted, we recommenced the combat on foot. His sword broke against mine; and he was at my mercy, when by a sentiment of compassion, for which I shall ever reproach myself, I granted him his life. Far from manifesting any gratitude for this act of generosity, he dreamed no longer but of vengeance, and such is also the source of his profound animadversion against our glorious Henry IV. After the assassination of the late King Henry III., I espoused the cause of the League against the Bearnais, and the Duke de Mercœur, although a fervent Catholic secretly promised his support to the Calvinists. More recently, Mayenne committed an irreparable fault in order to conceal his ambitious designs; he caused the Cardinal of Bourbon to be proclaimed under the name of Charles X., the seventh of August, 1589. Then, seeing into what an abyss of evils, anarchy was going to lead our dear France, and bearing in mind the usurping intentions of Philip II., who, under the cloak of religion, looked forward to nothing less than the monarchical unity of all Europe, and the degradation of the pontifical throne, I united myself frankly with the partisans of Henry. The Duke de Mercœur, on the other hand, turned about, entered into a coalition against that prince with the Dukes de Longueville, de Montpensier, d'Eperon, d'Aumont, the Baron d'O, and proclaimed to all who would listen to him that I was a renegade, a relapse, a heretic. But it was in vain that he distilled his venom of calumny to alienate from me the affections of the vassals of Brittany; my principles were too well known. I was able to say that I had a large part in the abjuration of Henry IV. The excommunication of Gregory XIV. did not frighten me, because I was sure to gain a soul for heaven, and a good sovereign for my country. And when Clement VII., yielding to the solicitations of my friends, D'Ossat and Duperron, accorded absolution to our well-beloved king, I blessed Providence for the favor vouchsafed to France by the interposition of the holy pontiff. But the jealousy of the Duke de Mercœur increased with all his failures. Furious at the triumph of the cause which I had sustained, he tried to pass himself off here as the heir of the ancient dukes, plotted with Philip II., and refused his allegiance to Henry IV. However, he feared me, and not daring to attack me openly, he disguises himself to attack me with a band of assassins at the corner of a wood."

"What!" said John surprised, "it was—"

"Hush! Let us advance nothing which we can not prove; the Church forbids it; and we, though excited by anger, must not sin; besides, to-morrow all doubt will be removed. But to conclude, you are informed of the hatred which animates the Duke de Mercœur against our house."

"That hatred I despise," warmly exclaimed the young man.

De la Roche shook his head with a sombre air.

"The duke is powerful," said he, "too powerful!"

"The credit of the king?" hazarded the equerry.

"The credit of the king is without influence over fanatics, and I confess I apprehend strongly that, notwithstanding the treaty of Vervins, the edict of Nantes, of the 13th of last April, an edict which insures to the Huguenots equality of powers, honors, and dignities with the Catholics, may seem wrong to the court of Rome, and entangle France in new religious wars. In a word—"

The marquis passed over his face his large hand, which was furrowed by a wound.

"In a word," he resumed, "I have the letters-patent which confirm me in the office of lieutenant-general of Canada. In eight days we shall start for that virgin soil, of which so many wonders are told, and Laura will enter the convent of Blois, where she will await patiently the return of her betrothed. If I succumb, John, you will protect her, will you not?"

"Oh!" exclaimed the young man with warmth.

CHAPTER II.

LAURA DE KERSKOËN.

IT was noon. Seated in a large sculptured chair, Laura de Kerskoën, lady of the manor of Vornadeck, turned over the leaves of her beautiful missal, printed on parchment and embellished with miniatures of the Byzantine style of art, enriched with a brilliant case, having clasps of embossed gold, with an Oriental amethyst at the centre, encased in a silver plate after the manner of St. Eloi, goldsmith of King Dagobert.

Laura de Kerskoën, heiress of Vornadeck, was at the age of illusions, seventeen summers, like a rosebud, ready to break the pod, of which the richness of its colors was jealous of the sweetness of its perfumes. Nothing so pretty, and at the same time so mutinous, as her countenance, where temerity and gentleness harmonized their features.

Opposite to this young lady sat her nurse, Dame Catharine, a native of Normandy, who, from the infancy of Laura, had taken the place of her mother.

"Tell me, nurse," suddenly asked the young lady, resting the missal on her knees, "do you know what o'clock it is?"

"I think it is near twelve," replied Catharine, "for I hear the bugle sound to relieve the guard at the castle. Pretty soon our good Marquis de la Roche-Gommard will be home, with his amiable equerry, the Lord of Ganay. I am sure that your heart pants for him. Viscount John is as handsome a young man as he is an intreped cavalier."

A slight disdainful smile rose to the lips of Laura, who replied after a minute:

"Were you not speaking this morning of going to see the fishergirl, who has broken her leg?"

"Yes, dear girl; I will go as soon as the great heat subsides."

"I think it would be better to go at once. If my uncle and guardian come home in the afternoon, it will hardly be possible to quit the castle, nurse."

"Very true, my daughter, you reason like an angel; I will go and get my mantle and immediately bring that poor woman the herbs and potions which the surgeon has prescribed."

While saying so, the old dame rose from her seat and started.

"Ah!" joyously exclaimed Laura, as she heard the door of the apartment close after her "duègne," as she called her. "Ah, I am then free at last! A few minutes more and perhaps * * After all, Catharine is so indulgent to me! She would not breathe a word of me to the Marquis de la Roche. It will not be long now until he comes, and that John de Ganay with him. * * What weariness! But she too will be soon here; she will come before them, my gentle messenger. What good luck!"

Bounding with gayety, the niece of the marquis ran to a narrow arch, embellished with colored glass, and raised the lower frame. An amorous ray of the sun enveloped her at once in the waves of its brilliant light, and extended softly on the ground.

For twenty minutes, Laura, with her arms resting on the window-stool, interrogated the extent of the azure vault, stripping the petals, so to speak, of an adorable meditation. She began to grow impatient, however; when, at the North, there appeared a black point.

"Addresse! my dear Addresse!" murmured the young lady.

The point enlarged insensibly, assumed proportions, a form slight and lank. It was a pigeon cutting the atmosphere with its wings. It approaches—it approaches! Already one can distinguish its white plumage and its slender neck, girded with a green band.

"Ah! dear Addresse," repeated Laura; "then it is you; I was not mistaken!"

Like a skilful pilot, examining the port after a perilous voyage, the bird redoubled her zeal since she saw the beautiful head of Laura extending over the embrasure of the window. It had passed the wall of the castle, and glided over the external ramparts, but had not time to receive the reward of its voyage, when suddenly a report was heard, and the young lady grew pale, then uttered a piercing cry. However, she immediately recovered her presence of mind. Then she projected her person outside the window-stool, and saw the bird flapping its wings, and entangled in the foliage of a moulding, a few feet above her. Below, on the wall, were soldiers laughing loudly and felicitating one of their companions, whose murderous arm had wounded the innocent creature. Delighted with his dexterity, the soldier who did the harm laughed louder than the rest; but at the sight of the niece of their lord all were silent, and soon disappeared. The young heiress could then without the fear of being surprised, lower herself more, stretch out her arm and seize the unfortunate pigeon; she took it softly, drew it to her, and returned to her seat.

The bird had its thigh broken. Laura could not restrain her tears.

"Poor thing!" said she, in broken accents, "it will never get well."

However, she washed the wound carefully, drew from the mangled flesh the bloody down which sullied it, and after having assured herself that the lead had only grazed some secondary tendons, she took from the neck of the pigeon a green ribbon, and brought it tenderly to her bed.

"Our Lady of good Succor," said she, "have pity on my little Addresse! I will burn in your honor four large tapers of perfumed wax, and give a beautiful napkin of Flanders linen for your altar, if you will preserve her to me in life and health, or else put to death the scoundrel of a soldier who has caused her death!"

This invocation being ended, Laura de Kerskoën unrolled the ribbon, which she had put into her bosom, introduced it into a bronze decanter, suspended from her waist by a chain of the same metal, and withdrew it at the end of five seconds. The original color had disappeared; it was brown and marked with brown characters. In the twinkling of an eye, the young girl had devoured these characters, and all her members trembled with fright.

At this moment the sound of a trumpet awakened the echoes of the manor. Laura precipitated herself to the window, her eyes riveted on the esplanade near the drawbridge of the principal entrance.

"The Marquis de la Roche and John de Ganay!" exclaimed she in a fright. "Holy Virgin! Bertrand is lost!"

CHAPTER III.

THE MANOR.

Built on the plateau of an abrupt rock, the manor of Roche was one of the most redoubtable fortresses in Brittany. Its general configuration resembled that of a trapezium, of which the axis was directed to the northwest, and of which the small side extended to the northeast. This configuration was described by a boundary of ramparts, with an elevation of thirty feet. In the rear was the chateau properly so called. Four large wings, composed of cut stone, united to each other by square towers, composed it. Still more to the rear, at the centre of a vast court, rose the citadel to the height of twenty toises, a sort of octagonal fortress, surmounted by a diadem of projecting turrets. It was here the arms and munitions were deposited, and where, in cases of necessity, the prisoners of war were confined to prevent their being rescued. A deep sloping ditch, cut in the solid rock, and a wall bristling with iron spikes, surrounded the fortress at the base. Five gates led to it; the two first situated beneath a vault in the exterior rampart, and separated by an intermediate portcullis, or herse; the two following being in the body of the inhabited edifice, equally separated by an intermediate portcullis; and the fifth placed at the base of the fortress. No surrounding ditch protected the first line of fortifications, which were founded on perpendicular rocks, impossible to be scaled. One could arrive at the chateau only by a zigzag path, incrusted, so to speak, in the flank of the mountain, and which crossed a drawbridge, under which a very deep well had been made. Two masses of granite, in the form of half moons, provided with numerous battlements and loop-holes, defended this bridge.

The chateau of La Roche had been constructed in the fifteenth century by Aymon de la Roche on his return from the crusades. To this it is needless to add that the building was of the feudal style of architecture.

At the time the bugle sounded, an archer appeared on the platform of the gate.

"Brittany and Navarre!" cried the marquis.

Immediately a rattling of chains on rollers was heard, and the bridge was promptly lowered. The cavalcade entered, the Marquis de la Roche taking the lead. Arrived at the court of honor, he halted, gave some orders concerning the captive, jumped from his horse, and made a sign to the equerry to follow him. Taking a large stairway, they descended to the armory and penetrated into an apartment of the narrowest dimensions, contiguous to the hall. This was the chamber of the Marquis de la Roche-Gommard.

It had a very sombre and very austere air; one might easily have mistaken it for the cell of a dominican. Nothing to gratify the eye. The furniture consisted of a camp-bed, simply covered with a bear's skin, two tables, covered with books, cards, stools, mathematical and astronomical instruments, some chests, and a sealed casket on the white-washed wall. The only ornament, worthy of attention, was a large crucifix, in black wood, and of exquisite purity of form. It was said that this crucifix was the work of the famous Michael Angelo, which had been taken away from the church of the Holy Spirit at the time of the civil wars in Italy, and sold for a hundred silver marks to the father of William de la Roche.

The Marquis took a seat, and drew from his pocket-book a parchment, sealed with the arms of France and Navarre; he glanced over the contents, while John de Ganay stood a few paces distant, in a respectful attitude. The parchment contained these lines:

"We, Henry the Fourth, of the name, by the grace of God King of France and Navarre, to our friend and faithful subject of the Mesgonnets, chevalier of our order, counsellor in our council, and captain of fifty armed men, the Lord de la Roche, Marquis de Cotemmineal, Baron de Las, Viscount de Caventon et St. Lo, in Normandy, Viscount de Travallet, Lord de la Roche-Gommard and Quermolac, de Cornac, Benteguyno et Lescuit, conformably to the will of the late King Henry III., have created Lieutenant-General of the country of Canada, Hocheleja, Newfoundland, river of the Great Bay Norembegne and the lands adjacent, on the following conditions:

"That the Lord de la Roche will have particularly in view the establishment of the Catholic faith; that his authority will extend over all the men of war, both on sea and land; that he will choose the captains, masters of vessels, and pilots; that he shall have a right to command them in all cases which he may deem necessary, while they can not, under any pretext, refuse to obey him; that he may put the ships and crews, which he will find in the ports of France, in a seaworthy condition, raise as many troops as he may wish, to make war, build forts and cities, give them laws and punish their transgressors or pardon them; grant to noblemen fiefs, lordships, manors, counties, baronies, and other dignities, subject to our sovereignty, according as he may deem conducive to the good of the service, and to the others of lower condition at such charge and annual rent as it may please him to impose, but from which they will be exempt the six first years, and longer, if he deems it necessary; that on the return of his expedition, he can divide between those who made the voyage with him, one third of all the gains and profits, retaining another third for himself, and employing the remaining third to meet the expenses of the war, fortifications, and other common expenses; that all the noblemen, merchants, and others who will accompany him at their own expense, or otherwise, can do so in full liberty, but that they will not be permitted to carry on commerce without his permission, and that under pain of the confiscation of their ships, merchandise, and other effects; that in case of disease or death he can, by will or otherwise, name one or two lioutenants to tako his place; that he will have the liberty in the whole kingdom to make a levy of workmen, and other men necessary for the success of his enterprise; finally, that he will enjoy the same powers, privileges, immunities, and authorities of which the Lord of Roberval had been gratified by the late King Francis I.

"Given at our palace of the Louvre, in our good city of Paris, this second day of January, of the year of grace one thousand five hundred and ninety-eight, and of our reign the ninth.

Signed,

"HENRY OF FRANCE AND OF NAVARRE." *

"John," said the marquis, when he had concluded the reading.

"Monseigneur!"

"You have read the narrative of James Cartier?"

The equerry nodded affirmatively.

"And you are still resolved to accompany me?" added William de la Roche, closely scrutinizing the yonng man.

"Yes, sir," replied the equerry without hesitation.

"The perils and dangers don't frighten you?"

---

* It will be understood that the letter, which we have given here, is but a very succinct abridgment of that which granted to William de la Roche the Lieutenancy of Canada. To have given the letter entire would have been a superfluity, which would be injurious to the dramatic interest of our recital.

"I have descended from a family in which the term fear has no meaning. On our coat of arms is engraved '*Audaces fortuna juvat!*' which signifies that a man should never be afraid *when he is engaged* in a noble enterprise."

"Well," said William, "I like to hear you speak of fortune. But you understand the object of our expedition?"

"To found a colony."

"This is not all," replied the marquis warmly. "Oh, it is not all! I say it is the least inducement! My son, we have to propagate the doctrines which Jesus Christ, our Saviour, transmitted to the world through the medium of the holy Roman Catholic and Apostolic Church; we must carry the torch of truth into the midst of ignorant and idolatrous people, who inhabit the forests of North America; we must work out our own salvation, to merit heaven in converting the Indians to our religion! we must "(De la Roche lowers his voice)" prevent the heretics—the Huguenots—you understand me, John—from distilling on New France the venom of their lying dogmas, as they have already tried to do at Charlefort, at the instigation of Coligny!"

After this sortie, dictated by the religious fanaticism of the time, De la Roche inclined his head on his breast, and indulged in profound meditation. But if he had cast his eyes on his equerry, he would have been surprised at the change he had undergone in a few minutes. John de Ganay was pale to lividness; his features contracted; his muscles trembled, he seemed to combat with himself against bitter anger, furiously bit his lips, as if to repress the words that flowed to his lips. By degrees, however, he recovered his self-control, so that, when the marquis had got over his revery, he was calm, or at least seemed so.

"You understood me?" asked the Marquis de la Roche.

"I did," coldly replied John.

"And you will come, the cross in one hand and the hoe in the other, and if I succumb—"

"I will undertake the accomplishment of your last wishes."

"Mark you, John," said the marquis, rising, and taking the hand of the viscount, which he found moist and cold: "thank you, you will one day be the glory of Christianity."

De Ganay retired, and William de la Roche went to prostrate himself before his crucifix.

CHAPTER IV.

THE UNCLE AND HIS NIECE.

Laura de Kerskoën was again seated in her chair, absorbed in thought.

"What folly! to write me that he will come this evening! Did I not tell him that I expected my uncle? But what signify these words: 'Fear nothing, my precautions are well taken; to-morrow, if you wish, we shall be united by indissoluble ties.' Oh, I tremble! What am I to do? Dear Bertrand! he is capable of all—he loves me so much! Why is it that a mortal enmity divides our parents? But no, no! I shall never be the wife of any man in the world but him! Oh, I would rather berry myself in a cloister! Is not my love just, is it not legitimate? Do I not owe my existence to this brave champion? Where should I be without him, good St. Mary? At the peril of his life he rescued me from the flames which devoured the convent of my aunt. How handsome he is, how brave! And yet so timid with me! confronting every danger, in order to come and respire one instant under the window of his queen! What a difference between him and that John de G nay, whose assiduities importune me! Besides, what can the Marquis de la Roche think of him? he seems to me not a loyal Catholic, the Burgundian. I cease to think of him, after I have made the sign of the cross, and he always finds some pretext for not being present at the holy sacrifice of the mass. On the contrary, Bertrand never fails to be present. Every Sunday, disguised as a serf, I see him piously humbled in a corner of the village church, where I regularly since the death of our worthy chaplain. * * To come this evening, what imprudence! Would that I could warn him! Impossible, Addresse is too seriously wounded! What resource then! Would that I knew where he * * And that equerry who is strolling incessantly on the ramparts, telling the Marquis de la Roche to double the guards, because that—because that—Bad plan, bad plan; my uncle would suspect at once. What fatality! Some magician has made a charm, that's sure. * * I must implore the aid of my merciful patroness!"

Having formed this design, the devoted young lady ran to kneel before her crucifix. While thus prostrated, William de la Roche entered, without interrupting her. Not wishing to trouble her meditations, he was about to retire, for the rigid guardian was far from suspecting that it was a mundane thought—a thought of a disobedient lover, which thus absorbed the attention of his ward; but suddenly the latter exclaimed:

"Oh, thank you, thank you, happy patroness, you have granted my petitions; he is saved!"

"Who is this?" asked the marquis.

"Monseigneur de la Roche," stammered Laura.

"Well, dear child, is it thus you receive your uncle, after an absence of two months?"

"Pardon, pardon," said Laura, blushing. "I ——"

"You did not expect me, naughty girl," replied William, tenderly kissing her forehead. "But, thank heaven, we have returned safe and sound, and all is ready for our approaching departure!"

"Your approaching departure!"

"Ah, my friend, you tremble because I take with me the object of your thoughts! John de Ganay will accompany me to New France. There, do not grieve, my Laura; do not lower your eyes to conceal your affliction. I prom return him to you in a year, at most."

"But, monseigneur ——"

"But what, mademoiselle?" said he, sitting down and taking her on his knee.

"But ——"

"Since I promise to return him to you, you are not going to be jealous of your old uncle. The separation will fortify you both, and you will like me all the better for having kept you asunder some time. You will pass your widowhood under the abbess of the monastery of Blois."

"But, uncle," said the young lady, who recovered by degrees from her emotion, "have you not told me that you had deferred the project of founding a colony at New France?"

"Ah!" replied the marquis, smiling, "it is less my project of colonization than the colonist, whom I take with me, that calls forth this insidious question."

"You have then obtained your letters-patent?" said she, with an agitation which escaped the attention of her interlocutor.

"Better still," replied he, "I have escaped the trap which had been set for me by the Duke de Mercœur."

Laura started.

"Dear child," said De la Roche, pressing her affectionately to his bosom; "you will pardon me for leaving you, but the voice of God speaks to my conscience—I must go. A new Peter the Hermit, I bear the banner of the Roman Church in the midst of infidels, and soon the opposite shores of the Atlantic will ring with the praises of the All-Powerful. Courage, my daughter! Offer your soul to God, this will aid you to support this trial."

Laura was sensible. Brought up by William de la Roche, who had spoiled her, she cherished him as a father. If the long expeditions of her guardian had never frightened her, at that epoch of civil wars, the idea of a voyage across the Ocean to countries supposed to be much more distant than they really were—this idea, we say, could not fail to make her sad. She burst into tears. Persuaded that these tears had his equerry for their object much more than himself, William tried to console her with caresses. Then, imagining that he supplied a sovereign balm for the grief of his niece, he said, when withdrawing:

"Never mind, my child; dry your tears. You will be betrothed before we embark."

As soon as he had left the room, Laura tapped three times on a gong with a silver wand. Her waiting-maid, a young, courteous, and handsome Picardian appeared.

"Luzette, who is the sergeant of the guard at the gate of the chateau?" The abigail turned her eye with a knowing air and replied:

"It is Goliath!"

"Go down to the office, and tell the butler not to forget his post to-night. You understand me!"

"Mademoiselle will be obeyed," said Luzette, bowing.

"Ah, I am indisposed—I will not go to supper!"

Luzette made a second bow and retired.

"By this means," exclaimed the niece of the marquis, "perhaps I may succeed in securing his safety."

CHAPTER V.

THE TROUBADOUR.

"COME, Sergeant Goliath, another glass of that generous cider with which we have been gratified by the noble Laura de Kerskoën."

"Fill up, fill up, Hare-Ear, for by the good day my tongue is as dry as charcoal, and my stomach resounds like an empty barrel."

"A brave demoiselle is our young lady of the manor!" added Hare-Ear, filling a wooden porringer, which he handed to the sergeant.

"By my life, you speak truly," replied the latter; "a brave demoiselle, without doubt!" He raised the goblet to his lips: but suddenly he stopped, and cocked his ear.

"What's the matter, Goliath? It would seem that you hear something."

"Surely I do, by jingo I hear——. Don't you hear?"

By the half-open door of the guard-house the evening breeze bears these well-known words, chanted in slow and harmonious style:

> . . . . Li Bretons
> Jadis souloilent par prouesce,
> Des aventures qu' ils oioient
> Faire des lais par remembrance
> Lu'on ne les mist en oubliance . . .

"Oh, oh, by jingo, this announces to us, if I don't very much mistake, the jovial troubadour who has given us so much solace and pleasure of late. This will be a precious windfall for us to receive into our chamber. He will recount to us the valiant histories of the brave Americans, and will not fail to relate to us once more the marvelous adventures of the Chevalier Bertrand of Guesclin."

"And also the expedition of the four sons of Montglave," said Hare-Ear. "At the end of winter, when the pleasant weather of summer commences, and one sees the trees flourish and the flowers bud."

"Not so fast, comrade—not so fast!" interposed a third halberdier; "let us haste and make merry—that's all very well, but let us enforce the countersign. The alarm is sounded."

"Oh, that's but a small affair," said Goliath. "Let our gallant minstrel be introduced. I will answer for all."

"No, indeed, sergeant; no, indeed," replied the other obstinately; "you will answer perhaps with your neck. That's your affair; but my intention is not to neglect on any account the duties for which I am responsible."

"By Jupiter, it is my opinion, old whiner, Balafiè, that you will not be satisfied until I cool your blood with the balm of my steel."

Balafiè was going to retort, but one of the halberdiers handed him the porringer, which still continued to go the rounds. The perfume of the sparkling liquor appeased the wrath of the trooper, and after having drunk, he said:

"At all events, do as you like; I will wash my hands out of it as Pontius Pilate did on the occasion of pronouncing judgment against our Redeemer."

"By jingo, you are right in consenting ——"

"But, sergeant," objected some of the soldiers, "if our redoubtable master, the Marquis de la Roche, came to know that we had received a stranger in our guard-house.'

"By my life, who would dare to tell him? has he a spy among us?"

This interrogation imposed silence on the reluctant. For the rest, the song of the troubadour was so poetical, so harmonious, that it would have softened a rock. At this moment he began to sing the old romance of Brittany, of which Thibault, Count de Champagne, has left us a translation,—accompanying himself on his fiddle:

Las! si j'avais pouvoir d' oublier
Sa beauté, sa beauté, son bien dire,
Et son très-doux, très-doux regarder,
Finirait mon martyre.

. . . .

"There are not two throats like that in all the world, by jingo; it is that of our bard; he will not sleep at the tavern, if for that act of charity I were to be flogged with rods until the blood began to flow. There, send for the sentinel."

In a few minutes the sentry arrived in the guard-room of the chateau De la Roche, where this scene passed.

"Ah, 'tis you, Courtevue," said Goliath, "who has been singing at such an hour under the walls of the chateau?"

"The American troubadour."

"Alone."

"Alone, sergeant."

"Let the bridge be lowered, by Jupiter! we have still a pitcher full, and we will spend a pleasant night."

After these words, the commander of the post went out to meet the host that chance brought him.

The enormous pannel of thick planks described slowly its quarter of a circle, and re-covered the well which was at the entrance of the fortifications.

"Qui vive?" cried Goliath, perceiving a shadow cross the darkness of night. In response to his query he received this stanza:

> "Pour débaucher, par un doux style,
> Femme ou fille de bon maintien,
> Point ne faut de vieille subtile,
> Frère Lubin le fera bien."

"Is it you, by jingo, my bard?" Squatted before the bridge, the shade continued its ballad:

"Je presche en théologien ;
Mais pour boire de belle eau claire,
Faites-la boire à votre chien:
Frère Lubin ne le peut faire."

"Ah, bravo! bravo!" exclaimed Goliath, wringing his hands. "Come, my gay nightingale, you will pump at another reservoir, than a cold fountain. And by the horns of the devil——"

But before he had finished this phrase, ten vigorous fingers pressed his neck with their steel muscles, a poignard was placed at his breast, and he fell into the well without uttering even a sigh.

CHAPTER VI.

THE ATTACK.

During this time Viscount de Ganay promenaded on the rampart, as well to assure himself that the sentinels were at their posts as to meditate.

The weather, delightful in the morning, became gloomy in the afternoon, and at this moment the dark heavy clouds glided lazily through the sky. The darkness was profound; but at short intervals a dazzling flash tore with sloping flame the thick mantle of the firmament, and illuminated the high towers of the chateau.

No breeze disturbed the air; one respired a thick atmosphere, charged with electricity.

In the distance the sea roared, breaking its waves against the beach, and betimes the hoarse cry of the screech-owl also disturbed the silence of the night.

The equerry felt himself overwhelmed with sadness.

"She has not come to meet me," thought he; "she has not presided at supper, under pretext of indisposition; and yet, I am pretty sure, I have seen her at the window when the marquis caused the bugle to be sounded for lowering the drawbridge. It is strange! Could I be deceived? Has she not loved me? Not to love me! Oh, it is impossible! A hundred times I have spoken to her of my love; never, it is true, has she avowed me. What an impenetrable mystery is the heart of a woman! Ah! I am foolish to make myself weary; is it not she that sprigged the scarf I wear round my waist? Is it not she that has given it to me? Still these cursed suspicions! Eh, who would she love then? Since she left the convent she has remained at the chateau, neither receiving nor seeing anybody. Bah, I am, indeed, foolish to——! What's this? It seems to me that some one calls."

John, who happened to be beneath the window of Laura, raised his head. This window, we have omitted to say, opens towards the south, opposite the outside gate of the manor.

"Bertrand, is it you?" said a voice. The viscount made a vain attempt to pierce the obscurity which enveloped him with its opaque folds; nothing; he distinguished nothing!

Nevertheless, he was about to reply, when suddenly the west was in a blaze of phosphorescent light, followed by a formidable rolling of thunder, and a cry of terror.

"Laura de Kerskoën," murmured De Ganay, who had seen the young lady crouching at the window.

But before he was able to account to himself for the impression made upon him by this incident, the celestial fire had vanished, darkness had resumed its place, usurped only for a moment, and a second cry, vigorous, wild, exciting, disturbed the echoes of the manor :

"Attention! attention! To arms! to arms!"

"What's this?" asked John of an archer that passed near him.

"The chateau is invested! the chateau is invested!" replied the latter, running as fast as his legs could carry him.

Without troubling himself, the equerry ran towards the upper guard-house, where was deposited the handle for raising and lowering the portcullis. The greatest confusion reigned among the soldiers.

"Lower the herse!" cried the viscount.

"But the enemy has already passed the fortifications," observed one of the guards.

"No matter! no matter! Let his retreat be cut off."

And while the soldiers hastened to obey this order, John ran to the staircase, which led to the gate of the chateau proper. It debouched on the southern part of the trapezium; the equerry pressed his steps in that direction; but, quickly as he went, he was outstripped by the assailants who rushed tumultuously towards the drawbridge.

Already the noise of the attack was heard all over. The big clock of the fortress sounded the alarm. Aroused from sleep, the garrison mustered into line, and made preparations for defence, while the marquis, interrupted in the middle of his prayer by the first rumors, precipitated himself into the court, where he was soon joined by the *elite* of his men. He was informed that a band of unknown persons had surprised and massacred the external guard.

"Raise the bridge, close the gates," said he with the greatest coolness. "Let a company proceed to the platform, another to the towers, and let the women, children, and domestics be confined in the fortress."

Immediately, without loss of time, he proceeded to the chamber of his niece, in order to take her to a place of safety, for the apartment which she occupied during peace served as an intrenchment for a detachment of archers when the fortress was besieged. But judge of the astonishment of the marquis! The chamber of Laura de Kerskoën was empty.

It was not the time to inquire into the motives of the disappearance of the young lady, since every second that passed aggravated the common danger. Suppressing his anguish, De la Roche flew to the salient gallery which projected over the gate of the chateau.

A troop of men were there assembled; some rained stones on the heads of the assailants; some shells; others boiling oil; others used cannon, mortars, etc., while archers and musketeers, posted at the port-holes of the neighboring towers, riddled the enemy with arrows and balls.

The scene was frightful, the combat sad as the tempest which roared in the distance! By the hazy light of some resin torches, frequently eclipsed by the lightning the eye caught the shadows of men running here and there, throughout the extent of the building, between the interior counterscarp and the earthworks of the rampart. Then were heard ferocious cries, moanings, imprecations, and, surmounting all, the solemn voice of the thunder rumbling in the distance.

The agressors had time to break the chains of the drawbridge before the alarm could be given, and, notwithstanding the projectiles of all kinds poured on them by the defenders of the chateau, they attempted resolutely to force the gate.

An enormous plank which they had found on the glacis, served them for this purpose.

Twenty robust men, placed at the sides of the plank, sustained it on their extended arms, and gave it a see saw movement in darting its extremity against the gate, which made a great noise at each stroke of the formidable ram.

"Forward! forward! Come, come, my braves!" vociferated a chevalier, armed to the teeth, whose helmet, adorned with a black plume, and who commanded this mob of demons.

"Courage! courage!" exclaimed in turn William de la Roche, who, having seized a swivel gun, fired incessantly on the enemy.

But notwithstanding the valor of the besieged, notwithstanding the streams of boiling pitch which they poured on the enemy, the latter did not hesitate for a moment. Wounded and dead were thrown into the ditch; new hands replaced them immediately, and the improvised ram did not cease to batter at the obstacle which they desired to upset. One of the hinges of the gate had given way; the others could not hold out long. The enemy was bellowing victory, when William de la Roche exclaimed:

"Throw the *thunderbolt!*"

The "thunderbolt" was a monstrous ninety-six-pounder, pointed at the angle of the platform.

All the men around the marquis commenced the work, and after some unheard-of efforts, the colossal of bronze was thrown from the top of the gallery on the human surge that struggled below.

First, there was a horrible crackling; then an exclamation of pain and terror.

The bridge was broken, and all who were on it were precipitated into the ditch below.

Then a panic ran through the ranks of the enemy. Those who were nearest wished to run; but, driven back by those most distant, who desired to take part in the action, they fell pell-mell into the ditch, where they were torn and lacerated by the spikes of iron which garnished the scarp. A large number were killed in this struggle, and the besieged availed themselves of the confusion by plying their adversaries with grape.

An impetuous wind had arisen, chasing the clouds towards the east. Between the streaks made by their dispersion, the moon now exhibited her silvery disk, and anon replunged herself behind an impenetrable curtain. These fluctuations of light and shade imparted to the siege of the chateau colors truly fantastic.

Meantime, the chevalier with the black plume had succeeded in re-establishing order among his followers. They retreated; but at the moment when they reached the gate a troop of musketeers, which John de Ganay had got together in haste on the rampart, made a violent attack on them. The musketeers, contrary to their expectations, were received with an intrepidity which compelled them to return. The viscount made a fruitless attempt to stimulate their ardor; they would listen to nothing, but dispersed in every direction, incapable of resisting the onset of those whom they had supposed they could cut to pieces.

Trembling with indignation, Viscount de Ganay was going to precipitate himself into the midst of the struggle, to perish sword in hand, when he perceived the chevalier with the black plume.

To strike two men who interrupted his passage, and to seek out the chief of this cowardly expedition, was but the work of a moment for our brave equerry.

"Between us both!" exclaimed he, extending his sword to stop his antagonist.

"Are you a chevalier?"

"Yes, I gained my spurs at the blockade of Paris."

Immediately their swords crossed, cracked, and struck a thousand sparks out of each other, and the trumpet resounded, announcing a momentary truce, in order that the noble combatants might be allowed full liberty.

For an arena they had the little esplanade in the rear of the principal gate; for a light the moon, which shone at this moment above the scene of the combat; for witnesses a circle of soldiers.

CHAPTER VII.

BERTRAND.

THE black chevalier, as our readers have decied, was Bertrand, the favorite lover of the beautiful Laura de Kerskoën. Having no hope of obtaining the hand of his mistress on account of the hatred between his uncle, the Duke de Mercœur, and the Marquis de la Roche, he had resolved to profit by the absence of the latter, in order to carry away the young lady of the manor. His plan was one of the most simple. Having in his pay a regiment of troopers, Bertrand was to present himself at the gate of the manor in the disguise of a troubadour, a plan, which he had often previously adopted for the purpose of securing an entrance.

A part of his soldiers were to follow him, concealing themselves among the rocks; he was to solicit hospitality, which was never refused, because the soldiers of the garrison knew that the troubadour was agreeable to the niece of their master, and thus render himself master of the fortress. This explains the message which he had expedited to Laura by means of the carrier pigeon. But scarcely had he sent this message, when a spy informed him that the marquis, then at St. Malo, was on his way back to the chateau. Made desperate by the disappointment which adjourned the accomplishment of his designs, our paladin resolved to seize the marquis. Having failed in this attempt, he proceeded, nevertheless, with his enterprise, in which, as we have seen, he suffered a new reverse.

Bertrand knew the Viscount de Ganay well, and if he required that he should renounce his title, it was only in jest. Nor was he less aware of the pretensions of John to the heart of Laura, which explains why it was that he attacked with such blind fury; for, stung with jealousy, he wished to humiliate a rival who had already distinguished himself by numerous exploits.

The duel lasted more than twenty minutes, with a fury which nothing could equal. The two antagonists were perhaps about the same strength, but to the passion of his adversary, John opposed an imperturbable calmness, and after the first passes it was easy to see that, except a lucky accident occurred, the viscount would be the victor in this singular combat.

In fact, the nephew of the Duke de Mercœur, exasperated by the coolness of the equerry, plied his sword at random without paying any attention to the thrusts of his antagonist; it was now that John awaited him; but as he desired rather to disarm than to kill him, he neglected many opportunities of striking him, now that it was easy to do it in all security. Finally, however, grown tired himself, he gave blow for blow, and after a parry or two, he made a feint and struck Bertrand in the opening between the cuirass and armlets.

The young man staggered and fell on his knees; his shoulder was completely transfixed.

This defeat put an end to hostilities. The assailants surrendered to the mercy of the besieged, who had come out of the chateau by a trap-door, in order to be present at the duel.

William de la Roche warmly embraced his brave equerry, caused the captives to be put in chains to the number of sixty, and had Bertrand conducted to one of the dungeons of the fortress. Then having given orders to double every guard, and to cover the dead bodies with quicklime, he brought John de Ganay to his apartment.

"Well," said he on arriving, "was I not right, my dear and brave friend?"

"I don't know, sir."——

"Then you did not know Bertrand de Mercœur, nephew of the duke?"——

"I had heard him spoken about, a good deal, as a valiant champion——"

"Valiant! Do not apply that epithet to him, my son, Bertrand is a coward, unworthy of the coronet he bears on his blazon. Do you wish a conclusive proof? It was he who attacked us this morning on our way from St. Malo; he who has attacked to-night by means of a conspiracy of which I don't know the plot; he who has provoked and wounded you!"

"Can it be possible?" murmured the viscount.

"Only too true," replied William; "but what course are we to pursue in regard to him?"

"To refer him to the justice of the king."

"So I was thinking—yes, it seems to me to be the best expedient; for his crime can not remain unpunished, and our security requires that we do not keep him here. The duke would not know how to rescue him. Come, good courage, John! In a few days we shall be on our way to defend a more noble cause—the holy cause of the Christian religion."

The Marquis de la Roche and his equerry exchanged a few words more, and then parted, the one to inform himself as to his niece, the other to assure himself that all danger had ceased.

CHAPTER VIII.

THE EVASION.

WHAT had become of Laura de Kerskoën? Why did her uncle not find her in her chamber?

At nine o'clock the young lady of the manor opened the sash of her window, and heard the noise of a footstep on the rampart; she said, as the reader will remember, "Is it you, Bertrand?" But the flash of lightning having shown her John de Ganay instead of him she expected, Laura suddenly retired in a fright, augmented by the war-cry which nearly at the same moment came to her ear. Trembling and terrified, she first thought of seeking refuge with her uncle. An instinct—the instinct of love—stopped her. Returning to her window, she saw through the darkness the black plume which surmounted the helmet of her lover.

"Bertrand!" said she, "merciful Heaven! is this done by him?"

But a thought struck her. Without reflecting any further, she descended into the court of honor; she hoped to be able to warn Bertrand that the marquis had returned to the chateau. Unfortunately all the means of egress had been barricaded, and she was obliged to return to her apartment. It was during this absence that William came to see his niece. Palpitating, lovesick, not daring to look outside, she sat on the side of her bed, and listened. It is more difficult to describe than to imagine the moral tortures she had to suffer during the siege of the manor. Every musket report reverberated through her heart like a funeral knell; and when the *thunderbolt* fell on the bridge, with a horrible fracas, the poor girl almost fainted.

What a sad situation for her! If her uncle was conqueror, her lover would without doubt be put to the sword; if, on the contrary, Bertrand prevailed, what might he do to the Marquis de la Roche, who had reared and cherished her like a father? *Mon Dieu*, what affliction for the unfortunate Laura! Distracted by the conflicting sentiments of duty, gratitude, and the anxieties of the passion of love, how deeply did this cruel alternative pain her. Her heart beat violently, and the blood rushed to her head, when Catharine entered with a torch in her hand. The good dame shuddered at every limb.

"Jesus, Lord, have pity on us!" she exclaimed. "They are going to seize, pillage, and sack us, as they did at the monastery of Rennes. Holy Mary, mother of God, protect us!"

"You are, then, so much afraid, nurse?" said Laura, in order to allay her fears.

"Fear, dear mademoiselle!—fear! Oh! let us pray, my daughter; let us implore the justice of heaven that right may triumph!"

Laura did not rightly know what response to make to this invitation; impelled by the example of her nurse, she prostrated herself, and both commenced to tell their beads, interrupting each other from time to time as the tumult increased.

When the duel between John de Ganay and Bertrand had ended, both the besiegers and besieged were silent.

"Mercy, sweet Saviour," said Catharine, supposing that Providence had heard her prayers, "the traitors are expelled."

"Hush!" said Laura, rising and approaching the window.

"Oh, demoiselle! demoiselle! where are you going?"

"Hush!"

Thrusting herself out of the window, the young lady looked about anxiously; then she shuddered and bounded back; then she advanced again, passed her head outside the sash, writhed her body, and with muscles quivering, and eyes fixed, she contemplated the drama which was being enacted on the esplanade. I leave it to be imagined what sensations she experienced during this long combat, which compromised the head she loved above all expression. Twenty times she tried to scream, but her emotion made her dumb; twenty times she wished to shut her eyes and to withdraw; but a power of attraction, more energetic than her will, held her riveted to that place.

Bertrand is struck—he falls!

Immediately the nerves of Laura distended—she was hurt at heart—she sank down on the floor! Catharine ran to her aid.

* * * * * * * * * *

The next night, between eleven o'clock and midnight, Laura de Kerskoën, lady of Vornadeck Manor, enveloped from head to foot in a dark mantle, stealthily crossed the court of honor of the castle, proceeding direct to the fortress. A sentinel was in the sentry-box at the entrance, but he had got a soporific, and he slept profoundly.

Laura penetrated into the tower, mounted the first flight, and drawing a large key from her corset, opened, after many difficulties, the door of a chamber of triangular form. This chamber is the prison of Bertrand.

Chained to a block of stone, the young man was suffering from a violent fever, occasioned by the wound he had received on the shoulder.

"Who is there?" asked he sadly.

The young lady uncovered the lamp which she had concealed under her mantle, and knelt by his side.

"Laura! Is it a dream?"

"Alas, poor Bertrand!"

"But what! I do not dream! It is you, really you! Oh, approach!—yet—yet—there—that I may touch your clothes, and respire your breath! My God, yes, it is she—it is my Laura—"

"Dear Bertrand, what a position you are in!"—

"Do not pity me, Laura, good angel, adored idol! I am happy since you have given me this proof of love. Now I will confront the worst tortures without a murmur."

"What do you say about tortures, friend? I have come to deliver you."

The prisoner smiled bitterly.

"Oh!" said he, exhibiting the irons, with which he was bound.

"Are you too feeble to sustain yourself?"

"How is that?"

"Wait," said Laura, handing him a little file.

A flush of joy brightened the pale countenance of Bertrand.

"But after?" said he.

"After! Fear nothing."

And with her tiny fingers the charming girl began to file the chain which riveted her lover to the wall.

This work was slow and painful; the white hands of Laura were stained with blood. But the courage of love animated her—that courage which has rendered so many women famous by their heroism—and at the end of an hour the chain was sawed.

"Now, let us hasten!" said she.

The hope of liberty gave strength to the captive; they descended the steps of the fortress until they arrived at the ground floor; here was a large square, in the centre of which was a well.

"Come," said the lady, pointing to the brink of the well, "we must part here. A few feet above the margin of this well a ladder is concealed, and lower down is a subterranean passage, which will conduct you to the northern flank of the mountain. Here is the stolen key of the postern; but swear on your honor that you will never reveal the secret which I have confided to you."

"Alas," said the young man in a plaintive tone, "I no longer feel any wish to leave, I would rather die!"

"Go, friend!"

"Without you existence—"

"Bertrand, I will never be anybody's, but yours. Take this ring; it is one bequeathed me by my dear mother—let it be the pledge of our betrothal!"

The young man took the ring, and pressed it to his lips.

"Come, let us separate, time presses," said Laura, her eyes filling with tears.

Aided by his mistress, Bertrand descended into the well, put his foot on the first step of the ladder, and bid the young lady adieu. But she stooped down, and kissed his forehead.

"Oh, you will be mine, my well-beloved!" exclaimed the prisoner with transport, and holding in his left hand the lantern which Laura had given him, he proceeded down in to the depths of the abyss.

By degrees the sound of his step faded away, and when it had ceased to resound on the humid stairs, the niece of William de la Roche stood up, saying:

"Blessed be my merciful patroness! Bertrand is saved!"

A few minutes after Laura de Kerskoën, Countess of Vornadeck, returned to her apartment without having been remarked.

CHAPTER IX.

BEFORE THE DEPARTURE.

A MONTH had passed after the events we have just related. Laura is at the window, where we have already seen her—she is expecting something. A pigeon arrives, its white plumage recalls our gentle messenger of love. In a word, it is Addresse; she brings a letter.

This letter informs her that Bertrand is safe, recovered from his wounds, that he proposes to carry her away, and wishes her to feign love for Viscount de Ganay, and declare to him that she has made a vow not to contract any engagement until she has attained her twentieth year; in a word, to determine him to adjourn, until his return from Canada, their betrothal, which was to have taken place next day.

After having read and re-read this note several times, she shed sweet tears—Laura proceeded to the armory. The equerry promenaded, absorbed in thought, and agitated by gloomy presentiments.

"You seem very sad," said the young lady, in her most agreeable tone; "has any misfortune befallen you?"

"Ah, mademoiselle," replied the viscount, "yes, a great misfortune! so great that I despair of being able to bear it."

"Indeed! should I be indiscreet in asking what is the cause of this deep affliction?"

"Then, are you not grieved yourself?"

"Me! Holy Virgin! yes, much grieved. There is no use in my saying that I can reconcile myself to the idea of his departure, and——"

"And——" exclaimed John.

Laura lowered her long eye-lashes with a gesture of modesty, but without making any reply.

"Do you regret only the Marquis de la Roche?" insinuated the equerry, while a prey to the most piognant emotion.

"Do you think I would forget my friends, Master John?" replied the lover of Bertrand, accompanying this question with so incendiary a glance that the poor viscount believed himself loved, and felt disposed to throw himself at the feet of the siren.

"But," said he, with a trembling voice, "do you number me among your friends?"

"What! Is it you that ask me such a question; you who enjoy the consideration of Monsiegneur de la Roche; you who have so recently saved this chateau; you——ah, it is too bad, John, to doubt me so!"

A liquid pearl, which sparkled at the corner of her eye, crowned this series of tender reproaches, already expressed by the significant emphasis which she impressed on her words.

Women possess a marvelous talent for simulating the sentiments which they do not experience. They are often even more eloquent in affecting passion than under its real influence.

Is it surprising, then, that the viscount permitted himself to fall into a snare thus strewed with roses.

"What! Is it true?" exclaimed he, with warmth. "I did deceive myself. You love me, Laura! You partake of the passion which overwhelms me, and you——Oh! joy makes me silly, I have been so long hoping for that avowal. Oh! *mon Dieu*, give me the necessary strength to bear such delight!"

He wished to seize the hand of Laura, and kiss it, but she resisted, gently smiling.

"Fie! The naughty chevalier will not put faith in the attachment of his best friends! You deserve, Master John, that for your pains I should burn the knot I have platted for your sword."

"A sword-knot! Ah, Laura, your kindness overwhelms me!"

"A sword-knot which I have here, and which I will attach myself, if you will permit me, to the guard of your rapier. Henceforth be less suspicious, or I may get vexed for good. But I have a request to make of you."

"Of me——a request! Oh, speak; be assured that I will do all in my power to prove myself worthy of the first mark of confidence you have deigned to accord me. Yes," pursued he, "ask of me my life, I shall be happy to offer it to you."

His complexion, usually pale, was suffused with an incarnate blush; his voice had sympathetic intonations; all in him exhaling the perfume of true love profoundly felt. The vanity of Laura was flattered by this triumph; but her heart was too profusely occupied to be moved by contact even with so ardent a passion.

"What I am to request of you would cost you much," replied she. "However, I will not take advantage of your kindness, to elicit in advance a pledge for which you would perhaps afterwards reproach yourself."

"No, no," interrupted De Ganay, with vehemence; "no! whatever you order, I swear by the guard of my sword to execute faithfully."

The lover of Bertrand could not repress a smile of satisfaction in seeing him fall into the net which she had so adroitly set for him.

"I fear you may repent of this precipitation," she objected again.

"Fear nothing; speak."

"Master John, my uncle wishes that we be betrothed to-morrow."

"And this is my sweetest aspiration."

"This is what I doubted."

"You——"

"Alas, sir, I have promised not to contract any engagement before I am twenty years, and I am not yet eighteen, do you know."

"And this promise," stammered De Ganay, plunged in the horror of disappointment.

"I have made to a person dearer to me than existence."

In pronouncing these words in a faltering tone, Laura rumpled the corner of her handkerchief.

"That your wish may be granted," said the young man, after having paused a moment to conceal the anguish which rent his heart. Then he added:

"A vow is sacred; I will respect vows in respecting my own. But, Laura, will you be faithful?"

"Oh, certainly," said the niece of the marquis, continuing mentally her perfidious falsehood. "Yes; I will be faithful to my last breath. To Bertrand," murmured she in an undertone.

"Ah, ah, my young friends, a tender romance of love!" interposed William de la Roche, who happened to be passing at the moment.

Laura availed herself of the opportunity to run away like a frightened hind.

Twenty-four hours after this conversation, a cavalcade, composed of ten armed men, a dominican, and two women, mounted on palfreys, left the manor of De la Roche.

It was Laura de Kerskoën, who set out for the capital of Blesois, where she was to remain in a convent until the end of the expedition of her uncle.

Standing at the summit of the fortress, John de Ganay followed for a long distance with his eyes the cavalcade, which winded about the flank of the mountain.

The equerry hoped that one of the women would turn about and beckon to him, but no one did, and when the two amazons, preceded by their escort, disappeared behind the massive trees, John crossed his arms sadly on his breast and exclaimed:

"Great God! has Laura deceived me—does she not love me?"

PART I.

AT SEA.

CHAPTER I.

GUYONNE, THE FISHERWOMAN.

AT some distance from the chateau of De la Roche, on the sea-coast, rose a cabin of a miserable and desolate appearance. Stones, cemented with slimy clay, formed its material, and it was rudely thatched with straw. Two small windows, glazed with panes of oiled paper, admitted to the interior a glimmering light. Before the cabin extended a small kitchen garden, generally but badly cultivated.

This was the habitation of Perrin, the fisherman, of his son Yvon, and of his step-daughter Guyonne, the fisherwoman.

One night, at the end of May, of the year 1598, Perrin the fisherman, an old man of sixty, but still robust, notwithstanding his wrinkles and silvered hair, sat on a ledge of stone at the door of the hut, repairing a net that was much damaged.

The fisherman was sad, anxiety and despair marked his countenance, which was bronzed by the heat and inclemency of the season.

Frequently he gave a sad look towards the chateau; then a tear glistened in the corner of his eye; he allowed the thread to fall, and crossing his arms on his breast, had a profound revery. He soon resumed his work, however, uttering some unintelligible words.

Suddenly a young woman appeared at the corner of the thicket, carrying on her head a wicker basket.

The old man uttered a cry of satisfaction.

"Well, Guyonne?"

"Console yourself, my father," replied the woman. "Yvon will be liberated, if it please God to second my project," added she, mentally.

"Liberated—my Yvon liberated!" said the fisherman, with a passionate tone. "Oh, my daughter! Guyonne, dear child, approach me, that I may embrace you."

"Good father," said she, abandoning her cheeks to the caresses of the old man.

"But," said the latter, "you have then seen him? You have spoken to him? The Marquis de la Roche has pardoned him, has he not? Oh, I will pray to our Lady of the holy Saviour to favor the enterprise——"

"Listen, my father," gravely interrupted Guyonne, "I no not wish to deceive you. I have not seen Yvon."

"What do you say?"

"No, I have not seen him. I could not see him. He is at St. Malo, since this morning."

"At St. Malo?"

"At St. Malo, with all the other prisoners, who are to embark to-morrow for New France."

"Then," said Perrin, terrified by this news, "our merciful Marquis de la Roche has promised him to you——"

"Monseigneur de la Roche is gone himself, with his squerry. They have escorted the captives."

The old man grew pale, and staggered.

"Fear not," said Guyonne, "I will surely save Yvon; I swear it to you."

"Ah!" exclaimed the fisherman, "can you trifle with me in this way, my daughter? I have never done you any harm, and still you reassure me only to plunge me deeper and deeper in affliction."

"I have told you, and I now repeat, that I will save him," exclaimed she, in a persuasive tone; and Perrin felt his hope revived.

"How? What is your project?" objected he still.

"That's my business. Confide in me, my father; I will keep my word. Before twelve hours Yvon will be here; but it will be necessary to place you under the protection of the Duke de Mercœur. Now, give me your benediction, for never again, perhaps, shall we see each other."

Whether it was that he did not hear this last phrase, or that he did not understand its meaning, Perrin continued interrogatively:

"What! in twelve hours I shall have recovered my brave Yvon; are you sure, Guyonne?"

"As sure as one can be. But time presses; give me your benediction, my father," replied she, kneeling at the feet of the old man.

"Where do you want to go?"

"To St. Malo—to Yvon. Pray to the Almighty to second my designs."

"Go, my daughter," said the fisherman, extending his hands over Guyonne. "Go, may God aid you. For my part, I commit all to your courage and prudence. Ah! if you succeed in saving Yvon, I cannot live long enough to prove to you my gratitude."

Standing up again, Guyonne threw herself into the arms of the old man; then, after having exchanged with him a few words more, she proceeded towards the sea-coast, detached the cable of a small boat, jumped lightly into it, and rowed off, making a sign of adieu to her father.

The bay, usually ruffled and foaming, was this evening as level as glass. No breeze disturbed its tranquil surface, illuminated by the last rays of the setting sun.

Leaning on her oars, Guyonne struck the wave with the skill of an accomplished waterman. Her little boat made a slight furrow in the sea, unrolling a ribbon of foam.

Miss Guyonne was a strong and handsome woman. It is impossible to imagine a more magnificent combination of masculine forms united to feminine graces. Her head, admirable in expression, surmounted a bust richly proportioned, and of attractive appearance. Her thick black hair floated on her shoulders in silken ringlets, rendering her fine countenance a perfect oval. The forehead high and large, the eyebrows well defined, the nose somewhat hooked, and, above all, the vivacity of Guyonne's eyes, denoted a resolute and energetic character. Notwithstanding her tall figure and masculine organization, her hands were small, though bronzed by hard work; her feet comparatively small. If her eagle glance repressed the rash, the amenity of her manners, the touching sweetness of her voice, seduced those whom she treated as friends. Proud towards the disdainful, submissive without humility to her superiors, affable to equals, Guyonne displayed towards her relatives a complete self-abnegation. Physical and moral strength, superior material attraction, amiability, ingenuity, chastity —such was the woman. Far from being a drawback, her herculean stature imparted an additional charm to her person, when by acquaintance one was enabled to appreciate the rare qualities which adorned her.

Miss Guyonne was twenty-five years of age. She was supposed to be the daughter of a coaster, who it was thought perished in a shipwreck on the coast of Newfoundland, and of a woman who had married Perrin for her second husband. This woman died on having given birth to Yvon. The fisherman contracted an affection for his own child which amounted to idolatry. He reared him with all the care which his precarious condition permitted. But Yvon, as often happens, did not repay the affection of his father. Thoughtless and indolent, he was soon numbered amongst the worst boys in the neighborhood.

One morning he disappeared, and remained several years absent. This flight proved almost fatal to Perrin. Such was his grief, that he attempted suicide; but Guyonne prevented him. Yvon, who had gone to the war, returned suddenly as he had left, and the joy which his return caused to the old fisherman, was also well-nigh proving fatal to the latter. Alas! this joy was not of long duration, for Yvon, whose inherent slothfulness had inclined him to the life of a soldier, and who saw in the Marquis de la Roche an enemy to the Catholic religion, enlisted in a troop of bandits, in the pay of the Duke de Mercœur.

Having taken part in the attack on the Chateau de la Roche, he was taken prisoner, with all of his companions, who had escaped the missiles of the garrison. The marquis, who was then recruiting men for the expedition which he had projected, asked and obtained permission to transport his captives to the colony of New France, most of them being fugitives from justice, or malefactors. Master Yvon was but little reconciled to the fate that awaited him. A voyage of twelve or fifteen hundred leagues, after that an unlimited practice at the hatchet, the spade, and the hoe, had but little charm for his imagination. Knowing that his father had formerly rendered service to the Marquis de la Roche, he informed Perrin of his situation, and begged of him to solicit his pardon. Certainly there was no need of supplicating the fisherman. At the news that his well-beloved son was about to be torn from him, he hastened to the chateau, and William de la Roche welcomed him with a cordiality which he was little in the habit of evincing towards his vassals. But as soon as the old man let him know the object of his visit, he lowered his eyebrows, and drily replied, that Yvon should share the punishment of his accomplices.

The fisherman returned heart-broken to his cabin. The attentive solicitude of Guyonne was needed to allay the bitterness of his grief, and to re-animate the hope of his heart.

"All is not lost," said she; "Dame Catharine loves me like a mother. You are aware that she is the nurse of our young lady, Laura de Kerskoën, and has great influence on the Marquis de la Roche. Let me speak to her; perhaps with her aid we may succeed in softening the marquis."

Like all who aspire to the realization of a wish, Perrin accepted this persuasion, and Guyonne proceeded towards the manor.

Dame Catharine, quite sad after the departure of her young mistress, wept with Guyonne, and finally promised to intercede with the Marquis de la Roche.

William was inexorable; such was his iron character that never he would modify a resolution once made. He made this inflexibility his point of honor.

"All I can do for you, my girl," said the nurse, "is to contrive an interview with this poor Yvon, when he goes to St. Malo. Viscount de Ganay has charge of the prisoners; he will not refuse to oblige us. I will have a talk with him; return to-morrow."

Guyonne spent the night thinking and praying; the dawn found her prostrated before the grave of her mother.

She was still melancholy; but the veil of anxiety which had covered her face for some days had disappeared.

An inconceivable determination germinated in the brain of the fisherwoman. She went up to the chateau.

"They are in route for St. Malo, and are to embark to-morrow, my child," said the old woman.

"Have you succeeded?"

"You can see him to-night by presenting this note to the sentinel."

"Oh, thank you, thank you, Dame Catharine! May God recompense you."

Guyonne descended the mountain running. We have already narrated the conversation which she had with her stepfather on her return.

Now, we will resume the thread of our narrative, and follow the young girl to St. Malo.

The curfew had not yet sounded, when she entered the port of St. Malo, and the stars were still to be seen in the firmament. Guyonne had no difficulty in finding the prison of the captives, for the streets were crowded with persons, engaged in discussing the probable chances of the La Roche expedition.

The highwaymen were confined in an old convent, situated at the south of the city. A sentry walked up and down before the door, musket in hand.

"Can I speak to the sergeant of the guard?" inquired Guyonne anxiously.

"To the sergeant of the guard?" replied the soldier; "yes, indeed, my pretty pullet. And what is the business of the sergeant of the guard?"

"I have a note for him."

"A note! By the hoofs of Beelzebub, what a fortunate mortal is our sergeant! Come here under this cloak, my angel."

While saying these words, the sentry advanced to put his arms around the waist of Guyonne; but the latter seized him by the middle, brought him to the ground like a feather, and dashed him against the wall of the monastery.

When the soldier got up he swore at her, and began to repeat his impudent familiarities, when the gate opened to make way for John de Ganay.

"Ah, master, it was heaven that sent you!" said Guyonne to the equerry.

"What do you wish?"

"Dame Catharine—" commenced the young girl.

"Well, my girl, I understand what you want," said the viscount with interest. "You are the sister——"

"Of Yvon, master."

"Enter, I will order that you be conducted to him."

After having addressed a few words to the commandant of the station, John de Ganay went out again.

"Follow me," said the sergeant to the young girl.

At the head of the stair-case, there extended a long corridor, whose sonorous flags re-echoed the noise of the steps, and they halted at a low door.

"Number 40," said the sergeant, "it is here."

He drew a bolt, laid the resin torch which lighted them, on the table, and retired observing, "In an hour I will come for you."

During this time Guyonne had precipitated herself into the arms of Yvon.

"Tell me, dear brother," murmured the young girl, after these warm greetings were over, "don't you long for liberty?"

"Yes, I should die before reaching that infernal country, where, it is said, nothing is to be got, but bruises and hard knocks."

"I am resolved to deliver you myself."

"You?"

"On one condition."

"One condition? speak; I subscribe to all in order that I may not be exiled to that cursed land of New France."

"If you will swear not to grieve our old father in future—"

"But what is your plan?"

"You will know it in due time."

"I make the vow you exact, Guyonne."

"Mark you, Yvon!" said the young girl, her eyes moist with joy. "Now," added she, "let us exchange our clothes. You will take my gown and mantle, and I will take your overcoat and pantaloons!"

"And you will remain a prisoner in my place!"

"Certainly," replied she with a smile.

"Have you thought of what you are saying?"

"Oh yes; I thought of it all last night at the grave of our mother; it was she that suggested to me this stratagem."

"Kind heart!" said the young man, embracing her; "but do not think that I would agree—."

"Yvon, think of your father; he can not live without you."

"No, no, my sister; I will not be guilty of such cowardice. You don't know what sort of brigands these troopers are, with whom I have been condemned."

"No matter!"

"What matter!" but you would be carried off with them."

"Child, do you forget that the Marquis de la Roche has refused to embark a single woman on his vessel?"

"To-morrow, I will declare my sex, and I shall be set at liberty."

This reasoning seemed very plausible; the love of liberty was so strong in his breast that he soon permitted himself to be convinced.

The two young persons were pretty nearly of the same height. They exchanged their costume, and Guyonne said to her brother while arranging her bonnet on his head:

"When the sergeant comes for you, pretend to cry, and hold this handkerchief to your face, in order that he may not remark the change. Once outside the monastery, you will easily get to the shore, where I have moored our boat."

"I understand," said Yvon; "but you?"

"Don't fear in the least. I shall know, with the aid of the Holy Virgin, how to get myself out of the scrape."

All passed as the noble girl had predicted. Yvon left the convent without the least suspicion of fraud, and when the outer door closed, grating on its hinges, Guyonne fell on her knees, exclaiming:

"I have saved my father and my brother! Lord, hallowed be thy name, on earth as it is in heaven!"

CHAPTER II.

THE EMBARKMENT.

At the first light of dawn the morning watch-bell sounded, and soon the prisoners were drawn up in two ranks in the yard of the monastery, in order to undergo an inspection. This band of persons belonged to all nationalities, and each wore his native costume, or at least the most characteristic part of it, forming a strange and picturesque spectacle.

Here stood the portly German with his bland face, flanked on the right by a slim Spaniard, dry, of an olive complexion; on the left by a gigantic, fat, red-faced Englishman, covered with a red helmet. There one distinguished a Swiss armed to the teeth, elbowing a Langudocian with a swaggering air, and a rough halberdier; further on was observed the slouched hat of the Italian, the green helmet of the mountaineer, the streaked doublet of the Tyrolean, the crafty snout of the Norman, the rubicund and jovial face of the Bourguignon. In short, it was a pell-mell of contrasts, an amalgam of heterogenities, a profusion of human antitheses, a variety of portraits of which no description could give any adequate idea. There was, however, one point of similarity between all—audacity was engraven on their countenances in indelible characters. With this exception, the troopers differed as much in their moral as in their physical characteristics.

A subaltern officer called the roll; no one was found absent, and as the officer terminated his report, William de la Roche, accompanied by John de Ganay, a mariner and a numerous suit entered the yard of the convent.

This seaman was forty years; his disposition was as hardened as his countenance; one forgot the Liliputian form nature had given him as if with regret; for his gray eye sparkled, his tapering face, his dejected chin, his prominent upper-lip, his nose, like the beak of a raven, gave him the grotesque air of a bird of prey.

He was clad with sordid niggardliness, with a straw hat pitched and tarred, a jacket torn almost to ribbons, and a narrow *broeck*. His foot-ware consisted of a pair of boots pieced at every seam. Rapacity flowing into the mould of avarice was clearly pourtrayed in this man; but, notwithstanding his physiognomy, the haughty Marquis de la Roche treated him with particular deference, as may be seen from the following dialogue:

"What think you of these fellows, Mr. Pilot?"

"Humph!" replied the sailor, "sad manure to enrich the earth."

"Do you think they will become acclimated?"

"Acclimated! These cattle will become acclimated anywhere, when they get sufficient of the leather thong."

"Then you don't approve of the cargo which chance has confided to me?"

"Humph! to tell the truth, I should have preferred twenty rustics from Brittany to the whole lot."

"Then you disapprove of my choice?"

"I disapprove nothing; you question me, I answer."

De la Roche, hurt by the tone of this impertinence, took a long step to the rear, but his interlocutor did not observe his gesture.

"Humph!" said he, pinching his nose, a movement which with him spoke volumes, "I believe the wind is veering to the southeast or northeast. It is necessary for us to hasten, if we wish to profit by the breeze in leaving port."

"Then let the clothes be distributed to these people," said the marquis in a loud tone.

Immediately chests, filled with clothing, were brought into the yard, and a sub-officer presented to each of the condemned a full suit of uniform.

This uniform consisted of a bonnet, a smock-frock, and pantaloons, all of brown linen, and marked with a figure, rudely worked.

In losing their liberty, the transports also lost their names; they became simply this or that number.

It was now about six o'clock in the morning.

A large animated crowd encumbered the streets of St. Malo, anxious to be present at the embarkment of the adventurers. On the balconies, at the windows, and even on the tops of the houses, were to be seen groups of the curious. It was no slight event in 1598 to witness the departure of a ship for America. Fifty years had scarcely passed since Cartier had weighed anchor in the same port to explore the part of the great American continent known as Newfoundland, had discovered St. Lawrence, and on their return from their different voyages the companions of the immortal navigator related so many wonders of the magnificent country of Canada that everybody wished to see those who were destined to civilize it. Thus every available place on their way was crowded; but it was particularly at the quays that the multitude pressed in tumultuous waves.

Among the transports there was one who attracted particular attention. The contrast between him and the one to whom he was chained, contributed powerfully to exhibit the nobleness of his behavior, and the manly beauty of his countenance.

"But, St. Theresa, how genteel he is," murmured a piquant Brittanian. "Is it not a shame, Martha, to carry so brave a youth beyond the ocean?"

"Ah, ma'm! yes, indeed; he is far too handsome to be beside these nasty bears who look as if they had just made their escape from hell."

"It seems as if an angel had been chained to a demon."

"Clear the dock!" ordered a cavalier, driving back the multitude with his lance.

Like a drop of water falling on burning charcoal, this little incident happily cooled the ardor of the two young women who had already become excited at the sight of the handsome transport.

When the column debouched on the esplanade, as we have described, a salvo of artillery saluted their arrival. The prisoners entered the inclosure prepared, uncovering their heads and kneeling. Soon after appeared a procession of monks, preceding a dais under which the Bishop of Rennes piously advanced—having been called upon to bless the departure of the adventurers.

The prelate mounted the steps of the altar, and said mass, which was heard with profound attention. Never was a ceremony more majestic, or more imposing, when in presence of this vast multitude, of this tranquil sea, of which the limits were lost in the azure of the celestial vault, the old gray-haired man in a voice, sympathetic and solemn, implored the divine assistance for the success of the enterprise, the audience feeling themselves moved even to tears.

The highwaymen themselves bowed the head, as Clovis had done in former times at the command of St. Remie.

William de la Roche, the pilot, and several sailors communicated, and received the consecrated host at the hand of the venerable prelate.

An observer remarked that not only did the equerry, John de Ganay, not take any part in the service, but also that he did not assist at the mass.

It is useless to conceal any longer, what my sagacious reader has already divined. Viscount de Ganay had embraced the doctrines of the reformed religion. If he did not dare to avow his faith at this epoch, when the abjuration of Henry IV. had fallen like an anathema on the Calvinists, John remained faithful to the doctrines of his convictions, and secretly conformed to the rites which he could not practice in public. It was easy for him to retire where there was such a multitude.

Mass being over, the embarkment proceeded.

The two ships Castor and Erable were moored at some hundreds of yards from the shore. In less than twenty minutes the passengers were transferred on board.

A discharge of cannon gave the signal for departure.

On the Castor were William de la Roche-Gommard, Governor-General of Canada; John Viscount de Ganay, his equerry; Alexis Chedotel, pilot-lockman; Guyonne, the fisherwoman, and a considerable number of future colonists.—

CHAPTER III.

THE CASTOR.

Even at the present day, wonderful as are the improvements made in the art of navigation, it is not without a sort of indefinable dread that we undertake a voyage across the Ocean; although the enormous and magnificent ships which literally furrow the seas offer almost as much security and accommodation as our houses and chateaux. What gigantic progress navigation has made during four centuries! What a difference between these immense vessels which are constructed at present, and those which then ventured intrepidly in search of unknown lands! When one remembers that it was with three vessels, of which two were *without decks*, and of which the third was one of only two hundred tons burden, that Columbus sailed from Palos the 1st of August, 1492, to discover America the 12th of October of the same year; when one bears in mind that it was with two miserable schooners of sixty tons burden that Cartier crossed the Atlantic, to be the first to explore the Gulf of St. Lawrence, Labrador, Newfoundland, etc.; when we bear in mind that it was with two vessels nearly similar, that the successors of these great men have achieved the discovery of the New World, how much does our admiration increase for the immortal regenerators of America!

The Castor, which bore William de la Roche and the greater part of the heroes to Acadia, was so small that a contemporary affirms that from the cords of the gunwale one could dip his hands into the sea. The capacity of the Castor was estimated at a hundred tons. For the rest, the vessel was handsome, solid at bottom, a fast sailor, and bearing her masts proudly, firm as steel, flexible as whalebone. She contained a hold, a steerage, and two cabins. The hold contained the provisions and munitions of war. In the steerage were packed the transports. The forward cabin had for a host the Marquis William de la Roche, the Viscount de Ganay, the pilot-lockman, Alexis Chetodel, and some others. The cabin of the prow was occupied by the sailors.

When she left the harbor of St. Malo, the Castor had on board ninety-two men, including the Governor-General of Canada, his staff, and some cadets from noble families.

Several transports had obtained permission from the marquis to remain on deck, in order to contemplate as long as possible the shores of that beautiful France, which they quitted, perhaps, forever. The others had descended to the steerage, so that they should not interrupt the movements of the sailors.

All, however, would have wished to enjoy the privilege accorded only to a few, for however vicious was their nature, however coarse their appetites, however hardened by the fluctuations of fortune, they were profoundly grieved by the thought of this tedious voyage so far from their country.

It is said that the love of place is a prejudice; but, oh, let us admit that it is a magnificent one, superior, in our opinion, to the most noble affections.

And the proof is that a man sometimes leaves his parents without regret; that he parts with his wife and children without remorse; that he will resist the storms of adversity as the rock does the fury of the tempest; that the loss of his property, of persons that are dear to him, does not afflict him; but that he will grieve and sob like a woman if he is forced to bid an eternal adieu to his country.

Guyonne inscribed under the name of Yvon, number 40, enjoyed the advantage accorded only to a small number of her companions.

Standing at the foot of the mainmast, she saw the shores of her adored Brittany fading gradually like a mist, whilst the sun shed its golden rays on the harbor of St. Malo, and the propitious wind filled the sails of the Castor.

Who could tell what were the thoughts of Guoynne? for, from time to time, a silent tear coursed along her cheek, and her head drooped sadly on her breast.

Noble girl, had she calculated too much on her courage, and already reproached herself with her heroic sacrifice?

No; Guyonne was as strong in mind as she was in body; the perils of her situation did not frighten her; the fate reserved for herself gave her but little anxiety; but she thought of the tomb of her dear mother; that tomb she used to watch with solicitude, and which she adorned daily with new flowers, and upon which the briars and thorns would now soon grow; she thought of her old father, who was going to be deprived of her attentive cares; of her young brother, without a guide to direct him over the sand-banks of life.

Poor Guyonne thought of her friends, of the evening song, of the lowing of her heifer, which she was to hear no more; of the chapel of the village, of her little chamber, to which, perchance, she would never return. Then she thought of—I know not what—of what is nothing, and what is all.

In front of her, leaning against the mizzen-mast, John de Ganay seemed also absorbed in profound meditation.

His reflections were full of bitterness. Had he not broken the tie which attached him to happiness? and did not each knot sailed by the Castor bear him farther and farther from her whom he loved?

Besides, a strange presentiment tortured the mind of the viscount. Notwithstanding the pledges of tenderness which he had received from Laura, he doubted whether she would ever redeem them.

All attempts to banish these painful suspicions were fruitless; they returned incessantly and overwhelmed him like a nightmare.

John remained six consecutive hours in this situation, motionless, and insensible to all that surrounded him. But when the earth is completely veiled, the equerry turns his attention to the prow of the vessel.

He perceived the pretended Yvon, who had not moved a pace since she got on board, but tried to pierce the horizon to distinguish a line that still indicated her country.

The serene beauty of the young man, his intelligent physiognomy, the softness of his features, the calmness of his demeanor, surprised the equerry to the extent of awakening him from his reverie.

He wondered by what chance this handsome youth found himself included among the condemned, when Chedotel, who ordered a change of tack, precipitated himself rudely from the forecastle on deck, and struck a violent blow with his telescope on the head of the spurious Yvon.

"Be off, you abortion of the devil!"

Stunned with the violence of the blow, the young girl obeyed slowly.

The pilot, furious, pushed her with such rudeness that she fell-on a large iron cable and cut her face.

"Naph" said Chedotel, continuing to give his orders.

This act of brutality revolted John de Ganay. He proceeded to reprimand the pilot severely, when he remembered that the marquis had invested Chedotel with full powers during the voyage. Repressing his anger, he bent down to afford assistance to the wounded, who rose with her face covered with blood.

"Do you wish me to call the surgeon?" said he, compassionately.

"Oh no, thank you, monseigneur; a little salt water will be sufficient to dry up these scratches."

The gentleness of this answer increased the interest which the equerry felt for the transport.

Drawing from his doublet a silk handkerchief, he presented it to her, saying:

"Wipe yourself with this. I will send for anything you want."

Guyonne, moved by a new and inexpressible sentiment, did not dare to accept.

"Take it," said the viscount, putting the handkerchief into her hand.

"Oh, monseigneur!" said the young girl.

"Well, you may speak of gratitude another time. Now, conform to my will."

The remedy of Guyonne had all the desired effect, save that there remained a few blue marks, she appeared more charming and fresher than before.

Her coarse uniform of gray linen, enhanced by contrast the fairness of her complexion.

The viscount could not repress a gesture of admiration.

"What is your name?" asked he, leaning against the side of the bulwark.

"Yvon, at your service, monseigneur," replied she, after some hesitation.

"Yvon! I heard that name pronounced before. Yvon! whose vassal were you?"

"Monseigneur de la Roche's."

"Ah, ah! In fact, I remember. Your father is a fisherman."

"A fisherman," repeated she, affirmatively.

"And what age are you?"

"I shall be twenty-five at Candlemas."

"Twenty-five years! You seem to be scarcely seventeen."

"I don't know how to lie, monseigneur."

"But you were with the bandits who assailed the chateau?"

The young girl stammered an unintelligible phrase.

"And you have a sister?" continued John de Ganay.

The reply of Guyonne was rendered inaudible by the clock of the Castor, which announced dinner.

The viscount parted immediately from his *protege* to proceed to the front cabin, where were already united the Marquis de la Roche, the pilot Chedotel, and the principal officers of the ship.

As to the step-daughter of Perrin, although she had taken no kind of food since the previous evening, she felt too much overwhelmed with grief to care to eat, and she remained on deck.

CHAPTER IV.

THE STORM.

TOWARDS the evening of the same day, Chedotel promenaded with precipitate step on the deck. His angular and coarse features were more repulsive than ever; he tormented his nose with his hooked nails with an inconceivable perseverance, and sounds frequently escaped from his throat which it would be difficult to translate.

At every instant the eyes of the pilot were attracted towards the sky, and he stamped with his feet like a man who foresaw danger without finding any means of avoiding it.

However, nothing in the atmosphere seemed to announce any change; the sun set illuminating the waters of the bay with his rays, and the wind whistled with unaltered equality.

The Castor cut the waves as rapidly as a bird, and to all others than an experienced mariner the night seemed destined to be as calm and delightful as the day had been.

All the convicts were shut up in the steerage; when the hatchway was opened a confused hum was heard as from a beehive. Lying about the masts, the sailors chatted, slept, and played at dominoes.

John de Ganay was seated on the platform of the ship, curiously examining the foaming of the waves as they broke, and darted liquid pearls at the flanks of the Castor.

The Marquis de la Roche had not quitted the cabin since dinner.

Suddenly he proceeded on deck and approached Chedotel.

"Well, Master Pilot, fine weather isn't it? God has blessed our expedition."

"Humph! fine weather—humph!"

"You——"

Chedotel, whose eyes were attentively fixed on the horizon, suddenly interrupted the marquis.

"Take in sail!"

"What's the matter?" said the marquis, astonished at this order, of which he understood the signification, but which, he thought, was not prompted by any apparent cause.

The sun had extinguished its last rays in the sea; one could remark that its disk had a copper hue.

"Tack to windward!" cried Chedotel, with a piercing voice.

The change of course had scarcely been effected when a violent blast whistled in the rigging of the Castor.

Soon after a rolling was heard like that of distant thunder, and the sky was streaked with sombre clouds.

All the sailors had suspended their pastime to run to the rudder, some to the sail-yards, some to the capstan.

"Furl the sails! furl all!" thundered the speaking trumpet of the pilot.

But before the manœuvre was executed, a second swell assailed the Castor, and gave her such a push to the larboard that the lower rigging plunged deep into the water.

This unexpected seesaw precipitated the marquis against the poop.

The works of the Castor cracked with a horrible clatter.

"Return, monsieur!" said Chedotel to the marquis; "return to your cabin, this is not your place."

In saying this, the pilot was no longer that man of astute and sulky countenance, whom we have presented to the reader: he became the mariner in his sphere, the mariner who measured his strength with that of infuriated nature, and recognized no other counselor than his eye, no other master than his own will.

On land the human being rarely forgets his character; at sea he debases or exalts it according to circumstances.

Lazy, drunken, libertine, vile, the sailor is, however, susceptible of accomplishing prodigies of labor, endurance, nobleness.

The commander of a ship, though he may be a stupid brute in calm weather, becomes a genius in a storm. His voice dominates even that of the tempest, his will controls the rage of the elements, and his person becomes incarnate with new life to struggle against the three formidable enemies—fire, air, and water!

Like an artist seized with inspiration, Chetodel, his speaking trumpet in one hand his telescope in the other, had grown ten inches taller.

The sea swelled more and more. The waves, high as mountains and fierce as unchained tigresses, rushed tumultuously against the carene and the gunwale. The squalls succeeded each other with frightful rapidity. It was said that the Castor danced a sort of fairy dance on the abyss. Now, she mounted on the extremity of an immense wave, and anon she plunged into a shroud of waves, nothing around her than humid plics; then, rushing above the water, panting, she freed herself from her aquatic winding sheet, and recommenced, after encountering a thousand perils, her checquered course.

Fortunately all her sails were closely reefed; four robust men had charge of the rudder, and Chetodel firm at his post directed the ship with the ease of a skilful equerry who dashes his charger through the middle of ravines, fords, and precipices.

The sailors forgot the danger of the situation in admiring the extraordinary coolness of the pilot.

The storm continued to rage with alarming obstinacy. It was to be feared that the Castor would strike against one of those numerous sand-banks with which the bay abounds.

Night approached apace, and the convicts in the steerage, with the exception of a very small number, surrendered themselves to all the transports of terror, when a terrible cry brought their anguish to a climax.

"Fire! fire!"

Almost at the same moment John de Ganay appeared at the top of the steps which descended into the interior of the Castor.

"Ten men with good-will!" asked he.

More than twenty precipitated themselves on the steps of the ladder.

The viscount made his choice rapidly, and ordered those selected to mount and close the panel.

In executing all this, he spent less time than we can describe it in.

The fire had originated in the kitchen, and already it was completely enveloped in flames when the convicts arrived on deck.

The wind redoubled its impetuosity.

The Castor flew over the foaming waves with such rolling and pitching that scarcely were the men employed at the pumps able to preserve their equilibrium.

"Reef the shrouds at the toggels!" cried the pilot, who with his quadrant followed the disordered movements of the bark without emotion, and displayed a presence of mind that was surprising, in the multiplicity of his orders.

When sometimes a wave, after having washed the deck, menaced the forecastle, furious and pale with rage, our pilot put his arms around the mizzen-mast, and without bowing his head, without constraining for a second the posture of his body, he continued to transmit the orders necessary to the safety of the ship.

Meantime the fire continued to make progress, the pumps, but ill-manned, were insufficient to combat its greedy appetite.

"I believe, we shall be burned," said one of the sailors.

"Fried like gudgeons in a stove," replied another.

"But the Erable should come to our assistance at least in an hour."

"Ah, yes," added a fourth; "but with such squalls of wind I defy her to come near us."

"Are we then lost?" demanded the Marquis de la Roche, who had left the cabin, and made his appearance on deck.

"Hum!" replied Chetodel; "Lost! Hum! It may be!"

"But——" De la Roche, whom his dry answers annoyed, was disposed to object.

"But," exclaimed the former, stamping with his foot, "Monsieur, retire! your presence interrupts me, your questions are unreasonable."

"What do you mean?" said De la Roche, wounded to the quick.

"Once more, I say, leave; or I will give up the direction of the vessel."

"This tone!"——

"But do you not see that every second you make me lose, compromises our safety?" said Chetodel with a determined voice, seizing and shaking in his hands the fist of the marquis.

"Clown!" objected the great lord.

A swell of the sea, as large as a mountain, as strong as an avalanche, struck the starboard in an oblique line, and in an instant covered the flames, cut short the speech of the marquis, and would certainly have carried him off, had not the steel muscles of the pilot disputed with it the violence of the shock.

Although all the men then on deck were carefully on their guard, two among them were torn from their embrace of the mizzen-mast by the irruption of the waves, and disappeared in the inexorable abyss,

"Without a grave, unknell'd, uncoffin'd, and unknown."

Surprised by the sudden arrival of this swell, John de Ganay who worked at the pumps, had only time to snatch the end of the halyard, in order to save himself from being precipitated over the bulwark; but the rope broke, and the unfortunate young man was about to die a frightful death, when Guyonne, supporting herself with one hand round the mizzen-mast, extended the other to him, succeeded, thanks to the extraordinary vigor with which nature had endowed her, in dragging him up the bulwark where he could easily enter the ship again as soon as the swell had passed away.

Guyonne then rose her head. Her long hair fell in dishevelled folds on her cheeks, and the water streamed from her clothes; but contentment was pictured in her beautiful face.

Before setting her foot again on deck she piously crossed herself, and carried to her lips a little leather purse, which probably contained some pious relic.

"Hum, it is only a squall after all!" murmured Chedotel, remarking that the rain commenced to fall, and that the fire had been extinguished by that enormous wave which might have engulfed the Castor if it had struck her either at the prow or poop.

De la Roche had prostrated himself in prayer.

Some of the sailors and transports imitated his example.

"Rise, rise, rabble!" cried Chedotel in a commanding tone; "and you, Monsieur," added he, addressing himself to the marquis, "I summon you for the security of all on this vessel to retire immediately into your cabin, for your acts demoralize my crew and aggravate the common danger."

The marquis left without uttering a word. The imminence of the peril from which Chedotel had rescued him was still too fresh in his memory not to impose silence upon him. But, nevertheless, from that day forward, he vowed mortal hatred against the pilot.

While he retired, the latter, profiting by the first symptoms of an approaching calm, caused the main-sail to be hoisted once more. At ten o'clock at night, the Castor, favored with a fair wind, had resumed her ordinary rate of sailing, and glided rapidly towards her destination. The sky was disengaged from clouds; the stars sparkled, and nothing was heard on board, but the step of Chedotel, who rapidly paced the poop, and the whispering of the two sailors who watched at the prow.

CHAPTER V.

THE CONSPIRACY.

Fifteen days had passed after the departure of the expedition for New France, and with the exception of the tempest of which we have just been speaking, the weather was almost constantly favorable.

The Castor and the Erable were in close proximity, and were approaching the Banks of Newfoundland.

On board of the first of these ships all seemed peaceable, and often the song of the sailors and convicts mingled with the murmurs of the waves; pleasant stories excited roars of laughter, and the sombre legends caused a stilness for hours together.

The calm was but apparent however. As the Atlantic conceals under its torpidity abysses and terrible anger, so beneath her tranquillity the Castor concealed abysses of frightful passions. The countenances are gay, but the hearts are sad; the lips utter kind words, but the mind cherishes sinister plots; some pray, some dance, some amuse themselves by other means; but the prayer is false, the dance is affected; the amusement forced; in the interior of the bark are inclosed the elements of discord; let only a spark be evolved, and the volcano would commence its eruption.

Meantime the Castor moved along this evening before the breeze, like a bashful maiden before her mother, to use the picturesque expression of the sailor Noel. Why then did Master Chedotel, seated near the cabin table, his elbow supported on the back of a chair, appear sombre? Why was the Marquis de la Roche loading his pistols in the neighboring cabin? Why did John de Ganay pace hurriedly up and down the saloon, heaving convulsive sighs? Why did Guyonne weep silently in the separate appartment which she occupied since the day after the storm? Why, in a word, instead of sleeping, did the bandits seat themselves around the main-mast in the steerage, and whisper? Before answering the first questions, let us hear what the exiles say; perhaps, we may thereby catch the thread of the mystery:

"My dear friends, I believe, it is time now, if ever, that we rid ourselves of that marquis clique, which shuts us up here like rabbits in a rabbit-hole. Does he take us for moles that he does not wish us to see the light of the sun by day, or the moon by night. *Sandiou!* this goes beyond all bounds of courtesy due to brave fellows like us. For my part I assure you that I am tired in this underground dungeon, like a mouse in a trap, and I am quite disposed to give a plunge to monseigneur, the Marquis de la Roche. What does my friend Tronchard think?"

"I," responded the Flemming; "by the beard of the burgomaster, I think that my friend Molin is right; and that we are fools to mould in this cabin like codfish in a barrel."

"*Der Teufel!*" objected a Swiss; "but we are without arms——"

"What?" interposed the German.

"Without some good carbines," resumed the other, "we should only be cut up into mince-meat. Prudence is the mother of safety, remember!"

"Arms! *pov dios*," said a Basque; "are we not in numbers, and can't we, by a sudden rush, make ourselves masters of the crew?"

"Then, by jingo, has not each a knife-blade?" added the Provencal.

"And arms?" pursued the Wurtembergian, exhibiting his athletic trunk.

"We are sixty against thirty, *mordieu!*" maintained Molin.

"All that is very fine; still," interposed the trembler, "but——"

"But, but; you have always buts. You mutton-hearted fellow!" retorted Tronchard, with an impatient air. "Come, quick! what signifies your buts? or I will hurl you by the starboard among the fish tribe."

"Hush! Let us not get excited at all, my very dear friend," said the Marseillais. "Anger is a bad counsellor. Let us chat like people used to good company."

"*Por dios!*" resumed the Basque, "it is time to commence the work."

"Yes, yes!" exclaimed several voices.

"I approve of you, my brave!"

"And after, what shall we do?" grumbled the reluctant Swiss.

These words fell like a refrigerator on the ardor of the rebels.

"After! Time enough for that; we will consult with each other. When the dish is served one eats; nothing more natural."

"If it is not a poisoned dish."

"How is that?"

"Eh! Suppose we have dispatched all the equipage *ad patres*, the pilot at their head——"

"The pilot, nonsense! It is not for the pilot we are preparing the sauce; quite the contrary. The pilot I love and esteem."

"Bravo, Molin, bravo, *por dios!*" said the Basque. "You have as much wit as a doctor of arts, and I promise you a crown of hemp as a recompense——"

"No jesting now," interrupted the Marseillais, who had constituted himself chief of the plot. "This is what I propose. Open your ears as wide as the hatches, my gentle lambs. We are to arm ourselves with all the pieces of iron we can find, then force the hatchway, and handsomely precipitate ourselves on the first cabin, while the remainder attend to the second cabin. The latter will seize the sailors. But no noise—no blood. The others follow me. Do all agree to this?"

"Yes," was the unanimous reply.

"Very well, my adored jewels," continued Molin; "you will await the word like angels, and I am sure we shall do up our little affair in excellent style."

"But all this does not tell us what we are to do," said the Swiss.

"By Bacchus!" replied the Sicilian, "what will the rats do when there are no more cats?"

"What will they do?"

"Yes, what will they do?"

"Oh, my faith——"

"They govern, imbecile."

"Superb. Pepoli! Your reasoning is superb. You are worth your own weight in gold," exclaimed Tronchard. "Come here, until I embrace you."

"It is not absolutely necessary. I have manners," retorted Pepoli, with the gesture of an offended maiden.

"Are all determined?" asked Molin, whom these digressions wearied.

"Yes," shouted the whole crowd of convicts. "Death to the Marquis de la Roche!"

"Silence, silence!" said the Marseillais, extending his hand. "Let us proceed without noise. This is the only way we can succeed. Come here, Wolf."

The German bowed his colossal form, the height of which would extend at least a foot above the steerage, and approached the chief conspirator.

"You see this pannel?" said the latter, indicating with his finger the lid of the hatchway.

A sort of grunt would translate the reply of the giant.

"Well, by jingo, my brave! don't you think this pannel will annoy us devilishly?"

"Oh, oh, *der Teufel*," said Wolf. "It is not difficult to remove it."

Pronouncing these words, he made an arch of himself under the trap-door, so that his broad shoulders touched the extremities of it. He expanded his lower limbs, and gradually straightening his spine, made the irons fly out of the boards. A crackling, and an "*ouf*" of satisfaction, announced his victory.

The clatter of the waves against the sides of the Castor, smothered the noise of the rupture.

While this terrible storm was accumulating in the steerage, Chedotel was the prey of a conflict scarcely less terrible. His hair stood of an end, large drops of perspiration flowed down his forehead, and his nails beat his breast. All of a sudden he seemed to arm himself with a desperate resolution; he left his cabin and proceeded to that of Guyonne.

Extended in her day clothes on a pallet, the young girl was falling asleep. A smoking lamp afforded a glimmering light. Chedotel trembled so much in entering that he was obliged to support himself against the wainscoting to prevent himself from falling. Here there was a minute of hesitation; his heart beat as if it would break his chest.

Struck by the glimmering light of the lamp, the profile of the pilot was frightful to look at; he might easily have been taken for one of those demons whose horrible figures are found sculptured in the granite of the old basilisks of the Middle Ages.

Suddenly the pretended Yvon moved herself feebly on her couch, her arm around her beautiful neck, a sweet smile played on her half-closed lips, which allowed the name "John," to escape.

Immediately the hesitation of Chedotel ceased, a wild enthusiasm seized him; he extinguished the light and precipitated himself towards the bed.

Awaking in surprise, Guyonne prepared for a determined resistance, when frightful imprecations reverberated above the cabin.

"Death to the Marquis de la Roche! Death to the Marquis de la Roche!"

CHAPTER VI.

REVOLT ON BOARD.

WELL, with sixty months shouted "Death to the Marquis de la Roche!" and the immensity of God, with its solemn voice, echoed "Death to the Marquis de la Roche!"

The night was still bright and beautiful, like a maiden on a holiday, and the Castor glided on gayly without caring any more for the frightful vociferations alluded to than the eagle does for the roaring of the tempest.

On land a revolt has always something in it that inspires secret fright; but on sea, it creates terror. On land it can be avoided or suppressed by a thousand different means; on sea, flight is impossible. The abyss is under your feet, the unknown over your head, and death around you. The revolt must be confronted, grappled, crushed by the force which produced it—by strength of mind, or its fury submitted to.

Behold! A thousand lightnings flash, red, like the sun, extinguishing themselves in the dark rage of an approaching tempest, stifle their smoky flames on the deck of the Castor, and spread over the vessel colors as lugubrious as those of a conflagration. Through this light appeared strange figures, savage types, which seemed as if vomited from the gloomy empire in an access of fury. These men brandished in one hand torches, in the other oars, bars of wood and iron, pieces of chain; instruments of every kind. In short, they might be regarded as a satanic assembly returning from an infernal orgie.

They surge tumultuously on the sides of the Castor, rush to the main-mast and divide themselves into two bands, one led by the German, Wolf, towards the forecastle, occupied by the sailors, the other by the Marseillais, Molin, towards the rear, occupied by the Marquis de la Roche and his suite.

Already the man at the helm, intimidated by the explosion of the revolt, abandoned his post, to seek refuge in the rigging. The barque, left without direction to the whistling of the winds, rolled about and threatened to founder, when Chedotel debouched on the deck.

William de la Roche, John de Ganay, several other gentlemen and Guyonne, arrived there at the same time.

"Death to the marquis! Death to the marquis!" shouted the piercing voice of Molin.

And a sinister voice replied: "Death to the marquis! Death to the marquis!"

"By Christ! we shall succumb to the band!" exclaimed Chedotel, remarking, that the Castor had come to the wind, and that the main-sail was half loose.

He ran immediately to the bar, and gave it a vigorous movement. By degrees the ship recovered herself, and continued her former course.

During this time De la Roche addressed the rebels.

"Retire, dogs! or I will have you all hanged to the yard-arm, to serve as food for the vultures."

The first summons was rendered inaudible by the howling of the insurrection.

"You do not understand this language," pursued the marquis. "Well, you will perhaps understand this better!"

In pronouncing these words, he fired with one of the pistols he held in his hand.

"By the beard of my respectable burgomaster, I believe I have received all," said Tronchard, extending his arm and leaning his face against the side of the ship.

Struck with fear, the crowd of insurgents retreated, but only to return promptly, electrified by the cry of their chief:

"Nonsense, are you going to retreat now like scabby sheep! Let us revenge our friend—our friend Tronchard, on this ruffian of a marquis, and his satanic company."

"Yes, *por Dios*," replied the Basque; "let us be revenged, let us be revenged, comrades!"

The clamors rose higher and higher. It seemed as if the Castor had been transformed into a pandemonium. Pressed by the human sea which mounted still behind him, Molin found himself suddenly transported to the halyard, within two feet of De la Roche. The former was armed with a long cutlass, the blade of which darted yellow scintillations by the light of the torches. William de la Roche, absorbed wholly in the attitude of the rebels, had not observed the movement of his enemy. The eyes of Molin sparkled like carbuncles, and he rushed at the marquis. But before he was able to perpetrate the homicide which he projected a stroke of a hatchet, energetically applied, cut off his arm; the pain caused the bandit to groan.

"Ah," murmured he, perceiving Guyonne, "it is you, snake, that has maimed me! You have a solid fist, my calf,—but——"

He fainted from loss of blood.

A discharge of musketry attracted the attention of the assailants at the same moment. This volley emanated from the prow, where the sailors sustained a violent assault from Wolf and his party.

At the first signal of the *emeute*, the man at the catheads gave a shout of alarm. All the sailors quitted their hammocks at once, and seized such arms as were nearest to hand. Then by order of the master of the crew they formed themselves in battle array, and waited in silence, broke the door of their cabin, in order to receive them with a cross-fire. Such a reception was well calculated to rout the uncertain people who had hoped that the sailors, far from opposing their enterprise, would join them. Five victims made by this volley, filled them with consternation. Some retreated in confusion, the band headed by Molin, others ran to take refuge in the steerage, others finally, with the Wurtembergian Wolf at their head, attempted to storm the entrenchment of the marines.

The disorder was at its height on the dock of the Castor; for in the *melee* the greater part of the torches had been extinguished, and the shades of night began to regain their predominance. Some pieces of rope, forgotten by the heroes of the drama, harassed them in turn, tripping them as they attempted fresh attacks on the sailors

"A *falot*," exclaimed the marquis.

Guyonne descended to the store-room, and returned with the object demanded. De la Roche lighted a match, and approaching a swivel-gun which John de Ganay had just pointed against the rebels.

"Now," said he, "let all return to the steerage, or I will fire this piece."

His gesture and accent were irresistible. To doubt that he was ready to accomplish his threat, would be folly. The rebels obeyed in silence, with the exception of Wolf, Pepoli, and five or six others. The latter, however, had not heard the injunction; but had they done so, they probably would have paid no attention to it. Rushing against the sailors, before they had time to reload their muskets, they were attacked with stocks and barrels. The only weapon the German giant had, was a bar of the capstan, which he used as a club, and with so much dexterity that each of his blows was equivalent to a passport to eternity. The Sicilian on his part did wonders with a sabre, picked up during the fight. Their other companions seconded them worthily, so that the victory would have undoubtedly turned in favor of the convicts, had it not been for the cowardice of those who retired.

"You, brigand, *der Teufel!*" said Wolf, raising his redoubtable bar over the cranium of the master of the crew.

"And you, ugly noddle-head!" said a cabin-boy, kneeling in his hammock, where he had secreted himself, and discharging his pistol in the very countenance of the Hercules.

"*Der Teufel*," still exclaimed the colossus, falling at full length.

It was his last breath, and with it expired the revolt.

CHAPTER VII

THE EXECUTION.

NEXT day in the afternoon the Castor presented a sad spectacle.

The day was, indeed, beautiful, the firmament pure and serene, the sun warm and viviying. The greatness of God displayed itself in all its magnificence around the ship, but the very contrast of these majestic beauties enhanced the melancholy of the scene which we are about to describe.

Seated on an estrade, dressed in his costume as Governor-General of Canada, and having at his right the pilot Chedotel, at his left Viscount de Ganay, the Marquis de la Roche passed a sad glance over the ocean. At his feet, chained two by two, and guarded by sailors with loaded muskets, were all the convicts, with the exception of Yvon. Above their heads, suspended from the rigging, were eight corpses, among which were observed those of the Flemming, Tronchard, and of the German, Wolf.

Birds of prey hovered around the ship, piercing the air with their cries, and in the foamy furrows made by the Castor one could distinguish a dark, scaly object, following the bark with stubborn persistence. It was a shark that scented the dead.

After two hours the drum was beaten; thenceforth the undertone conversation and whispering ceased; all eyes turned towards a trap-door at the prow. First Pepoli, the Sicilian, was seen with his hands tied behind his back, then the Marseillais Molin, carried by two sailors, and finally the Basque, and a Burgundian, named Francis, nicknamed the "Toper."

Molin, notwithstanding the loss of his right arm, retained his full consciousness. His features, contracted by suffering, still bespoke pride, and a sardonic smile played on the corner of his discolored lips.

"Pepoli and Francis," said the Toper, "are always fond of jokes."

"Rope for rope," said the former, "it always seemed to me that I must finish with a rope; but, on my soul, I had no idea that I should have the chance of dying in the arms of a virgin."

"In fact," said the latter, "there is some hemp that does honor to the soil where it was produced."

"And to the shuttle where it was twisted."

"Just see, Pepoli, how the brave Wolf draws up his tongue! Will it be said that he is waiting for a draught of beer to quench his thirst?"

"The drunken German goes!"

"And that animal, Tronchard, who has caused himself to be fanned by the birds of heaven."

"Still more refinement than that!"

A second rolling of the drum put an end to these low jokes.

De la Roche stood up and ordered: "Numbers 31, 43 50."

"Present!" replied Molin, Pepoli, and Francis in turn.

"You are each condemned to be hanged," replied the marquis. "Recommend your souls to God. You have but half an hour. May this example serve as a lesson to those who would in future attempt to revolt against my authority."

On the delivery of this inexorable sentence a shudder of fright passed over the crowd of convicts; the victims alone manifested no emotion.

"This is what I call precision," said Pepoli.

"In my view of it, it is a good way to prevent people from languishing," added Francis.

"*Por Dios*, it is long since I wished to have a *tete-a-tete* with Monsieur Satan; how things will come about!"

"Holy Bacchus, my divine patron, that the wine below may be as generous as in Burgundy!" added Francis.

A third rolling of the drum announced that the fatal hour had arrived. All the exiles kneeled, and two minutes after the grating of pulleys, the croaking of frightened birds of prey, and some inarticulate sounds, formed the funeral knell of the criminals.

Meantime the day was beautiful, the firmament pure and serene, the sun warm and vivifying, and the greatness of God displayed itself in all its magnificence around the ship.

CHAPTER VIII.

THE LOVE OF A FISHERWOMAN AND THE LOVE OF A PILOT.

WE now return to one or two of our principal personages whom the incidents we have just related have forced us to leave under a sort of veil.

It will doubtless be remembered that Guyonne had saved the life of Viscount de Ganay during a storm; it will also be remembered that she saved the life of William de la Roche during the revolt. These two traits prove that to the heroism of the heart the step-daughter of Perrin united the heroism of courage, and presence of mind: a trinity of virtues which unfortunately are not common among men.

The viscount and the marquis paid, in turn, to the pretended Yvon the debt of their gratitude. The former in admitting her among the waiters of the cabin; the latter in rendering homage to her bravery in presence of the whole crew, by promising to send her back to France free.

The young girl had, therefore, attained a better position than she had ever dared to hope for; and she could contemplate the future without much apprehension. But, too often, fortune does things by halves. In giving us a full hand on one side, she clips our wings on the other. Two passions already struggled with each other in the thoughts of Guyonne: she loved Viscount de Ganay, and she hated the pilot Chedotel.

These two passions were engendered in her breast at the same time, took root together, and gained strength in supporting each other.

The day of embarkation, Chedotel had brutalized the young girl; John de Ganay had taken her under his protection; such was the commencement of this double sentiment.

First, Guyonne misunderstood herself as to the nature of her penchant for the equerry. She regarded it as the result of a lively gratitude, but she had passed the age at which one can not comprehend himself; if her soul had remained free from all tenderness, foreign to her family, a penetrating intelligence had taught her to seek and find the cause of the feeling she experienced. Guyonne, in short, discerned promptly that it was love which made her fear and desire the presence of John de Ganay; and that it was love which impurpled her cheeks when she spoke to him, and caused her voice to tremble when she replied.

This discovery filled her with fright.

What an abyss separated her, the poor daughter of a fisherman and of a serf, from the wealthy Viscount de

Ganay, son of one of the most powerful lords of lower Burgundy—how was this abyss to be crossed? To think of it seemed the climax of insanity; besides, did not John love another, the beautiful Laura of Kerskoën, the manoress of numerous vassals, the unrivaled beauty, the pearl of Brittany? Surely it seemed impudent effrontery on the part of a poor girl like Guyonne to aspire to the hand of the equerry of Monseigneur de la Roche.

But love reasons in vain; when the object which excites it is worthy, the more it accumulates reasons to extinguish itself, the more it acquires life and consistence. The less reason it has to be, the stronger it is; the greater the social distance between the lover and the beloved, the greater the force of attraction between the former and the latter.

Guyonne sought a remedy in prayer; prayer inflamed her imagination, and exalted her love. But the course of that love had changed. She resolved to devote herself to the happiness of the young man. This determination restored calmness to her mind; without, however, establishing lasting peace. She accustomed herself to the idea of one day serving the wife of the viscount, and nursing their children. Certainly, it required robust piety, and a resolute character to consecrate one's self to such a martyrdom; but as we have already said, Guyonne was the type of incarnate moral purpose.

It is not strange, then, that in the course of two weeks, the love of the fisher-girl for the viscount assumed such vast proportions. At sea, where the circle of impressions is limited, all the movements of the heart are for this very reason more violent, and the most illusive circumstance acquires over our faculties the power of a veritable event.

The Viscount de Ganay was ignorant of all, even of the sex of his liberator. Perhaps, had he not been under the influence of another passion, that he would have been astonished at certain movements of Yvon; perhaps he would have remarked, that sometimes when he thought he was not seen, he regarded him with languid and moist eyes; but the image of Laura always interposed between the equerry and the pretended bandit, and never did the idea occur to him that the heart of a loving young girl beat under that masculine costume. Nevertheless, having one day surprised her before a crucifix, and in an attitude of devotion, which attested the warmth of her religious sentiments, he could not help saying:

"Then you believe in God?"

"In God, monseigneur! Who does not?"

"Too many ingrates," replied the equerry; "but when we believe in God we are afraid of offending him."

"This, indeed, is my greatest fear."

John de Ganay smiled, and this smile brought the purple to the cheeks of the young girl.

"How, did you ally your fear of God with your relations to these miserable wrecks of vice and debauchery?"

At this question the countenance of Guyonne changed from purple to crimson, and burning tears sparkled on her eyelids.

"It is all the more strange," pursued he, "because you belonged to an honest family, in the midst of which you had only to imbibe good principles."

One can imagine the wound which this accusation gave poor Guyonne, unfortunately justified as it was by appearances. Incapable of restraining herself any longer, she sobbed aloud.

"Come, don't cry, child," said he, interpreting, erroneously, the expression of her affliction; "try to repent, and God will pardon you, as those you have offended on earth have already done."

A painful sign was the sole response of the poor girl.

The accusation under which she labored, was, however, the least of her sorrows; she had a much heavier burden to carry; her aversion for Chedotel, and the absurd passion of the latter for her.

This passion commenced the very day they embarked.

It is necessary, in order to understand our narrative, to relate here some anterior events.

When John de Ganay was wrested from death by Guyonne, the clothes of both were drenched with water. The equerry, having changed his costume, ordered another uniform to be given to Yvon. The latter hastened to take off the wet clothes, and to put on those brought her by the valet of the viscount. This done, Guyonne returned on deck, in order to set her smock-frock to dry. A pocket of the frock contained the note given her by John de Ganay, to visit her brother Yvon, at the prison of St. Malo. By chance this pass, which simply contained the name of the applicant, written with red ink, and the coat of arms of the viscount, by chance, we say, this pass had dropped from the pocket which concealed it, on the rigging, where it remained all night. Next morning, Chedotel, while having the deck washed, perceived the object, picked it up, and swore an oath on seeing what it inclosed. At this moment, Guyonne came for her frock. Master Chedotel was struck with her fine form and beauty; of which certain appearances indicated a feminine nature. Recalling then, his own remarks on the name he had seen on the pass, he conceived some suspicion. The espionage cost him nothing; he watched the disguised convict, and the same night his suspicions were justified. He knew the sex of number 40.

The idea of a generous sentiment can no more germinate in some minds than a grain of corn can grow on sand; and Chedotel's was one of those minds.

Guyonne could be nothing more in his opinion than a prostitute, who, weary of the streets of Nantes and St. Malo, had desired to transport her miserable existence, and her common favors, into another hemisphere. The first idea of the pilot was to put the marquis on his guard, in order to obviate, by an immediate incarceration of the girl, the disorders which her presence would occasion if she happened to be discovered. Then a thought occurred to him:

"Hum!" said he, scratching his head, "God pardon me, she is not ugly; she has a tempting form—it would be a good idea if I could reserve this pullet for myself!"

But he soon discovered that he was strangely mistaken in regard to the young girl. To his infamous propositions she replied with a firmness that stupefied him. Resistance transformed his caprice into a passion, the passion into a delirium. We will not report either his promises or his threats to Guyonne. It has been seen what a crime Chedotel would have committed, in order to satisfy his brutal lust, had not the breaking out of the insurrection just at the moment cut short his odious attempt. It is now easy to understand the hatred of Guyonne for the pilot. Had she not even loved John de Ganay with that pure and enthusiastic love which we have endeavored to portray, his gross sensuality would have revolted her. This brute, with a human face, could inspire nothing but contempt; whether he loved, or hated, he could only inspire invincible disgust.

Poor Guyonne! She often wished to discard the aversion against this monster; yes, one hour after the revolt of the convicts, she implored God in favor of the scoundrel, who had done his best to make her his victim. Her situation was frightful—to love and not be known to detest and be loved!

There are moral tortures a thousand times more cruel than physical tortures.

CHAPTER IX.

FAMINE.

It seems as if misfortune had extended its sable wing over the expedition of the Marquis de la Roche, as over the majority of those that preceded it. As much as the discovery and colonization of South America were favored by fortune, as much were those of North America disfavored by fate.

It is not surprising that the French Government treated with great negligence, not to say ill-will, efforts to found establishments on the banks of the St. Lawrence. When Cartier sailed from St. Malo, the 20th of April, 1534, to explore Labrador, it was generally thought that, according to the example of Columbus, Cortez, Vespucius, Pizarro, etc., he would plant the flag of his king over countries, rich in mines of gold and silver; when, on his return, he brought nothing but chagrined, exhausted sailors who, as they said, had only found "black forests, deep snow, and thick ice." Francis I. felt so much annoyed that he refused the bold navigator a private audience. Thanks, however, to the solicitations of Philip de Cabot, Charles de Mouy, and some other noblemen, Cartier was able to resume his explorations the following year. It is sufficiently known what dangers he confronted in the course of this second voyage, which led to the discovery of the country, since known under the general name of Canada; it is also known what a terrible winter these adventurers passed on the banks of the St. Lawrence, and what a concert of maledictions saluted the disembarkation of their chief in France, whither he hastened to return the following spring. Certain authors, Champlain among others, pretended that he was disgusted by this check, but this is not probable; if he conceived any disgust, it was not because he did not succeed to his wish, for his mind was too strongly fortified to permit him to be discouraged by reverses, and he had too much wisdom, not to understand what a source of wealth he had bequeathed to posterity.

At all events, as Charlevoix remarks, it was useless for him to boast of the country he had discovered, the little he had brought from it, and the sad condition to which his people were reduced, by cold and by scurvy, persuaded the majority that he could never be of any use to France. Particular stress was laid on the fact that he had seen no appearance of mines; for then much more than at present, a foreign land that produced neither gold nor silver was worth nothing.

Nevertheless, four years after, in 1540, Cartier triumphed over all difficulties, and again set sail, accompanied by Francis de la Roque, Lord of Roberval. This expedition had no better fortune than its predecessors. Cold and famine decimated the ranks of the colonists, and James Cartier disappeared from the theatre of history.

Political quarrels and religious dissensions caused North America to be forgotten until 1549. At this time Roberval, encouraged by his previous efforts, fitted out a ship, and sailed in the vestiges of his predecessor; but the vessel was lost, including men and merchandise, and nothing was heard of him after.

This was sufficient to divert public opinion from the project which had occupied him for some time. About half a century passed, before any one thought of trying again.

We have depicted the departure of De la Roche; we have seen him, aided by Chedotel, struggle against the fury of the elements, and of men; now, we are about to see him battling against a still more redoubtable scourge, against famine.

The Castor had brought provisions only for fifty days; he had calculated on the Erable, whose cargo included a vast supply of munitions of all kinds. But attacked by the tempest, she deviated from her course, and forty days had already passed without there being any sign of land. As a climax of misfortune, the Erable was lost in a storm. It was necessary then to diminish the rations of water, and soon after the rations of flour. These measures, commanded by imperious necessity, could not be carried out without exciting serious discontent among the convicts; but the fate of the leaders of the first revolt had intimitated them too much to venture to rebel a second time. Besides, the crew knew that the marquis and his staff shared their miseries; this was sufficient to stop the most seditious. Such is man's nature: he suffers voluntarily with those who suffer, but does not excuse his privations, when surrounded by those who revel in abundance.

All our existence is past in speculating on comparison.

Sorrow had then extended its crape over the Castor; none were met but emaciated and sunken countenances.

William de la Roche rarely left his cabin; he feared that his thoughtful physiognomy might betray the anguish which agitated him, and he consumed his hours in prayer and meditation. John de Ganay was not less sad than his master. In proportion as their position became more critical, the equerry regretted more and more his having abandoned the mild sky of France. He dreamed of the idol of his thoughts. Sinister presentiments gnawed on his heart like asps. A thousand circumstances passed unperceived, while the rays from the beautiful eyes of Laura dazzled him and pressed on his memory. Now, feeling himself not loved, he sighed with grief; anon believing his love reciprocated, he mourned the folly which had drawn him so far from the object of his passion; then, to these poignant emotions were united the remembrance of his cherished Burgundy, with its climate so temperate, its fields so green, its sun so pure. He recalled the manor where his infancy and early youth were passed; he sat in imagination under the great mantle-piece, heard the recital of the brave deeds of his ancestors; supported his head on the knees of his mother, and went asleep with the song of caressing romance.

Two only of our personages had preserved the moral force, indispensable to defy adversity. These were Guyonne and Chedotel. Brought up side by side with want, having frequently felt the pangs of hunger, the sister of Yvon did not feel, like her companions, that want of nourishment, which was increased by the shackles that opposed its being satisfied; and although the convicts were reduced to a few ounces of biscuit a day and some salt meat, she was as fresh and as serene as the day she took her departure from St. Malo.

As for the pilot, what he was at the commencement of this recital, he was the same when the famine was at its height; hardened, morose, sarcastic, vicious, as the genius of evil. Unable to gratify his infamous desires in regard to Guyonne, he resolved to be revenged. But Chedotel was not a man to revenge himself in an ordinary way. He wished an atrocious, frightful vengeance.

In the morning, after having made observations with his quadrant, and found that the Castor approached the parallels of 42 degrees longitude, and 53 degrees latitude, a fiendish smile lurked at the corner of his lips.

Having given some orders relative to the movement of the vessel, he hastened to the Marquis de la Roche. The latter was engaged in a conference with his officers, among whom was included John de Ganay. Chedotel approached them, affecting an air of great consternation.

"What's this, now ?" exclaimed the marquis; "will not the wrath of Heaven cease to oppress its humble servant ?"

"Hum!" replied Chedotel. "At sea, one must be prepared for the worst. The fact is, that never had I less chance than on this occasion."

"But what's the matter?" asked the marquis.

Those present examined the countenance of Chedotel with avidity.

"Truly, if that damned Erable does not come to our relief, we are in great danger——"

"Well?"

"It is difficult to digest, although our stomachs are as supple as inflated bladders."

"No such jests in my presence!" exclaimed William de la Roche, in a loud voice. "Master pilot, I order you to speak, and not to conceal anything from me."

"Hum! I did not suppose, monseigneur, that you would be in such a hurry to hear bad news; but since you wish it I submit to your will. The steward assures me that we have not more than a barrel of water."

"More than a barrel of water!" exclaimed those present.

"Only one, alas!" rejoined Chedotel, laying particular emphasis on the figure.

"Oh, 'tis impossible!" said De Ganay.

"And" continued the pilot, with a diabolical intention, "provisions for one week—scarcely."

"What?"

"By diminishing the rations," added he.

A cry of fright rose from every breast.

"But," said Chedotel, who greatly enjoyed the anxiety of his auditors, "perhaps there is still a means left whereby to escape the frightful death which menaces all; for it is a horrible thing, gentlemen, to die of hunger, between sky and water. Hum! I remember a time, when we had a shipwreck—it was on board of the Amphitrite, and in order to save ourselves from the frightful death of which I speak, we were obliged to eat one of our comrades——"

"That's enough, pilot. Keep your reminiscences for yourself and your equals. Are we far from land?"

"Hum! One can not tell precisely. The sounding gives twenty-four fathoms, and a bottom of shells. Stop! do you hear the sailors shouting, *Vive le roi!* This announces the Banks, and that we are banking, which means, that we are entering on the Banks of Newfoundland."

"Then, the shores of Acadia——"

"Monseigneur, the currents are numerous in these seas; the winds very variable. I can affirm nothing—at least until you consent to adopt a plan."

"Let us see what it is? Be brief."

"At some hundreds of knots from us, there is an island, which contains a small lake of fresh water. We could disembark this rabble there, if such were your good pleasure, and go to procure provisions among the savage tribes of Acadia. Then we could seek a favorable place to found the new colonial establishment, and afterwards return to our people."

"By the mass! this is wisely thought, Master Chedotel," said one of the noblemen.

"Yes," replied De la Roche, crossing his arms; "but what will support these people during our absence?"

"Hum!" rejoined the pilot, "they will not want; the island abounds with game and fish!"

The marquis rose from his seat, walked about three or four times, and addressing himself to Chedotel:

"May God assist us! Do as you think best!"

CHAPTER X.

LAND.

Five days after this conversation the dawn appeared through cold and compact fogs. A strong favorable breeze whistled in the rigging of the Castor, and the faces of all the passengers looked joyful; for already those silver globules ranged in parallel lines, which indicate the proximity of land, were seen to bubble around the vessel.

At the same time all dangers were not avoided; the Castor pursued a course that brought her into the middle of ice-mountains, which at every moment threatened to overwhelm her. But the news that they were near land, and would soon disembark, was sufficient to reanimate the spirits of those most discouraged.

Let us contemplate the scene which is now being enacted on the deck of the Castor. The fog envelops the barque with an impenetrable veil; it is fifteen hours since all these unfortunate people have tasted a morsel; the horizon is hidden from their view; yet some sing, some leap, some run about, weep, embrace each other—all because they have learned that they have arrived at their destination.

"By St. James, I salute thee, the happiest day of my life, although your face looks as gloomy as that of a draper who has surprised his wife, sinning *tete-a-tete* with a cornet of light horse," exclaimed a Spaniard, agitating his blue linen cap.

"I will burn three candles in honor of my patron," said a native of Brittany.

"And I," added a German, "will make a vow not to drink a single pot of beer this year, if we arrive at a good port."

"I imagine, my boy, this abstinence will not be very difficult," said the mate; "do you suppose that beer flows here like the waves?"

"It is not the less true," said the son of Germany, somewhat cooled, "that if there be hops we can brew beer; that if one can brew it he can drink; that if one can drink——"

Chedotel, whose peevish and jealous humor made him the enemy of the amusements of others, wished to prevent the fun of the exiles; but De la Roche interposed, and although the pilot alleged that the noise and confusion they made embarrassed the crew, the marquis did not like to interrupt the slender amusements of the unfortunate people.

"The ship sails well," said he; "the wind is propitious. It will cause no inconvenience to allow them to divert themselves for an hour or two."

"No inconvenience!"

At this moment, Guyonne, attracted by the discussion, appeared on deck.

Chedotel, perceiving her, went direct to her, and taking her rudely by the hand dragged her along towards the forecastle.

The young girl could easily have torn herself from his grasp, but her false position on board of the Castor precluded her from making any resistance. She resolutely followed Chedotel.

"Listen to me," said he, in an earnest, passionate voice, "and remember what I tell you; for in two hours my determination will be irrevocable. I love you, and you know it. For one word of love from you, I would sink this vessel and all it contains; for one kiss from your lips, I would give worlds; for your possession——"

The voice of the pilot became tremulous; all his muscles quivered like the chords of an instrument of music during a storm.

"For your possession," continued he, "for your possession, Guyonne, I would damn my soul! I would sacrifice all humanity! You see how I love you—you are in my power—and I respect you! I, who have in my hands the fate of a hundred individuals; I, before even the proud Marquis de la Roche bends the knee; I, who despise the fury of men, disdain the fury of the waves; I, who am more a master here than the king is in France—I implore your pity I implore your compassion, Guyonne! I supplicate you to consent to be my wife, to give me one word of hope. Come, do you wish me to prostrate myself at your feet, in presence of the whole crew? Say, do you wish it?"

"No," coldly replied Guyonne.

"What, then, can I do to please you?" exclaimed the pilot, impetuously attempting to embrace the young girl by the waist.

"Nothing," replied she, starting back.

"Then you don't love me?"

Guyonne made no reply.

"And you never will love me," continued Chedotel, wiping away the cold perspiration which bathed his temples, "and you will never consent—you vile outcast of society, to be the legitimate——"

"Never!" replied she, firmly.

"Do you not know that you are under my absolute authority; that by a word or a gesture I can sign your death-warrant?"

"Never!"

"Ah! have I not sovereign command here? And you dare to say never! Have I understood you aright? But, unfortunate woman, who must be tired of life! Never! Lunatic! Then you feel yourself strong against torment? Never!——"

In articulating these imprecations, the pilot pressed her hand as if he would break it.

There was a pause of a few seconds in this solitary drama in the midst of a crowd; in that drama, of which the dance and noise rendered the vociferations inaudible, an observer would have been able to see then that the pilot struggled between two divergent passions, each exalted to a paroxysm.

"You do not love the old sea-wolf, my fine girl?"

"I detest you!" retorted the young girl, her patience being exhausted.

"Hum! you detest me! This frankness rather pleases me. By the rigging, confidence for confidence, I will be as frank as you, demoiselle. Do you distinguish this point at the west?"

"Yes."

"There, then, know from this moment will be your grave, and Satan may have you under his protection!"

Soon after this blasphemy Chedotel went to rejoin the Marquis de la Roche, who paced up and down the quarter-deck, chatted for some minutes, and went in person to the rudder.

The sun mounting to its zenyth, had, by degrees, disengaged its dazzling face from the veils which covered the empyrean. Some clouds still wandered here and there on the foamy waves; but already the celestial dome unveiled its splendors, and in the distance were grouped blue masses which assumed various forms, scattered and again re-united at each knot made by the Castor towards the shore. This was cape Canceau, the island of Acadia, now Nova Scotia.

CHAPTER XI.

THE ARRIVAL.

Chedotel, without quitting the helm, seized one of those little telescopes which had recently been invented by a German, named Jansen, and examined the shore.

"Hum!" murmured he, "this devil, Castor, knew her way; but I am not satisfied to disembark my freight on this side."

Then returning the glass to its place, and raising his voice:

"Another tack!" he cried with a piercing cry.

The chains were heard to grate on the pulleys; the sails, loosened, flapped heavily against the masts; the sun seemed rapidly to describe the arc of a circle; the chains grated again on the pulleys; the sails caught the wind, and the barque resumed her former gait.

The amusements had ceased, and for some minutes the convicts, mute and palpitating with hope, were eagerly examining the shores. The turn of the Castor filled them with surprise, but attributing it to an urgent cause, they abstained from all comments, and contented themselves with feeling a little disappointed at seeing the shore of New France vanish like an illusive mirage.

William de la Roche consulted one of the maps, drawn by Cartier, and of which the fidelity was truly inconceivable. He was quite astonished at the course steered by the pilot.

"Are we not proceeding after the manner of the crawfish?" said he with a smile, "I thought we should keep the cape to the north; and here the needle of the compass turns towards the south."

"To the north," replied Chedotel, "hum! yes, our course is to the north; but the shortest way is not always the best."

"Nor, is it the promptest, is it, pilot?"

"Hum!"

"Nevertheless, I should like to know, why it is that we are returning. Are there reefs or sand-banks?"

"Hum! reefs, sand-banks, you are right, there are both! the coast is surrounded with them."

"It is the coast of Acadia, is it not?"

"Hum! the coast of Acadia; no, it is not the coast of Acadia," replied Chedotel cooly, "it is an island!"

"An island!" said the marquis.

"An island!"

"What do you call it?"

"Hum! I don't know that it has received any name."

"It is strange that neither Cartier nor Roberval have distinguished it."

"Hum! that need not astonish you; this island is a mass of sand which is most of the time covered with water. The navigators whom you cite might have sailed by it without observing it."

But it was too late. With the exception of a point almost imperceptible, the Governor-General of Canada distinguished nothing at the horizon.

"Are we going to the other shore of which you have spoken?"

"We shall be in range of it in about four hours," replied Chedotel.

"Then have you passed it?"

"Several times!"

"And are you certain that our people can live there during the few days we must be absent?"

"Live there! By the cross, the ruffians were never in a place where they could be more jovial. They have only to stretch out their hands, in order to have cod-fish, hares, rabbits, partridges, etc."

"Do you remember, pilot, that you will answer to me for them on your head?"

"On my head? Hum! I value my head more than a million of these profligates; but no matter, I will answer for them."

Whether it was that he did not understand, or whether he did not hear, he took no notice of this impertinence; he descended into the interior of the Castor, while Chedotel muttered with a sinister sneer:

"Take care whether they will get food; the island is as barren as the deck of a vessel. Ah, monseigneur, you have treated me rudely during the voyage; you have treated me like a clown! I, Chedotel, who have been at sea thirty years. Ah, Mr. Governor, you will govern—the Hurons and the Esquimaux—if you can * * And that abigail! Ah! ah! Hum! if I could be witness * * Come, what does he want?"

A rolling of the drum had drawn this exclamation from the pilot.

At this summons the transports assembled in order, and William de la Roche, followed by his staff, appeared on the quarter-deck.

"Reef the top-sail and the bow-sprit," shouted Chedotel, whose vigilant eye lost no movement of the Castor.

While the sailors executed the order of the pilot, William made the following speech to the convicts:

"Boys!

"You know that, notwithstanding all my cares, misfortune has hitherto marked our expedition. Provisions came short on board. Had we been some days longer at sea, we should have been reduced to the last extremity. I have shared your miseries and privations. Like you, I have suffered from famine; and had I not entire confidence in the goodness of God, I might, perhaps, have given way to hopeless despair. But, he who believes in the infinite mercy of the All-powerful, he who disposes every night the burden of his tribulations at the feet of the Redeemer of the world, is strong even in adversity.

"We now approach land, not the continent, as you may have supposed, but a fertile island, where, with a little labor and ingenuity you can provide for your natural wants. I will explain to you here that the want of provisions, an imperious necessity, has forced me to land you on a neighboring island. I will disembark with you provisions for two days, divers tools, bedding, hunting and fishing implements; then the Castor will set sail again to seek on the shores of New France a suitable place for the establishment of the colony which I have projected. As soon as I have found it I will return for you, and take you thither."

As De la Roche proceeded, a loud murmur, the precursor of a storm, rose in the ranks of the convicts. A spark was sufficient to produce an explosion, nor was the spark wanting.

"It is intended to abandon us in the middle of the ocean!" shouted an individual, lost in the crowd.

"It is intended to abandon us!" exclaimed the echo of twenty voices, with an accent of terror, and of unqualified menace.

"Yes, to abandon us!" rejoined the first voice; "to abandon us on some unknown shore; there, to become the victims of famine and wild beasts."

A formidable roar welcomed this declaration; and in less than a second, as if impelled by an electric shock, all the convicts were pressing tumultuously under the poop, with the intention of scaling it.

Chedotel laughed in his sleeve, and continued to steer towards the northeast.

De la Roche felt that it was necessary for him to lay aside his habitual pride, in order to put down the insurrection.

"Listen," said he, "I have every right over you; the punishment of the ringleaders of your first mutiny must have convinced you of this. But I am opposed to violent executions, and I pardon you this moment of insubordination, but with the understanding that any similar attempt in future will be punished with death."

"Yes, with hangings, like those of Molin, Tronchard, and others!" interposed again the same individual in a tone of bitterness which revived the irritation.

"In order to show you," continued the marquis, "that I have no intention of abandoning you, as certain suspicious persons among you fear, my equerry, Viscount de Ganay, will remain among you, and command you in my absence. Are you satisfied?"

"Yes, yes," replied several bandits.

"Well, then, return to the steerage, and make your preparations.

This promise immediately suppressed the effervescence which rose in every head.

"Lord de Ganay, I shall depend on you," said the marquis, turning towards his equerry, "four sailors will serve you as a guard."

"I will obey, monseigneur," replied the viscount with indifference.

Chedotel reefed the sails, with the exception of the mizzen, and with sounding-line in hand, steered the Castor across the *battures* which encumbered the passage where he was then sailing.

Soon after some miles, an island was observed covered with small trees, which in the distance produced an agreeable effect.

The order was given to bring the vessel to and cast anchor. Then William de la Roche, accompanied by his principal officers, descended into a small boat, and landed. He was the first to disembark, plant a cross, and the flag of France and Navarre in the sand, and take possession of the island in the name of the king, his master.

The sun set behind a thick gray cloud, which stained the azure of the firmament as a spot of ink would stain a holiday robe, when the small boat bringing back William de la Roche came for John de Ganay, the four sailors, charged with watching over his personal safety, and the pretended Yvon who served him as a domestic.

In this capacity Guyonne proceeded to cross the bulwark to take part in the landing, when Chedotel seized her by the hand, and exclaimed with concentrated fury:

"Woman, it is your wish! Well, you will be the prey of antiches who await you yonder. Adieu!" added he almost biting her fingers. "Do not forget the first and last kiss of your lover, Chedotel!"

Guyonne trembled with fright under the infernal gaze of the pilot, and mechanically jumped into the boat which set off at once.

It had but touched the shore when a sudden gust of wind whistled in the rigging of the Castor. A rolling of thunder succeeded to this sinister presage. The bark made three successive lurches, and receded as if driven by an irresistible power.

"Blood and death!" said Chedotel, "hell seconds my designs! We will weigh anchor.—Raise the anchor, and take a reef in the mizzen-sail!"

"What's the reason of this?" asked William de la Roche.

"Do you see these phosphorescent egrets which dance at the extremity of the cacatois?" replied Chetodel; "it is St. Elme's fire. It is necessary to regain the deep sea at once, if we don't wish to be wrecked on the shoals, or against the rocks.

Forty persons, including Guyonne and John de Ganay, remained on the island of Sable.

PART II.

CHAPTER I.

THE ISLE OF SABLE.

The Isle of Sable, a wild and arid plain, is situated in latitude 43 degrees, 56 minutes, 42 seconds; and in longitude 60 degrees, 17 minutes, 15 seconds, on the great oceanic route taken by vessels to gain the northern ports both of the Old and of the New World. Its distance on this side of Neadie (Nova Scotia), and Cape Britain, is about eighty-five miles. As its name indicates, hills of sand, indented by the waves, compose it. It scarcely rises above the elevation of the sea; although it contains some hills which consist also of sand. The best known at the present day is Mount Lutrell, situated at the western extremity towards the south. The Isle of Sable is in the form of a crescent. Its greatest length from east to west does not exceed ten leagues; its breadth five leagues. Placed at the north of the St. Lawrence, in the Atlantic, it is surrounded by large banks, such as are generally to be found at the confluence of rivers. A broad beach, covered by the sea when the tide is in, and left dry when the tide is out, surrounds the island throughout its whole circumference. If nature had made it productive and habitable, this wonld have proved a better and more formidable defence than a line of ramparts and bastions, for not only are large ships precluded from approaching; but even coasting vessels can arrive only with the aid of their boats. At the centre is a lake, now called Lake Wallace, which is five miles in circumference. The shores of this alone enjoy a sort of sickly fertility. Here are to be seen some stunted, consumptive trees, or rather shrubs, and occasionally shreds of down; also some plants of pale color and weak stems. It is, in short, an utter desolation, forgotten by some fatality, in a corner of the Atlantic.

"Never," says Charlevoix, in his *History of New France*, "was land less fitted to be the abode of men."

From time immemorial, the Isle of Sable has been the terror of mariners engaged in fishing, or in collecting furs in the waters of Acadia. Long before the expedition of John Cartier it was known and feared by the Basques, the Normans, and the Britons. The sea constantly pours its stormy waves around its coast, and the impenetrable fogs which brood over it render landing on it a difficulty almost insurmountable.. Even at the present day, it seems a sombre presage to all who approach it. The mariners, in their figurative language, have given it the name of "Hell Avenue."

In 1804, the British Government, actuated by a philanthropic solicitude which cannot be too much praised, established a station there, the object of which was to pick up any that happened to be shipwrecked; and in 1853 it erected houses, supplied with all things necessary to afford assistance to the ill-fated persons cast on its shores every month, nay, every week.

With the exception of a few sea-birds, no kind of game is to be met with on the Isle of Sable.

Let us now return to the forty individuals whom the Marquis de la Roche had left in this frightful solitude.

CHAPTER II.

THE FORTY.

As the Castor, after having veered about, steered with rapidity towards the east, a cry rose from the Isle of Sable.

A spontaneous, terrible, immense cry; a cry of despair, which drove from their retreat a flock of sea-gulls, and rose for a moment above the rumbling of the angry waves.

It was a cry from thirty-eight human breasts; one that concentrated the apprehensions of thirty-eight human beings; expressed the anguish of thirty-eight human souls, which saw departing the last tie which united them to civilized society.

Then were seen frightful individual scenes.

As many in a rage as there were men; as many violent clamors as there were voices; as many imprecations against heaven and the ship which was disappearing as there were arms!

The pencil has not sufficient colors, nor has the pen sufficient graphic force to reproduce this horrible picture.

After long days of suffering and privation in the entrails of a vessel, where they were huddled together like negroes at the bottom of the hold; after having seen land, and having saluted it with the enthusiasm of a prisoner saluting the hour of his deliverance; after having formed a thousand projects of future felicity, tasted the imaginary pleasures of soon being able to eat and drink at discretion; after so many emotions, to fall suddenly on an unknown shore, to all appearance sterile, at the beginning of a storm, without any covering against rain, without food to revive their strength, exhausted by famine! Could stoicism incarnate have resisted assaults so made?

To try to calm them, or make them listen to reason, was like casting oil on a blazing fire in order to extinguish it.

Viscount de Ganay, notwithstanding his youth, had too much experience of men and things, to excite still more those savage natures by any precipitate effort. Believing, besides, that the Castor had only weighed anchor to seek a safer mooring, he waited calmly until the effervescence should appease itself.

The predictions of the equerry in regard to his companions were realized.

Wearied with blaspheming and swinging their arms, in vain the best disposed concluded to make the best of their situation. Accompanied by Guyonne, and the four sailors that served him as an escort, John, believing that the time had come to act, approached the groups.

The bandits, in their excitement, had not remarked the presence of the viscount amongst them. When it was known, hope revived in those susceptible hearts; and they instantly gave way to the most divergent sensations. John de Ganay appeared to them as a sacred hostage; as a certain proof that the Governor of New France did not intend to abandon them. Towards them, reproved by the world, a great and powerful lord had the right of perfidy; but the viscount was a true nobleman; his arms attested the fact; and certainly the Marquis de la Roche would not have had the audacity to play such a nasty trick on a member of the distinguished Burgundian family of the De Ganays.

These natural reflections soon found expression, and the viscount found every ear ready to listen to him, and every hand ready to obey his orders.

The night rapidly unfolded its gloomy mantle; the rain fell in torrents, and the wind took masses of water from the surge, and dashed them about on the beach.

"Come, my braves," said the equerry to the exiles who surrounded him, "as it is not likely that we shall hear anything of the Castor before to-morrow morning, we had better encamp here as best we can. Form yourselves in groups of ten each; my sailors will give each group rations of wine and salt-meat, which I have landed in my boat; then, by cutting some branches, and inserting them in the sand, and covering them with your linen sheets, you can construct tents which will be passable for valiant troopers, more accustomed to lie under the canopy of the stars than under decorated wainscots. *Vive* Monseigneur de la Roche, Governor of New France!"—

"*Vive* Monseigneur de la Roche, Governor of New France!" unanimously repeated the convicts; for in appealing to the valor of the bandits, John de Ganay took them at their weak side. To flatter the self-love of the masses is the secret of the eloquence of the great popular orators.

The rations of wine and provisions were scrupulously distributed, and promptly swallowed, and each group commenced the duty of preparing a refuge against the storm which still raged furiously.

Enveloped in his mantle, John de Ganay superintended the works, while his sailors and Guyonne prepared a tent in the centre of the little camp. Towards nine o'clock all that was necessary, was done, and the rain ceased by degrees; but it was succeeded by a piercing cold, so that the poor bandits, drenched to the skin, had a very disagreeable night in perspective, when an old mariner, who had taken part in the expedition of Roberval, asked suddenly, addressing himself to the viscount:

"Would monseigneur permit us to light a fire?"

"Light it, my brave," replied the equerry, "but I am afraid, you cannot succeed. The two barrels of powder I have brought here from the Castor are damaged; and as it may happen that I may require my pistols for some more pressing business ——"

"No matter for that, monseigneur! I learned from the savages of Acadia how to light a fire without either powder or flint."

"Truly, that is curious! How do you do it?"

"Nothing more simple, as you will see."

The sailor retired, and, guided by the moon which emerged at intervals from behind a curtain of thick clouds, succeeded in discovering in the cavities of the shore some dry sea-weed and two branches of rotten beech.

Having brought both into the tent of the viscount, he cut a hole into the thickest of the pieces of wood, sharpened the other, and introduced it into the whole which he had made, and rubbed the two branches against each other simultaneously, until they began to emit sparks.

At the sight of the sparks the bandits were astonished. Some believing it witchcraft, and devoutly crossing themselves; others resolutely crying out a miracle; others, still more fanatical, denounced it as an exhibition of the black art—a terrible charge in that age of superstition, when physical phenomena were considered as magic, and those who produced them were punished with butchery.

Fortunately for the ingenious sailor, John de Ganay did not partake of the prejudices of the precept: "Be aware of exhibiting your science to the ignorant; for of ten who will witness it, there will be nine who will deny it, one who will refute it, and ten who will be jealous of it."

With the exception of the viscount, of the three other sailors, and of Guyonne, all refused for a long time to warm themselves at this fire, "kindled by hell." Finally, however, the cold increasing in intensity, a few ventured, the rest imitated them, like the sheep of Panurge; but the equerry, having advised them to take some coals out of the fire, and light others for themselves, none dared to venture. These men, who, as they said themselves, feared neither God nor the devil, and who cared little for divine or human, had all horror of the supernatural.

From this night forth, as will be seen in the course of our narrative, the sailor Philip Francœur, surnamed the *Maleficieux*, was an object of aversion, dread, and respect to the entire troop of convicts.

CHAPTER III.

FIRST DAY ON THE ISLAND OF SABLE.

THE night passed without accident. Early next morning the convicts, standing on the heights on the shore, sought anxiously a glance at the ship that had brought them. Vain attempt, although no fog extended its mantle over the face of the Ocean; although the sun shone brightly, nothing interposed between the eye and the impenetrable *bariere* of the horizon.

"Venison stomach!" said an ex-lancer who had served under Mayenne, and affected the manners and the favorite expressions of the celebrated covenanter. "Venison stomach! I believe, we are closer prisoners than paroquets in a cage."

"Do you believe it, Grosbec?"

"It is my melancholy opinion. No more of the Castor, on the plane liquid, as M. Virgilius Maro said."

"Yes, but she is coming."

"Who is?"

"The Castor."

"Calculate on that, my brave German, and in the mean time hold your tongue."

"Ah, I perceive ——'

"What do you perceive?"

"Down there, at the South!"

"Ninny, it is a sea-gull."

"Yes, it is a sea-gull," gravely observed a large man, a sort of Hercules, who had hitherto remained silent.

"A sea-gull," repeated the ex-lancer, "and I am afraid! What do you think, father Francis Rivet?" said Brise-tout.

"What I say, is," said the colossus, striking his foot against the ground, "that you are right, Grosbec, we are left like rats in a trap, brutally abandoned here to perish with hunger. Ah, Molin, although the devil may have him, predicted rightly. Do you know, said he to me, that we are to be abandoned, in order that our carcasses may serve as food for fishes, or ravens; not a doubt of it?"

"From the point of view in which he regarded it he was not deceived, poor Molin," said Grosbec; "but, venison stomach, we are not yet reduced to that?"

"Not yet, possibly, and to-morrow—"

"To-morrow," said another personage, lost in the crowd, "the Castor will have returned."

"Who says that," asked Grosbec.

"Nabot," replied several voices sneering.

"Nabot is an imbecile," said Brise-tout with impatience.

"An imbecile! who is he that has called me that name," exclaimed a little man, scarcely three feet and a half high, stepping over the legs of the spectators, and advancing towards the giant.

"The imbecile who has given you his name, is I," rejoined Brise-tout.

"You?" said the dwarf, striking his fists proudly against his haunches.

"Alas! yes, my fine miscarriage."

The face of Nabot grew pale with fury.

"Then you imagine, you are very strong."

"*Mordieu!*" I am as strong, in any case, as an embryo like you."

"Yes, but say that again!"

This was received with general laughter.

"You do not know, perhaps," said Nabot, "that, small as it is, the hatchet fells the largest oak, and the sword-fish kills the whale."

"After?—"

"After?—let you take care!"

In finishing these words, the dwarf jumped on his belly, seized Brise-tout by the leg, and before the latter had thought of opposing his design, threw him at full length on the sand to the great amusement of the lookers-on.

The colossus rose, muttering menacing words between his clenched teeth, and proceeded to chastise his tiny adversary; but Nabot prudently hid himself.

The murmurs suspended by this joke, recommenced with renewed bitterness. Brise-tout, as much to cause the trick played upon him, to be forgotten, as from natural taste, constituted himself the mouthpiece of these murmurs.

"Since we are abandoned," resumed he with that guttural accent, characteristic of him, "I think, we ought to divide all the munitions, and that afterwards each person may make what disposition of himself he may think proper, living here or leaving it."

"That's right, that's right!" replied several bandits, giving serious glances at the tent of John de Ganay. "No privilege, no chief, let us divide!"

"Yes, divide, pack of dogs!" said a sailor who suddenly made his appearance in the midst of the mutineers.

"What is he muttering there?" said Brise-tout, breaking a round shuffle-board between his fingers as a pastime.

"I am muttering that you are more beasts, than the porpoises, you especially, descendant of Goliath," continued Malificieux. "What, you grumble because the Castor is not yet returned! But do you not know that a squall may chase a vessel a hundred leagues out of her course? And I, who have been twenty years at sea, told you that the Castor could not be here before to-morrow. But, here comes Lord de Ganay, I advise you to keep quiet, if you value your skin. Come, silence in the ranks! Do you not remember the dance of Molin, Tronchard, Pepoli, and company, eh?"

This question, asked with sarcastic irony, was more than sufficient to impose silence on the mutineers who feared that their conduct might be regarded as a revolt. So when Viscount de Ganay made his appearance in the midst of the groups, he found the bandits generally disposed to listen to him.

The equerry had profoundly reflected during the night. The conclusion he came to was that he must act with energy towards the perturbed and vicious spirits placed under his control, if he wished to make them obey him in the end. Consequently, having assured himself that his four sailors would devote themselves to him to the last, he resolved to explore the island, then to establish his camp in a convenient place.

He then divided his men into four bands of ten, each of which he placed under the authority of a sailor.

A half a dozen pairs of pistols, as many hatchets—such were the only arms and impliments possessed by the exiles. These arms were divided between the commanders of troops; then a rallying cry was agreed upon to be used either in case of danger, or for the purpose of waiting. It was decided that towards two o'clock in the afternoon the various bands would take up their march to return to the point of departure, and that at least three scouts should be sent in advance, one to remain, to receive the Castor, if, perchance, she should re-appear during the absence of the explorers.

One band proceeded towards the east, another towards the west, the third between these two, that is towards the presumed centre of the island.

This third band was commanded by John de Ganay in person, with Malificieux as lieutenant. Among those who composed it, were included our acquaintances Guyonne, Brise-tout, Nabot, Grosbec.

The day was luxuriant in charms. Nothing could equal the purity of the sky which looked like a cupola of saphire, in the midst of which was set a sparkling carbuncle. The sands on the beach, reflecting a thousand fires under the rays of the sun, seemed to form round the island a collar of pearls and rubies; there was nothing even to the meagre brushwood, and shrubs seen in the distance which did not impart to that desolate shore an air of deceitful gayety which at first dissipated the sinister apprehensions of the convicts.

"Venison stomach!" said Grosbec, addressing himself to Brise-tout, "it is my opinion that we are wrong, after all, in regarding ourselves as desolate; we are in a good country. Provided that the savage demoiselles do not show themselves too particular in the chapter of manners. —By the way, where the devil do those ladies conceal themselves? I have not yet had the pleasure of a glance at one of them!"

"The savages! nothing more is wanting now!" swore Brise-tout.

"Monsieur Grosbec, mind your nose," interposed Nabot.

"My nose!" replied the ex-lancer, raising his hand to that organ, which was unduly prominent.

"Eh! without doubt, the Indians have a great fancy for the nose; ask Malificieux."

"Be silent, you insect," replied Francis Rivet, pulling the ear of the dwarf.

"Ah!" exclaimed the latter, "do you think, I am deaf?"

"Stop, earth-worm," said Grosbee, "venison stomach! what famous odor one respires at home."

"Excuse! the odor of a corrupted spouse," said the dwarf.

"Some vervain, brute!"

"That depends on the nose."

"On what?"

"On the nose, venison stomach!" retorted Nabot, imitating the Gascon accent of Grosbec.

This bad pun had a foolish success, and elicited peals of laughter.

"Silence!" interposed Malificieux, "this is neither the hour nor the place to joke in school-boy fashion. Let us see, what is that?"

At the call of the sailor John de Ganay stopped, and was imitated by the other man, whose eyes turned anxiously towards the point which Philip Francœur indicated with his finger. There, among the branches of some junipers, appeared a white body, which passed along on the grass with the utmost tranquillity. John de Ganay loaded a pistol, adjusted it, and fired, but without result; for the animal was seen to bound off at once. The march, interrupted by this incident, was immediately resumed. At noon, the convicts reached a lake, and a halt was ordered. No human trace was remarked; and at the places visited by John de Ganay, the island was not only deserted, but destitute of everything necessary for the subsistence of our race. However, the sight of the lake reanimated his hope; the shores were found green; and their soil seemed suitable for culture. Desirous of pursuing his observations, the equerry lounged on the bank of the lake, while his companions rested themselves, or made war on the inhabitants of the water. He arrived thus at a grove of birch; having passed it, he suddenly found himself before a hut, coarsely constructed of branches. At the noise of his footstep, an individual, covered with skins, who had been squatting on the threshold, uttered a sharp cry, and plunged into the lake. John knew not what fear was; but a wise prudence counseled him not to venture any farther, suspecting that the beech grove might be haunted by a tribe of savages. He even determined not to make his discovery known to the bandits for the present, in order to avoid increasing their discontent. On rejoining them, he partook of a modest repast of fish, which they had prepared, and then brought them back to the camp of the previous evening, but little impressed in favor of what they had seen.

Already the two other troops had returned. Their report was unanimous; the island produced nothing but sand

The roll of the convicts was called; there was but one wanting—number 40. Guyonne!.

CHAPTER IV.

BRISE-TOUT.

John de Ganay alone felt some uneasiness for the absence of number 40. The rest of the band were naturally too selfish and too well used to the vicissitudes of fortune to care about her. Besides, the pretended Yvon, far from inspiring the affection of the bandits, had rather excited their jealousy, on account of the interest which the viscount did not cease to take in her welfare. In all places, in all positions, man sees with displeasure one of his equals more favored than himself; but it is epecially in the heart of the unfortunate that envy has established the seat of its empire. As to the equerry, two reasons caused him to regret the disappearance of Guyonne; first, the attachment which he felt towards the pretended young man; then the fear that her disappearance was to be attributed to the personage he had seen at the brink of the lake. However, he concealed his fears, and tried to seem gayer than usual, in order to reassure the convicts. Those who had remained at the encampment had spent the day in constructing as comfortable tents as possible. The debris of a wrecked ship had served them for this purpose; and when the explorers returned, those tents were in a state sufficiently advanced to inspire the hope that they would pass a better night than the first. Each of the departments had procured some edibles during their expedition, some ordinary fish, and others shell fish. The supper was prepared, and it was disposed of merrily; for before commencing his repast, Maleficieux made the remark, that the wind having veered to the southeast, it was to be presumed that the Castor would reappear next morning.

"If your prediction proves true, sailor," said Grosbec, "I swear to make you king——of libertines."

"And I," said Nabot, "I demand that the very illustrious Brise-tout be nominated pope of fools."

"Well done!" exclaimed the guests, who suspended their noisy mastication to give a mocking look at the hideous countenance of the colossus.

"Omelette!" said the latter, without losing a mouthful. "He will pay for it to me."

"In monkey coin!" retorted the dwarf, with a look of scorn at Brise-tout.

"Let you take care of yourself," said Grosbec; "when the elephant is tired playing with a cur he crushes him."

"Pshaw!" sneered the little man, "his character of my friend Brise-tout is too delicately conformed to his face.

There is no danger that he will take my sweets for absynth. Not the son of Venus the Ugly!"

"*Satane diabolieu!*" said Philip Francœur, tapping Nabot on the cheek with the handle of his knife.

"Yes, a devil, whom I'll reduce to the state of an angel," grumbled the colossus.

"Plague! the reduction will not be the more to be disdained. I, who have never been worth a farthing, shall not see myself metamorphosed without pleasure. Oh, what's the matter? A bucket of water! Master Polyhemus finds himself unwell. Quick, quick! Don't you see he puts out his tongue like one balancing on the gallows?"

Nabot spoke truly. Brise-tout, whose anger could not restrain a frightful voracity, had just swallowed a fish-bone, and was making unheard-of efforts to deliver himself of the bone stuck in his throat. He gesticulated, became enraged, perspired, wept, frothed, but in vain. The bone, far from yielding to his attempts to expectorate, stuck deeper and deeper into the flesh.

I leave the reader to imagine how great was the hilarity of the spectators.

"A pair of pencils to aid our Hercules," said one.

"No, do not deprive him of the merit of accomplishing alone, and without assistance, this third labor," replied the ex-lancer.

"*Sacramente!*" added the German, "he is just going if you don't unbutton him."

"Poor dear," continued Nabot, laughing to tears, "don't be discouraged. Valor! Yet another grunt! Stronger! there—well—that's the way!"

"He will conquer!—He will not! I told you he would conquer!—I told you not—Let. us bet——There, he is choking!"

"For God's sake, my love, at least do not break that bone. I will keep it; I will preserve it as a relic, in order to make a tooth-pick!"

The peals of laughter were redoubled.

However, the affair was not laughable in itself; and Francis Rivet did not laugh. His countenance, livid, and marked with red spots, contracted with pain, his mouth open and inundated with saliva and blood, his large staring eyes, of which the pupils hid under the lids; his body agitated with spasmodic movements, presented a horrible picture, whilst the cavernous sounds which grated in escaping from his breast, would have frozen with fright any other spectators than those which surrounded him.

"What a head!" said the incorrigible dwarf. "Is there no painter among us?"

"Why is Signor Titian dead?" added a Piedmontese.

"Ah, but," pursued Nabot, "Christian charity requires us to pray for those in pain. Let us, then, pray for our unfortunate companion drawing his last breath."

"*De profundis clamavi*," stammered Grosbec. "To die of a fish-bone is a lamentable destiny. Regretted Brise-tout, I will compose an elegy on his death. I will sing of his stoicism in suffering. I will deliver his funeral oration with the accompaniment of a Jew's harp and a wooden corn-creak."

"There is your epitaph, dear cherubim," said Nabot. "Hear and judge, before sacrificing yourself in the prime of life, to the worms of the grave."

Gross as this buffoonery was, it had the effect of bringing to a climax the good humor of the bandits, who clapped their hands with frenzy; for nothing is more acceptable to the vulgar than that which humbles a superior being.

But the thing had been carried too far. Irritated by excrutiating pain, the victim of their farce suddenly pounced on his tormentors, like a bull exasperated by the lances of the picadors, seized Grosbec by one hand, and Nabot with the other, lifted them off the ground, held them a moment in the air, and with his eye covered with blood, his lips with foam, he was going to knock their heads against each other, when an insupportable spasm forced him to loosen his grasp. Brise-tout returned, uttering a suffocating cry. Behind him stood Maleficieux, who, armed with a burning stick, thought it well to apply the extremity to the cheek of the giant, as the only means of saving the imprudents fallen in the power of his rage. Insanity commenced to gain on Francis Rivet. He saw no more; heard no more. The veins of his temples were swollen beyond measure. A delirious fever raged in his brain. Incapable of reflection, guided only by the instinct of an irritated animal, he leaped at the new enemy who dared to brave his fury. But Philip Francœur was as agile as a squirrel. He threw away his brand, precipitated himself on Brise-tout, leaped on his back, seized him vigorously by the neck, and aided by some other bandits who wished to join him, threw the giant on the ground. There a terrible struggle took place, the struggle of a bear attacked by a pack of hounds; but succumbing in the end to the number of his assailants, Brise-tout made a desperate effort to free himself; and while all his muscles were distended, all his physical faculties in full play, a terrible bellowing burst from his larynx, with streams of blood. The bone had disengaged itself in this supreme convulsion, and Francis Rivet signalized in his own way the termination of his suffering. Nevertheless, he got rid of one evil only to exchange it for one a hundred times worse; for his adversaries, exasperated by the blows he had given them, were by no means disposed to abandon him; but the arrival of John de Ganay was the signal of his deliverance.

The row had attracted the attention of the viscount, who was promenading alone on the beach. He hastened to pacify the combatants; and returned after having been assured by Maleficieux, that order would be maintained.

The night had already veiled the Isle of Sable. However, the convicts felt no inclination to sleep. The scene jnst referred to had excited them too much to compose themselves so soon. The fire was revived; each took his place around it with the exception of Brise-tout, who persisted in grumbling in a corner; and yielding to the solicitations of his comrades, who begged him to tell a story, the sailor, Philip Francœux, expressed himself in these terms:

CHAPTER V.

THE LEGEND.

"WELL, by boys, open your hatches, for I am going to unfold a long cable. Not to bewilder you in a maze of phrases, there are no doubt some among you who have beat about the Rue du Possédé, at St. Malo; a narrow, tortuous street, as sombre as the steerage of the Castor. By Neptune, it is well named the Rue du Possédé (Street of the Possessed). When one sees its delapidated worm-eaten houses, he feels ready to commit his soul to God. What stench! What a foretaste of hell! And it is haunted even at the present day only by emissaries of the devil. It is here, then, we are about to cast anchor for a moment.

"Forty years have now passed since the Rue du Possédé was the terror of the brave, devoted people of St. Malo, who regularly paid their tithes, and never failed, on returning from a sea-voyage, to offer a large yellow wax candle to our Lady of Good-Succor. But Lucifer is a cunning chap. No doubt you have heard how he bewitched the soul of a poor fisherman of the Rue du Possédé.

"Well, by the trident of Neptune! You will see how the fisherman became amorous, yes, amorous, my boys; and of the most beautiful girl in St. Malo! But she was as proud as a duchess. Yes, indeed, by the trident of Neptune; and James tried in vain, he could not anchor in the heart of his beloved. This rendered him sad and sombre as a tempest; so much so that he finally shut himself up in his steerage of the Rue du Possédé, and that it was soon discussed in the neighborhood every Sunday. Yes, indeed, by the trident of Neptune!

"In the mean time, Dame Louison permitted herself to be courted by the son of a currier, who was very rich, and so good a fellow that it was regarded as a real pleasure to see them dance together Sundays, after vespers.

"It had been agreed that they would get married after Easter; but when the old people were spoken to about the marriage, they shook their heads, saying:

"'The poor children! the poor children! Ah, it is much to be feared that Jacot will play them a bad trick!'

"Ay, and the old people were right; for do you see, my boys, those who have navigated on the ocean have an experience of which youth is ignorant. Yes, indeed, by the trident of Neptune.

"The fact is, that those who remarked Jacot, could not be mistaken in regard to his designs. One day he was as pale as a new sail; another, green as the leaves of a sapling; another, as red as blood; and always, always his eyes sparkled like coals of fire.

"Some went so far as to say that streams of sulphur and bitumen flowed from his mouth; others had it that peals of thunder issued from his house at night, even when the sky was pure and serene; some had seen him make the sign of the cross with his left hand; so that the Rue du Possédé was abandoned by degrees, and he remained alone, in company with demons. Yes, indeed, by the trident of Jupiter!

"It happened that on the Sunday evening before she was to be married to the son of the leather dresser, he invited her to take a sail with him in his boat.

"The weather was delightful, and Dame Louison had the misfortune to accept. They started at two o'clock, gay and joyous, in a little bark almost covered with ribbons. But the moment they quitted the beach, a black boat was observed in the distance, which hoisted sail, and seemed to watch the young people. Immediately all at the shore were overwhelmed with fright.

"The black boat was that of James.

"Dame Louison who was the first to distinguish it, felt the chilness of death running in her veins.

"'Let us return, let us return to land,' said she to her lover.

"'Return to land, why?'

"'I tremble!'

"'But ——'

"'See,' said she, showing him with the point of her finger the skiff, from the hull of which flowed such a stream of light that it made the rays of the sun seem pale—

"What, sacramento? the skiff burned in the midst of the sea!"

"Burned!" replied Maleficeux, "who has told you that it burned?"

"Since it was on fire!"

"Ah! novice, does the fire of hell burn the demons?"

"Brute of a German," said Grosbec, shrugging his shoulders. "You have never seen anything. Continue your story, sailor."

"Yes, indeed, by the trident of Neptune," resumed Philip Francœur, "burning flames streamed from the black skiff; and James stood up in the middle of it as tall as the mast of a man-of-war; his mouth vomiting torrents of smoke.

"All on the beach saw him, with the exception of the currier's son, who, far from listening to the prayers of Louison, commenced to row exactly in the direction of the black skiff.

"The latter receded towards the north, and the currier's boat followed. The black skiff having tacked about, the other tacked also. It was said that the former must be loadstone, and the latter iron so faithfully did they perform the same evolutions.

"However, the boat approached the black skiff by degrees, and after an hour's manœuvring in the bay they turned suddenly towards the north, and both steered in that direction.

"In a short time they almost touched each other. The agitated sea roared on the rocks, and flocks of griffins, larger than vultures, cut the air with their wings, uttering lugubrious cries.

"The two boats still appeared; but only like a camp-fire at the confines of the horizon. Then all of a sudden, a frightful peal of thunder was heard, and after that nothing was seen—except the sea white with foam, extended along the beach.

"The people of St. Malo went to the church, and prayed to the Holy Virgin to save Louison and the son of the leather-dresser. The day passed without any news having been heard in regard to them; but towards midnight, when the storm was at its height, the mariners remarked by the flashes of lightning that a small boat entered the harbor. It was observed to contain two persons, a man and a woman. In landing, the man put his arm about the woman's neck, and said: 'You will swear to me, on the salvation of your soul, that you are mine.' 'Yes, yours, nobody's but yours; always yours!' replied the woman. The unknown then stooped his head, and embraced the woman. She uttered a cry, and the sailors saw a glistening circle at the place where the man had put his lips. The sailors fled horror-stricken.

"Next day it was reported at St. Malo that, swallowed up with his boat during the storm, the son of the currier had perished, and that Louison was saved by James the Possessed.

"Some believed the recital; others regarded the fact as a magical charm; yes, indeed, by the trident of Neptune!

"What is certain is, that in one month after Louison married James, the poor fisherman became a rich captain, and received from the king a commission to go with two ships to reconnoitre the shores of Newfoundland.

"Not possible!" said the German.

"It was, then, James Cartier," added Grosbec.

"It was James, and that's all I know of it, my boys," replied Maleficieux with a knowing air. "My grandfather, from whom I got the story, did not tell me any more."

"But what way did your James die?" asked Nabot, who had listened attentively to the legend of the sailor, with his elbows on his knees, and his face resting on the palm of his hand.

"In what way did he die; yes, how did he die?" added the ex-lancer.

All eyes were turned towards Philip Francœur.

"Ah! there it is," said he, with the complaisance of a narrator who has captivated the attention of his audience; "that is something that has never been found out, and never will be; yes, indeed, by the trident of Neptune!"

Each of the bandits made a gesture of disappointment.

"However," resumed Maleficieux, seeming to collect his souvenirs, "I will relate what I have been assured by my grandfather, who was well acquainted with James:

"A certain evening, the fisherman having met Louison, begged her to consent to become his wife.

"'I will accede to your wishes when you can give me a hundred crowns in gold,' replied she.

"A hundred crowns in gold! it is more than James could amass by twenty years' labor." He returned to his cabin in despair, and decided to commit suicide. But just as he was passing his neck into the cord which was to deprive him of a life that had become insupportable, a little man, clad in black, suddenly entered his chamber.

"'What's that you are doing?'

"James made no reply. The appearance of the little man terrified him.

"'You want to hang yourself, imbecile,' continued the stranger. 'Much rather burn that rope, and marry the one you love.'

"'Marry Louison!'

"'Yes, certainly, would you not prefer that?'

"'Oh! yes but—'

"'But you want a hundred crowns in gold, do you not? and I will give you a thousand.'

"'You!'

"'Why not?'

"The looks of the little man were not well calculated to inspire confidence: for through the port-holes of his black coat was to be seen his dirty, hairy skin; then he felt ill.

"'Well,' said he with a sort of titter, 'follow me.!'

"James hardly knew whether he was dead or alive, however, he approached the stranger.

"Where will we go?' asked he

"'Get on my shoulders.'

"'I am too heavy; I shall break your back.'

"'Never mind that—get up!'

"He obeyed. The little man tittered again, and said:

"'Are you up?'

"'Yes,' replied the fisherman, trembling all over, for in crossing his arms round the neck of the stranger it seemed as if he had applied them to a red iron; James wished to jump on the ground; he could not; his fingers were riveted to each other, and his thighs fastened to the haunches of the little man, who immediately blasphemed the name of God, rose to the ceiling, which opened to make a passage for him, and in less than a second transported the poor fisherman to the top of a precipice twenty leagues from St. Malo; yes, indeed, by the trident of Neptune!

"There a crowd of monsters of all kinds growled about a large pot in which the members of a human being were cooking.

"The little man placed James near the pot, and said to him: 'Look!'

"The unfortunate man, although half dead with fright, looked and recognized the head of the currier's son, his rival, which the water, in boiling, caused to rise to the surface.

"'Horror!' exclaimed he.

"'You will drink a part of this broth, my friend,' said a hideous old woman, covered with wrinkles, who skimmed the pot.

"'No, no! never!'

"The monsters broke out into vociferations, and commenced a satanic dance around the fire.

"A cold perspiration suffused the limbs of James; and, strange to say, the blood ran through his veins as cold as frozen lead.

"'I am thirsty,' stammered he.

"The imprecations of the monsters redoubled.

"'Here is some broth; drink!' said the old woman.

"He jumped back with horror, but in an instant after exclaimed:

"'Some drink; oh, give me something to drink!'

"'The broth is ready; drink!' repeated the old woman.

"James lost his senses; his burning lips calcined his teeth, and his saliva was transformed into vitriol.

"'I want a drink; give me something to drink!'

"'Here, drink, my love!" said the old woman, presenting him a spoon filled with the infamous beverage; 'drink, and you will wed the beautiful Louison.'

"James, not knowing any longer what he was doing, took the spoon raised it to his lips, but seized with a remorse of conscience, he threw it away, as far as he could. But alas, it was too late; a drop of the broth which fell on his tongue sealed for all eternity his compact with the demons. Yes, indeed, by the trident of Neptune!

"Immediately the monsters approached James, kissed him in turn on both cheeks, and disappeared in the midst of a frightful clatter.

"James found himself alone on the precipice, with the little man.

"'Well, now, what do you wish?' asked the devil; for it was Satan. Yes, indeed, by the trident of Neptune!

"'To wed Louison,' replied the fisherman, who no longer entertained any fear of Satan.

"'You will wed her; but then?'

"'To be rich.'

"'You will; but then?'

"'Cause me to be spoken of throughout the world for centuries to come.'

"The Prince of Darkness made the usual sneering grimace.

"'It will be done according to your will; but then?'

"'Nothing.'

"'You are not ambitious, indeed! Rarely have I got any soul so cheap as yours. But as short accounts make long friends, first sign this paper.'

"'What is it?'

"'Oh, a trifle! Only the sale of your soul for love, fortune, and glory. Sign, please; time presses.'

"James shuddered. Two pictures unrolled themselves before his eyes. Here his mother and his guardian angel conjuring him not to abandon the path of virtue; there Pleasure, showing him her allurements, leaning on the arms of Luxury and Renown.

"James signed!

"'Get on my back once more,' said the devil.

"Raising him like a feather, they crossed the bay, the ocean, and arrived at a savage country, covered with snows and ice, inhabited by men who no longer resembled other human beings any more than a land wolf resembles a sea wolf. When they had arrived, the devil said to Jack:

"'Do you know what this country is?'

"'No.'

"'It is a country into which I have not yet extended my dominion, but into which I shall extend it in two hundred years, with your aid. You know your route. Return home; for it is not good for me to be here yet a while; and when you wish you can immortalize yourself. Dig under the gate of your garden, and you will find the thousand crowns of gold I promised you. Yours, then, be love, glory, wealth. Mine, your soul!'

"Fear returned to James. He made a violent effort to separate from Satan, and found himself alone in his house in the Rue du Possédé.

"It was broad daylight. Yes, indeed, by the trident of Neptune!

"Satan had not deceived him. Having dug in the garden, as directed, he found a casket containing a thousand crowns of gold.

"I have told you how he married Louison; how he set out to explore the Banks of Newfoundland. At present, it only remains for me to tell you, that, having refound the country to which the devil had shown him the way, and amassed innumerable treasures, he had undertaken his eighth voyage to New France, when Satan appeared to him in a storm.

"James grew pale at the sight of him.

"'Have I kept my word?' said the Prince of Darkness.

"'Yes.'

"'And you have been happy?'

"James shook his head, white with age, by which he meant no.

"The devil smiled with a sardonic grin.

"'So much the worse,' said he. Your soul is mine; the hour is come!'

A flame scintillated at the extremity of the main-mast; a wave, high as a mountain, struck the prow of the vessel. Ten minutes after, she had disappeared with all she contained."

"And James?" exclaimed Nabot.

"James! I don't know. Yes, indeed, by the trident of Neptune!" replied Philip Francœur. "Now, good-night, my boys; don't have bad dreams; and may God preserve us from the devil! Yes, indeed——!"

Malificieux did not finish his oath, of which a glorious snoring took the place of the *finale.*

He was sound asleep.

CHAPTER VI.

THE SHIPWRECK.

The next and following days it rained so incessantly that the convicts were obliged to remain in the vicinity of their encampment. John de Ganay would have preferred that the weather would allow him to reconnoitre the whole island, but finding it impossible to do so, he wished the bandits to occupy their time in some useful labor. If nothing proved that the Castor would soon return for them, it was equally true that nothing proved the contrary. Who knows? Weeks might pass before her return. It was important, therefore, to prepare for the worst. Besides, John knew that idleness is a bad counselor. When occupied, his men reflected less on the uncertainty of their fate, and habituated themselves by degrees to colonial life and labors.

He commenced by causing a sort of intrenchment to be made around the tents. Large piles, sharpened at the end, hardened in the fire, and intertwined with flexible branches, served for this purpose.

The equerry would have wished to dig a ditch for more security; but all his efforts were fruitless. The soil on which he operated was sandy, and every blast of wind filled the opening he had made.

Several times John conceived the plan of going farther into the interior, and encamp on the banks of the lake; but on each occasion some fear prevented him.

In order to guide the course of the Castor, in case she approached the island, he planted in the most elevated spot a mast, from which floated a piece of red stuff; and he established a sort of guard at the foot of it, which was to remain day and night to watch. Four men, who relieved each other successively at every hour, composed the post. Another post was formed near the camp, and John de Ganay confided the command of it alternately to such bandit as was found to conduct himself best. These plans were as judicious as they were able. It accustomed the convicts to military discipline; they invited them to conduct themselves well, so that they might obtain the favor attached to good behavior; and at the same time obviated the danger of surprise, if, perchance, the island was inhabited by savages, or by wild beasts.

The convicts occupied themselves at this work until Sunday. During this interval they supported themselves with fishes which they captured in the following manner: having dug deep holes on the beach while the tide was out, they surrounded them with osier hurdles, and waited for the return of the tide; then, when the water retired, they ran to their nets, which they generally found filled with cod, herrings, soles, crabs, and other fishes, abounding on the shores of Acadia.

Several sea-birds were killed besides, which, prepared by Maleficieux, the inventor of the mode of fishing we have just described, did not seem the least palatable dish to those who tasted them.

In general, the bandits did not evince a very rebellious disposition. Whether it was that they were aware that a mutiny would not, in any respect, ameliorate their condition; or whether the four sailors inspired them with salutary fear, they implicitly obeyed the orders of John de Ganay.

Sunday was clearer than any of the five preceding days, although the sun had not yet appeared above the horizon. Clouds, tinged with gray, covered the sky, and an impetuous wind whistled from the southwest.

In the morning, John de Ganay gathered around him all his companions, and made an affecting speech, exhorting them to patience. Afterwards he read them some passages from the Bible. They listened to him eagerly, and several of them were moved to tears by the consoling maxims of the Holy Scriptures.

After these pious instructions, John advised his subordinates not to go far from their tents, for the tempest threatened, and as they had not yet any certain knowledge of the island, it was to be feared that they might lose their way in the course of an excursion.

But there was no need of these recommendations; the bandits, fatigued with their previous labors, felt much less disposed to absent themselves from camp than to repose on their beds of pine branches, whether to sleep, or to plot between themselves.

A few, however, proceeded to the Mast Post, as they called the corporal's guard, of which we have spoken, where Maleficieux was required to tell stories.

Towards three o'clock, in the afternoon, the wind, which had not ceased to agitate the air, redoubled its violence.

"By the trident of Neptune," suddenly exclaimed Philip Francœur, interrupting himself in the most dramatic part of his story, "does Monsieur Boreas wish to take us on board, in order to transport us to the other side of the Atlantic. This would not be a bad manœuvre. How he does scream there, the old fellow. Hum!"

"What squalls! what squalls!" said one of the assistants.

"They are quite strong enough to upset our tents," added another.

"And us with them," continued a third.

"Come, now," said Grosbec, with his usual self-sufficient air; "venison stomach! have you ever seen the wind strike a man like a branch of poplar? This would do in fairy tales, but—"

"Ah, is that your opinion, good lancer," said Maleficieux, leering at Grosbec with a dissatisfied air. "Is that your opinion? And if I said that I who speak to you, have seen with my own eyes what is called—"

A sharp gust, followed by a crackling and an irruption of air in to the cabin, cut short the speech of the sailor.

The storm had already carried away the roof of the guard-house; and almost at the same moment the convict who was on sentry at the foot of the great mast, shouted:

"A ship! I see a ship!"

Surprise and joy responded to this exclamation.

All who happened to be in the guard-room rushed out.

The quarter-deck of a ship appeared in front towards the west. But the condition of this vessel, whatever she might be, was evidently frightful. Three cannon shots and a black flag, displayed from the extremity of a poll, announced almost immediately the distress of those on board.

"By the trident of Neptune, she looks like the Erable! yes, indeed!" said Philip Francœur.

The reports of the three cannons had resounded through the tents, occupied by the bandits. Sleep, conversations, songs, stories, all were immediately interrupted, and every body ran to the beach.

The storm foamed with fury. Large copper-colored clouds chased each other through the sky with fearful rapidity. Occasional flashes of lightning lit up the meridian with their forked tongues. The wind, impetuous one moment, was silent the next, abandoning the atmosphere to a mortal silence, and the water to its own convulsions; then, panting, irritated, burst forth like a thunderbolt, whirled in immense columns, mixing, confounding, annihilating, raising mountains of sand, elevating the waves, breaking against each other, or transporting them to considerable distances.

John de Ganay was one of the first to arrive at the ruins of the guard-house.

"What's the matter?"

"A ship was in view a moment since," replied Maleficieux. "The waves hide it just now, but it will soon show itself."

"Is it the Castor?" asked the viscount, adjusting to his eye a little telescope he held in his hand.

"I do not know, sir; but I rather think it is the Erable."

"The Erable, that, God pardon me, would be excellent luck!"

The satisfaction of the equerry brightened up every feature; and certainly it would have been very great to have elicited from him such an exclamation, a severe Huguenot as he was.

"Yes, she must be the Erable, by the trident of Neptune," continued the sailor. "Is not her bulwark red?"

"Red, bordered with blue, I remember her perfectly;" replied John de Ganay.

"Red bordered with blue; it is she then; you can be as certain of it as that my name is Philip Francœur, surnamed the Maleficieux."

"Let us go an our knees, and thank the Lord, for we are about to be saved," said John.

"Saved? not so fast master."

"What do you mean?"

"I mean that it is necessary to make a sign to that ship at onco to avoid—if that is now possible. Otherwise—"

The sailor raised his eyes to the sky.

"Otherwise she is lost!" exclaimed the viscount.

"Lost, yes, I can assure you."

"But how are the signs to be made?"

"It is very easy, master."

Closing his right hand, Philip Francœur whistled between his fingers, and in half a minute after the three other sailors, his companions, were at his side.

They conferred briefly together, then one of them climbed up the adjacent mast, and attached two poles to it, in the form of a cross, to the ends of which were fixed pieces of calico of various shades of color, and cords that reached the ground; and having finished the work, he descended.

In the mean time the vessel had re-appeared on the foam of the waves.

John de Ganay saw her fully.

It was, indeed, the Erable; but in what a sad state! Her masts broken, her bulwark washed away, her rigging in pieces, her prow fractured—all told of a long and terrible struggle with the elements.

Groups of men encumbered the deck. Among these men were some who danced like demons; others who cried like women; others who, prostrate, seemed to implore with crossed hands the aid of Providence; others who, armed with large jugs, were drinking to intoxication; others who laughed fiercely, or rather grinned; others who struck each other, and yet others who vainly endeavored to pacify them.

The viscount, horrified at this spectacle, imagined he had seen a cargo of the damned. His face grew pale, and his eyes filled with tears.

"See!" said he, handing the telescope to Philip Francœur.

The latter examined carefully, but his countenance continued as immovable as marble. Stooping to the ear of the viscount:

"Not a word, master," whispered he, putting his finger on his lips. "They must have revolted on board of the Erable, and made themselves masters; but if it be the will of God that they land here, we can make their heads pay for it, provided that our people suspect nothing."

"Does anybody direct the vessel?" asked the Burgundian.

"I distinguish nobody; however, there may be a pilot at the helm; for the bark does not roll very much. I am going to arrange a signal."

But as he finished this remark, a gust of wind, as sudden as it was formidable, broke in two the mast, at the top of which he had established his telegraphic materials.

"No chance, by the trident of Neptune!"

"What a clatter!" added Grosbec.

The Erable approached nearer and nearer to the shore.

The night began to fall, and while one distinctly perceived the disabled hull, a monstrous wave bore her over the mouth of an abyss to another wave; anon she is precipitated into a deep gorge, pressed by swellings of the sea which seemed bent on her destruction

"Can we render them no assistance?" ventured the viscount with a melancholy apprehension.

"The weather-side! the weather-side!" shouted Malificieux, putting his hands before his lips as a speaking tube.

Nothing was heard from the ship.

A gigantic wave struck her prow on the larboard side, and, almost at the same instant, a mournful cracking was heard, which told that the vessel had struck on a sandbank.

An awful cry of savage energy struggled with the cries of the tempest; at the surface of the water were to be seen unfortunates whom the ocean tore against the rocks, as if for amusement, until the darkness covered with its veil the death struggle of the Erable.

CHAPTER VII.

THE WRECK.

The sun, beautiful and radiant, raising its golden globe from the waves of the Atlantic, illuminated on the Isle of Sable a still more desolate spectacle than that of the previous evening, displaying all the horrible features of the *denouement.*

The air was fresh, and perfumed with penetrating exhalations. Above the sea or land not the smallest cloud floated—not the lightest fog. The sky, blue as the iris, and transparent as a mirror, formed an arch like that of an immense dome, whose transparent limpidity reflected its splendor and brilliancy. The shrubs, ruffled by the tempest, rearranged themselves with the first kisses of the sun, their leaves, wet with the dew, sparkled like emeralds; and a few small birds, concealed in the brushwood, saluted melodiously with their melodies the promise of a beautiful day. What a difference between the rising of that sun, and the setting of that which it succeeded! Yesterday, the elements raged against themselves, as if they had wished to replunge themselves into chaos; this morning they smiled with their most harmonious smile, rivalling in attractions, in coquetry, pressing themselves amorously into each other's arms, like a newly married couple awakening for the first time in the nuptial couch!

But there remained sinister traces of their passed wrath—traces all the more sad, because in proportion as the weather is delightful, and Nature is adorned with her gayest colors; for beauty and gayety grieve the heart of man more when chagrin has distilled into them some drops of her poison.

Behold the beach on the Isle of Sable, near the camp of the convicts. The tents are torn down, or dispersed; a mountain of sand has risen where a ditch had been dug, and a ditch had been formed at the place from which the mountain had risen; the soil is scored with winds; trees are broken, split as if by lightning, uncrowned or uprooted, exhibited everywhere their wounds.

But a very different scene on the beach recalled but too eloquently the storm of Sunday.

In the midst of innumerable fragments of the shipwreck, are groups of human bodies. All, with rare exceptions, wore the same uniform as the convicts on the island; and the greater part are cruelly mutilated. One seemed as if he had been beheaded; another as if his limbs had been cut off; a third as if his body had been lacerated with sharp pebbles; in short, all seemed as if they had been disfigured on purpose.

They were huddled pell mell with chests, barrels, fragments of sail, yards, or spars, and as the sea retired, it left behind it new victims of its wrath. These bodies, boxes, and barrels, it is almost needless to say, came from the Erable, whose hull was still visible, ensconced between two rocks, at about a hundred perches from the shore. It was all that remained of the poor ship, lately so spruce under her light rigging. No living being escaped the catastrophe which had engulphed her; none to relate the drama which preceded, and no doubt preceded her last moments; for it was in vain the companions of John de Ganay passed the whole night on foot, and lit fires along the shore; the violence of the tide rendered all efforts at saving fruitless. Then, when, towards one o'clock in the morning, the ocean reposed from its fury as from lassitude, when its surface was levelled, its huge inequalities—vomited by the sea, the fragments of the wreck, men and things, from the Erable, are drawn to the beach of the Isle of Sable.

Unfortunates! to die so far from their country, in the prime of life, and such a death! But at least they had Christian burial; for the new islanders had already opened a deep ditch in the bosom of the earth; and with tears in their eyes, and prayers on their lips, they piously disposed those who were to have shared for ever their good or bad fortune.

Heart-rending obsequies these were! One sobbed, another tried to distinguish the features of a friend in the cold, inert, and lacerated body; and at the same time removed from him his miserable convict dress.

John de Ganay presided at the funerals. His countenance was pale, his eyes were red and dry. He did not weep; but what efforts he made to suppress the burning tears! Sensibility would have been weakness under such circumstances; he knew this, and imposed silence on the emotions which wrung his heart.

"Come, friends," said he, "let us hasten to accomplish this melancholy duty, and let us avail ourselves of the low tide, in order to secure such objects as high tide has brought us. Philip!"

Malificieux approached him respectfully.

"Has the body of the captain, or of any of the officers been found?"

"No, sir," replied the sailor, bowing.

"Do you think they have escaped from the wreck?"

"Escaped the wreck, master!" exclaimed Philip, with surprise, which was equivalent to the most energetic negative.

"It is singular, however," murmured the viscount, "that the waves have cast up the remains of most of the convicts who were on board the Erable, without as much as one of the crew. It is singular!"

"Let us not accuse those who are no more," said Malificieux, in an undertone; "but I have seen what I have seen. We shall soon have low tide, if I mistake not; and then, if you wish, we can clear up this mystery."

"How is that?"

The sailor indicated with his finger the red line traced by the Erable in the surface of the Atlantic.

"Well?"

"I will undertake to go with a raft; and if the walls don't speak, perhaps the planks would."

"I understand," replied the equerry, thoughtfully.

The burial being terminated, the convicts knelt on the brink of the ditch, and the ex-musketeer intoned the prayers for the dead, the remainder of the band making the responses, without noticing that the viscount did not kneel as they did.

After this sad office, solemn even from its simplicity, a wooden cross was planted temporarily at the head of the ditch.

This work was superintended by the three sailors, and a guard, composed of sure men, had the mission of seeing that none of the various articles scattered about would be removed.

The viscount had rightly deemed it necessary to take these precautions, in order to prevent the pilfering of precious effects, and to prevent quarrels and loss of time. The convicts were under the influence of a deep melancholy; but by degrees their light and jovial nature resumed its wonted hilarity, and they commenced a characteristic dialogue.

CHAPTER VIII.

THE ERABLE.

By unexpected good luck, a large quantity of carpenter's and smith's tools were found among the articles saved from the wreck. An inventory of these articles brought also the discovery of several weapons, and many barrels containing seeds and grains of various kinds.

Malificieux commenced immediately to construct a raft with which he proposed to conduct John de Ganay to the wrecked vessel. The raft being finished tolerably, the two launched it, and the viscount having charged the three sailors to be careful in his absence, they embarked and steered towards the wreck.

In ten minutes the viscount and Malificieux reached it in safety.

It was with profound regret that the former approached the ship, where he had seen embark and perish so many brave men, among whom, at the time of sailing, were included several scions of the most illustrious families in France. But when, after having attached their raft at the starboard side of the Erable, they commenced to climb up on the deck, the equerry was so much affected that he was obliged to have recourse to the aid of the sailor to succeed.

Philip Francœur himself, hardened as he was by a long life of perils, shed tears in setting his foot on the quarter-deck.

"Poor devils!" he said, "they have paid dearly for their revolt."

"What do you say?" asked the viscount.

"Alas! sir, the suspicions which I conceived yesterday evening are confirmed. There has been an *emeute* on board; and probably it is to this we are to attribute the loss of the Erable—See!"

In pronouncing this word, Malificieux extended his hand, and indicated with the finger to John de Ganay the body of a man fastened with iron pins to the forecastle.

"The captain!" exclaimed John de Ganay, recognizing the uniform on the body.

"Yes," said Philip, in a tone of emotion, "the scoundrels have assassinated him."

"Poor captain!" resumed the viscount. "But great God, what has happened?"

"There has been a revolt," replied the sailor; "the rebels were the strongest; they killed the officers, garroted the commander, and abandoned the vessel to the mercy of the Ocean."

"Let us bring this body to the island," said John, "and bury it."

"Pardon, master," objected Francœur, respectfully; "we have but little time to spare. The returning tide will finish the vessel. It is much better to secure such valuable effects as we may find in the cabins, not yet submerged."

This advice was worth taking; and accordingly the equerry responded with an affirmative nod. Leaving, then, the unfortunate victim of a probable drama, they entered the rear cabin. Frightful disorder reigned throughout. Although the sea had swept away and washed a large part of the traces of the revolt, it was easy to see that it must have been horrible. Fragments of vessels, arms, and potteries; barrels, broken in by the hatchet, pieces of torn clothing, and broken furniture, told but too plainly, that after having massacred the crew, they indulged in a disgusting debauch, and that death had surprised them in the middle of an orgie.

"Fools!" said John de Ganay, in a mournful voice, "they have cruelly expiated their crimes. May the Lord, who has punished them in this world, pardon them in the next.'

"Do not pity them, master," replied the sailor, abruptly; "they have only had their deserts."

"The holy scriptures teach us that we should pardon those who are no more," said the viscount, with pious severity. Which of us can say that he will continue always innocent before God. But tell me how has it happened, that with the exception of the captain, we find no vestige of any of the officers who were on board!"

The convicts either shut them up in the hold, or threw them into the sea.

At this moment the timbers of the vessel shook from stem to stern.

"Let us hasten, master!" exclaimed Malificieux.

"Hasten!"

"Yes, the Erable threatens to fall asunder altogether.

"Let us leave, then, for I see nothing here—"

"In the captain's apartment perhaps—"

"You are right."

John made his way through a mass of rags, but only went a short distance, where he saw at a glance that there was nothing there, but a broken trunk. He was going to leave, when the sailor who had observed the trunk, called him, telling him that it inclosed a small chest, and plunging in his hand, he took out a coffer which he put into the hands of the viscount. The latter took it, examined it with a sort of curious satisfaction, and said to Philip:

"Without doubt, the steerage is entirely submerged."

"Entirely, master, even to the wing-transoms."

"Then let us go on shore, and take the body of the captain with us. It is my wish that he receives funeral honors."

Philip Francœur carried to excess the sentiment of obedience to his chiefs. Although he did not relish the idea of burying the captain elsewhere than from the deck of the Erable, he abstained from making any remark, and, seizing a sabre, he cut the cords that fastened the corpse to the rigging. He then knelt down, put it on his shoulders, and said to the viscount who saw him do so, with his arms crossed, and his head inclined mournfully on his breast:

"Now, if you will deign to believe me, master, we should not remain here one minute longer. Do you hear that crackling in the interior of the vessel?"

The advice came in good time. Shattered by the terrible shocks she had received, and incapable of longer resistance, the keel of the Erable was disjointed by the returning tide, and already the water had rushed in with a crash.

John de Ganay went on the raft with a bound. Notwithstanding the weight of his load, Malificieux made an effort to leap also; but whether he had miscalculated the distance, or whether his load was too heavy, he fell into the sea.

The viscount gave a scream.

"Let go the cable! for the love of heaven, let go the cable, master!" said the sailor, re-appearing on the surface.

The equerry obeyed mechanically, and almost immediately the hull of the wrecked vessel broke into a multitude of fragments which became the sport of the waves.

Philip Francœur still clung to the body of the captain. With one hand he dragged it along; and with the other he swam vigorously towards the raft. When he reached it, he caught hold of one of the pieces of wood which composed it, and tried to place himself astride on it with his load, but this was out of his power.

"Abandon the body!" said John de Ganay.

The sailor allowed the inert mass to go, which floated for a few seconds, and then disappeared in the abyss.

* * * * *

The sun, like an immense blazing furnace, illuminated the confines of the horizon, and embraced with red tents the plains of the Isle of Sabre, when John de Ganay and Malificieux rejoined their companions who awaited them impatiently along the shore.

CHAPTER IX.

THE COFFER.

In the mean time the convicts had not remained inactive. Directed by the three sailors, they had repaired their tents, and constructed a sort of pavillion for John de Ganay; a coarse one, it is true, but very comfortable, considering the circumstances. John thanked them heartily for this attention which he had not expected.

After supping in common, our hero retired into his new lodging, followed by Malificieux, whom he regarded henceforth rather as a friend than as a vassal.

Misfortune has this one good quality that it brings together the most opposite characters, equalizes the most diverse conditions, and levels the most distinct classes. In proportion as riches and happiness form lines of demarcation between individuals, misery and misfortune have a tendency to cover the abyss which separates them. "Grief," says the Abbé Constant, "is the fatigue of humanity in its progress." This profound and just opinion confirms those we just expressed. In order that humanity may march rapidly in the road to perfection, it is necessary to destroy secular prejudices, to extinguish the firebrand of hatred, lighted by the division of castes, to write in one harmonious whole all the scattered fragments of a community, and equapoise their forces; and for this purpose it is necessary that the members of that society suffer; that the best provided may have need of those who are called the disinherited. The latter can rarely elevate themselves at a bound; but the former can always descend. Generally the moral faculties are more developed in the one than in the others, —their sensibility is greater. When they suffer from an evil, they suffer doubly in comparison with others. This is the reason they call them, or go to them; for we always seek to rid ourselves of the burdens of our afflictions on those who seem to us stronger to bear them than ourselves, and even to prop them up with the indifference of others.

Overwhelmed with fatigue, Philip Francœur immediately entered the pavillion extended himself in a corner, and fell asleep. The viscount, too, was tired; but his mind, excited by the various emotions which he had experienced for the last two days, did not allow him to commit his body immediately to repose.

Malificieux continued to sleep soundly. In pausing to contemplate his calm and open countenance, which reflected a tranquil mind, John perceived the casket which he had brought from the Erable, and placed under the tent on his arrival. As much for curiosity as to divert his melancholy, he took the casket, approached a torch, and began to examine it. It was simply a box of violet ebony, chased with silver, and bearing two initials, chiseled in relief, and intertwined on a plate.

"This coffer belonged to the captain of the Erable, M. de Pentoëk," murmured the viscount at the sight of the figure which surmounted the coronet of a count. "It is very light! What can it contain?" added he, poising the object in his hand; "some papers, doubtless. Perhaps I may find in them some account of the first acts of the drama. * * Upon the other hand, if it contains anything private, I will burn it, or I will preserve the whole, in order to present it to his family, if ever ——"

A long sigh terminated the phrase of the young man; he resumed after some moments of hesitation.

"Yes, my duty is to open the coffer; neither honor nor delicacy will be offended at my doing so."

But the opening of the casket was no easy matter. The viscount had only his trouble for his pains, when the noise he made in trying to force the lock wakened Philip Francœur. Divining at the first glance the intention of the viscount, he said:

"Pardon, master; but if you will confide this box to me, I think I know the secret of opening it."

"You, Philip! how is that?" asked he smiling.

"Yes, I understand lock-smithing. My father was a locksmith, and when I was young—a good while since—he made me practice at the trade."

"Try then, but I fear you will not succeed," said John de Ganay, handing him the casket.

Malificieux took it, examined it attentively, turned it about in his fingers for nearly a quarter of an hour, and already the equerry had begun to laugh at his vain efforts, when suddenly Philip exclaimed with joy

"Ah! I have found it!"

"Indeed!" exclaimed John de Ganay, in a half incredulous tone.

"Wait, master," replied Francœur triumphantly.

"Let us see," said the former, approaching the sailor, who, by dint of fingering, at last found a small, almost imperceptible button in the middle of the chasing, and pressed it with his thumb.

"Well?" asked John.

"Well, I have found it. Here is your casket opened."

At the same moment the lid, disengaged by an internal spring, suddenly rose.

"Give it to me!" said the viscount in an excited tone.

Francis handed him the casket, and discreetly withdrew a few steps.

John de Ganay ran to the table, and looked into the coffer. First he only found some yellow papers, which he took out. They were parchments; then some letters which must have been read and re-read many a time, judging from the folds and the spots with which they were stained. The viscount asked himself, if he would read them in turn. He hesitated; but the address of one of them attracted his attention, in reminding him of the name of the De la Roche family, into which he was to enter. Overcoming his scruples therefore, he opened the letter, glanced over it with feverish avidity, then devoured all the rest in a similar manner. From his demeanor, and the exclamations which escaped him from time to time, it was easy to see that he was surprised to stupefaction.

After he had finished, he paced rapidly up and down his chamber, then he returned to the coffer, plunged his hand into it, as if to search for other papers, and took out a medallion, richly mounted with gold and precious stones. This medallion contained a portrait. Scarcely had he seen the latter, when he exclaimed:

"How beautiful she is!"

In a moment after, he added, with emotion:

"Poor Guyonne de la Roche! so noble, so charming, so unfortunate!"

It was undoubtedly a beautiful and noble woman he had before his eyes. Of majestic form, she had that dignified and imposing air peculiar to the old families. Her features were well defined, but of graceful outline. Her black hair, blue eyes, and the melancholy expression of her mouth, imparted to her physiognomy a sympathetic character. Dressed in the fashion of the time of Charles IX., she wore a robe of figured taffeta, with strawberry lace, and velvet hood. All about her respired elegance united to simplicity, sadness, and resignation.

Under the portrait was engraved the date, 1573.

John de Ganay contemplated her for a long time. He seemed as if he could not withdraw himself from that picture. By times he slapped his face; and seemed to try to collect fugitive and vague *souvenirs*, and murmured:

"It is strange! I know some one, who, if I don't mistake, greatly resembles this person. It is not the mother of Laura de Kerskœn; no, she was more slender, more delicate. Who is it, then? But where—where——?"

Resuming the portrait, he examined it again with redoubled attention, buried his face in his hands to reflect, and inadvertently let the medallion fall.

Philip, who observed him silently, hastened to pick up the object, upon which, in presenting it to the viscount, he cast a glance, which elicited from him an exclamation.

"Is she not very beautiful?" said the latter, responding to his own thoughts.

"Good master, but one would almost say that it is Yvon," replied the sailor.

"Yvon! that exile. Ah! I know!" rejoined John de Ganay, like a man who had found the thread of an idea, vainly sought for a long time.

"Is it not, master?"

"Yes, in fact, there is a resemblance—a striking resemblance. It is truly extraordinary. The more I look at it, the more I am persuaded—It seems as if this lady was his mother; and that young man was a female——"

"And why not, master?" said the sailor, with a knowing look.

"What do you say, Philip?"

"Eh, master, I can smell well; and I will wager ten years of my life against nothing, that our Yvon would make a finer figure under a bonnet than under a helmet."

"Ah, bah! foolish dream of my imagination," exclaimed the viscount, making a sign to Philip to go to bed.

The latter stretched on his bed, and was soon fast asleep.

John de Ganay would gladly have imitated him, but in spite of himself he was the prey of a thousand preoccupations, and he could not close eyes during the rest of the night.

CHAPTER X.

MYSTERIOUS.

The sleepless nights, added to incessant fatigues, moral and physical, undergone since his disembarkation on the Isle of Sable, had considerably subdued John de Ganay. Sleep claimed its rights imperiously. Nevertheless, since the perusal of the papers found in the coffer, the young man's mind was agitated with so exciting an idea, that, repressing the desires of nature, he awoke Malificieux at sunrise, and said:

"Philip, I think we had better resume our explorations. Although the wreck of the Erable has furnished us some provisions, it would be imprudent to consume them before we can feel assured of being able to procure others. The sea-shore is not suited for cultivation. You, as well as I, have doubtless remarked that the shores of the lake where we have already been appear fertile. It would be desirable, therefore, in my opinion, to return there as soon as we can, and try to cultivate a part. What think you?"

"Your opinion, master, seems judicious. So far as I have been able to see, game does not abound on the island, as that satanic pretended——"

Interrupted by a grave look of the equerry, he resumed;

"I mean the pilot Chedotel. Well, master, I may be mistaken, but this devil of a mariner——"

Another expressive look made him pause.

"Come on," said the viscount, curtly.

"In short," continued Philip Francœur, obstinately, "this Chedotel had always seemed to me like a lynx. Yes, indeed, by——! To return to the affair in question, I see it, master, in the same light you do. There are more ravens here than partridges, and more sand than hares, and the fish will not last long."

"Then it is best to set to work as soon as possible. Here, the same as in New France, the season will not wait."

"This is my plan," said John. "We will leave ten men here; they will be directed to finish the tents, to prepare food, and to watch the camp. With the others, I will commence the work."

"But the instruments?" objected Philip.

"Instruments, that's true!" replied the viscount, striking his forehead; "instruments! we have none—at least—"

A glance of hope lit up his countenance.

"Call Pierre!"

Pierre was one of the three sailors, ordered to guard the chests left by the tide on the beach after the sinking of the Erable, and since removed, as we have said, to the camp of the convicts. He ran.

He was a man of middle size, of a downcast and sullen countenance—one of those beings who must have inspired Shakespeare with his type of Caliban—a surname with which he was decorated.

"What do those chests contain?" asked John de Ganay.

"Some flour and some damaged grain."

"Are there not also some instruments?"

"Yes, sir, carpenter's tools."

"Is that all?"

"Some shovels and pickaxes."

"Ah!" exclaimed the equerry, as if relieved from a heavy burden.

One chest contained arms, and two barrels of powder. But Caliban was very careful to say nothing about this to the viscount. He had hidden with his own hands during the preceding night, unknown to all his companions, the chest of arms, and one of the barrels of powder.

Caliban had his design.

"Very well," said the equerry, "you can withdraw."

The sailor saluted humbly, and retired, giving a stealthy look of malicious jealousy at the viscount.

"Heaven may grant my prayers!" murmured the equerry, after Caliban left.

"Philip!"

Malificieux who had remained standing, approached.

"You will remain here, and in my absence you will command. Better than anybody else you are capable of fulfilling that duty. If Providence permits the Castor to return, you will let me know at once. I have confidence in your fidelity."

Francœur bowed.

"Perhaps," continued John, "I may not return for some days. Send me a courier every morning, with an account of the situation; I will transmit you my orders by him."

Although he was sorry that he could not accompany the viscount in this enterprise, he replied:

"Yes, master."

"And," still added the Burgundian, in reminding the sailor of the coffer, from which he had taken the papers, without removing the portrait, "you will take care of this casket; I will confide it to you."

He said no more, but the tone of his words, and the emphasis he placed on them, were equivalent to an injunction.

"It will not leave me night or day," replied Malificieux, taking off his hat.

"Thank you, Philip," exclaimed the viscount, extending to the former his hand which, at first, he did not dare to touch, but which he shook warmly, throwing himself on his knees, when De Ganay said:

"What, Philip, do you refuse to give me a token of friendship?"

The preparations for the expedition were promptly made. Those of the convicts who were sick, or least robust, were left at the camp; and the rest, armed with provisions, agricultural implements, hatches, and pick-axes, set out gayly on their march.

John de Ganay advanced at the head of the column, with his musket on his shoulder.

In the ranks they sang, laughed, and chatted. The indefatigable Nabot teased his good friend Brise-tout, who swore, raged, and threatened. The ex-trooper attempted to adapt an impossible air to a verse, not less impossible; in short, notwithstanding the gloominess of the weather, which was cloudy and moist, the little troop seemed almost satisfied with its fate.

John de Ganay alone did not participate in the general loquacity. He reflected. The viscount seemed growing tired of life. In his animated eyes there was, I know not what that was mysterious, like the titles of certain books. Without doubt, John's was no vulgar mind. Singular and critical as was his situation in the midst of that band of dissolute and furious convicts, he had shown no weakness.

It was natural, however, that discouragement should relax his energy, and darken his countenance. Why then did a feverish anxiety impurple his cheeks; whence this fire in his eyes? Why does he look about so eagerly from one side to another? Why are his steps now slow, now precipitate? What is the reason of these hurried movements, this uncertainty? What emotions give him pain? What does he wish? What does he doubt?—

CHAPTER XI.

DISCOVERY.

SUDDENLY, the ex-lancer interrupted himself in the middle of a chromatic gamut, and running from the front to the rear of the column:

"Pardon, monseigneur!" said he, in approaching John de Ganay.

"What's the matter?" asked the viscount, somewhat sharply, feeling annoyed at being interrupted in his reverie.

"Look, master, if you please," replied Grosbec; "there, in the direction of my finger."

The troop halted, and was silent.

"I see nothing," said the viscount.

"He has hidden behind this bush; but he will soon reappear. Wait—now do you see?"

"Well," said John, ordering him to be silent by a gesture of the left hand, while with the right he seized his musket.

At a distance of fifty paces an animal was distinctly observed eating grass.

The equerry adjusted his gun and fired. The quadruped bounded on its four feet with a cry of pain, and fell on the mossy carpet. It was dead.

"A sheep! it is a sheep," exclaimed one of the convicts, triumphantly, who immediately after the shot was fired, rushed forward to seize the game.

Nor was he mistaken; it was a sheep, and one of a magnificent breed.

The cry of joy elicited by this discovery can easily be understood. Never were spoils won by a conqueror more welcomed than the body of the poor member of the ovine race.

Evidently it was not alone. One pretended that he had seen the marks of a large flock; another was sure that he had seen several running through the bushes; but that fearing to lure his companions with a false hope, he said nothing on the subject.

John de Ganay did not know what to think; although his satisfaction equalled, if it did not surpass, the wild joy of his subordinates. A painful fear had ceased to corrode his mind; since the island contained sheep, they were no longer in danger of dying of hunger.

"Forward!" said the equerry. "Let one of you take charge of this animal; let it be skinned and roasted, on the brink of the lake."

Then he reloaded his musket, and the little troop resumed their march.

By the time they reached their journey's end, the sun had disengaged itself from the humid vapors which had veiled it. Covered with sparkling dewdrops, the shores of the lake reflected from between the blades of grass millions of diamonds, lit up as they were by the first rays of the morning sun. This sight, especially after they had traveled through such sterile tracts, was truly enchanting; it was like an oasis in the desert.

After some moments of repose, the viscount, having given orders to prepare breakfast, called Grosbec to him.

"You are going to accompany me," said he; "arm yourself with a hatchet."

"Yes, monseigneur."

Then they proceeded along the shore, in the direction of the hut which John de Ganay had seen during his former excursion. They were not long in reaching the thicket, in the midst of which it was. The equerry renewed the priming in his musket before proceeding any farther, and warning Grosbec to be on his guard, advanced with cautious step across the wood.

"Oh!" suddenly exclaimed the ex-lancer, discovering the cabin. "What's this?"

"Hush!" said his guide, redoubling his precautions.

The zephyr caressed the foliage of the trees with a soft trembling, and a streamlet mingled its silvery voice with the murmurs of the air. No other voice was heard.

With one hand on the hilt of his sword, and the other on the trigger of his musket, the viscount arrived at the door of the hut. It was wide open, and John de Ganay entered courageously.

No window illuminated the interior. First the equerry found himself enveloped in thick darkness; but by degrees, his eyes becoming accustomed to the obscurity, perceived the objects which surrounded him. These consisted chiefly of rude fishing implements.

John de Ganay was not a little surprised, when the sound of agitated respiration made him aware that he was not alone in the cabin. Turning towards the place whence the sound proceeded, he observed a person lying on a bed of branches.

"Be careful," said he, to Grosbec, who remained at the door.

Then he approached the bed, coughing loudly. The individual, who was asleep, awoke.

"I am suffering," said he, with a feeble voice.

"Who are you?" asked John de Ganay.

"Ah! Monseigneur de Ganay!" exclaimed she, endeavoring to sit up.

"Can this be you, Yvon?"

"Yes, monseigneur. Oh, heaven, what happiness! My holy patroness has granted my fervent prayers."

"But how?—What are you doing here?"

"Monseigneur, oh, how happy I am——" said Guyonne, overcome with joy, and forgetting her assumed character.

"Finally——"

The young woman covered the hand of the equerry with kisses.

"Finally?" resumed he, when she was somewhat calmed.

"Yes, monseigneur! How good the Almighty is, to have accorded me the favor—"

"Speak, Yvon," said John de Ganay in a tone, somewhat severe. Then he added more gently:

"What has become of you?"

"In returning from the excursion into the interior of the island," said Guyonne, "I was left behind, and hastened to join you; but in running, my foot slipped, I fell, and my leg was broken."

"You have broken your leg?"

"Alas, sir, I must have offended the Lord. Let his holy will be done!

"I passed the night where I fell—incapable of making any movement; so I resigned myself to die of grief, or hunger, when next morning I saw a strange being approach who seemed to me a demon. Believing that it was death, I asked pardon of God for my sins; but as soon as he saw me, he concealed himself, then returned slowly, then he concealed himself again, returned the third time, advancing nearer and nearer."

"It was a savage?" anxiously inquired the viscount.

"No, monseigneur; he is a Frenchman."

"A Frenchman!"

"Yes, he is completely mute and insane, the poor man! I believe, he must have been ship-wrecked many years ago, and had succeeded in gaining this island, where the instinct of preservation taught him the means of providing for existence."

"And you—Yvon?"

"Oh, master, your kindness to a poor serf is too much. He brought me into his cabin, and supported—"

"But your fracture?"

"My leg still causes much suffering," replied the young woman.

"Is the bone set?"

"Yes, master, he set it himself. It was not without pain; but I have prayed to God so much to preserve my life and health that I might consecrate them to you that he has deigned to accord me his powerful aid."

"Where is this man?"

"He has gone out to fish, sir."

"Will he return soon?"

"I could not say; but the sight of you will make him—"

"Run away," said the viscount, observing that she was loath to proceed.

"I fear so, monseigneur."

John de Ganay reflected for a few seconds.

"It is impossible for you to walk."

"Impossible, monsieur!"

"Wait till this evening; I will come back for you to bring you to the camp."

After having again exchanged some words with the pretended Yvon, John de Ganay left the tent, and returned towards his companions, telling Grosbec to say nothing about the adventure.

CHAPTER XII.

DEATH OF BRISE-TOUT.

As Viscount de Ganay and the ex-lancer approached the place where they had left the bandits, he remarked that the latter were greatly agitated. Formed into a circle, they seemed engaged in a warm altercation. Thev stamped, talked loud, swayed to and fro—in short, had all the appearance, even at a distance, of people ready to strike each other.

Grosbec was the first to distinguish this extraordinary scene; he called the attention of his master to it.

"Monsieur!" said he.

John de Ganay whose ideas wandered in the region of the imagination, started, and raised his head.

"Master," resumed his interlocutor, "I believe that there is something unusual passing there below."

The young lord looked in the direction in which his attendant had pointed his finger.

"A quarrel, doubtless," said he; "come, let us hurry."

They silently redoubled their steps, and soon attained the first rank of the circle, formed by the exiles.

The minds of the latter were so much absorbed in other matters that they continued their clamors and gestures without paying any attention to the presence of the viscount, who was under the necessity of calling on them to separate, in order to ascertain the cause of trouble.

At first his order had no effect; but Grosbec, having reiterated it in a commanding tone, they thought it best, to yield, and John entered the actual scene of the difficulty.

A most tragical drama was on the point of being acted, whilst the speakers howled diabolically round two individuals whose aspect was as different as the employment in which they figured.

One of the personages was no other than our old acquaintance, Brise-tout; but the second was a stranger, singularly acoutred with a dress composed of divers' skins, sewed together. He wore this costume like a mantle; his head, his legs, and his arms being naked. Nothing could be more grotesque than the physiognomy of this individual. Thick, curling hair covered his head and descended in long, uncombed tufts on his shoulders, tanned by the heat. It served as a frame for his meagre gruff countenance which had an infantine appearance, although age had already marked his features with an indellible stamp.

The position of the unknown was that of one condemned to death.

His hands were tied behind his back, and a coarse repe was round his neck, the end of which, thrown over a branch of oak, was held by two robust convicts who awaited the signal to draw the cord, and strangle the victim at the other extremity

Whether it was that he was not aware of the sort of punishment designed for him, or that he despised tortures, the unfortunate man made no movement to attempt to escape from his executioners, but looked at their preparations with an air of indifference. Before him was the body of Brise-tout. The bowels of the colossus were open to view, and there was a large wound above his left breast, from which thick blood flowed. Francis Rivet had not yet breathed his last; but his last hour had come.

At the moment when the viscount made his appearance, Brise-tout raised himself on his elbow, like a lamp that is re-animated before it is extinguished, and cast a hideous menace at the spectators.

* * * * * *

This scene was enacted in a much shorter time than it has taken us to describe it; its last phase had been so rapid that the convicts had almost forgotten the stranger who, with the rope about his neck, contemplated the whole scene with the utmost indifference. But as soon as Rivet breathed his last, the cry "Hang him! hang him! hang the murderer!" was shouted on every side.

Already the two improvised executioners, in order to show their good-will, pulled the fatal cord which was to launch a human being into eternity, when the equerry, drawing his sword, cut the rope with a blow, and the unknown man fell to the ground with a cry of suffocation.

"Let none of you touch this man!" said de Ganay with an irresistible gesture.

Observing that, notwithstanding his order, the sailor, Pierre, manifested a disposition to proceed, he walked towards him with his sword uplifted, and said to him resolutely:

"One word more, and you are dead!"

Certain of their obedience, the viscount ordered one of those near him, to untie the victim, which was immediately complied with. The unknown got up quickly, bounded between those who surrounded him, and before any one thought of opposing him, he had precipitated himself into the lake.

There he soon disappeared from the eyes of all.

John de Ganay recovered from his surprise, easily divined that this individual was the proprietor of the tent who had lavished his good offices on Yvon; but there remained a mystery to be cleared up, that of the death of Brise-tout.

The equerry questioned his people. He learned, that after his departure, Francis Rivet, being gone to explore the southeastern part of the island, saw a man fishing. Supposing him to be a savage, the giant rushed at him with the intention of making him a prisoner. A struggle ensued, during which the individual attacked struck his adversary with a sharp instrument. Feeling himself wounded, Brise-tout called for aid, but without letting go his hold. Some convicts, who happened to be near, ran to him. They seized the stranger, garotted him, conducted him to the camp, and prepared to hang him, in order to avenge their comrade, in compliance with his dying wish, when the sudden arrival of the viscount prevented them.

This story seemed plausible enough; John de Ganay was satisfied with it for the moment. He caused a grave to be dug, aud had the unfortunate Brise-tout buried, whose premature end caused but little regret.

As a funeral oration, Nabot recited over the grave of the defunct, with a slight variation a stanza which he had composed some days previously.

Passant, sous cet amas de sable amoncelé,
Git la pourriture d'un goinfre ensorcelé
  François Rivet, surnommé Brise-tout
  Passé maitre dans l'art de faire atout,
    Qui, faute de soudure
    Creva d'une blessure.

CHAPTER XIII.

A PERPLEXITY.

The end of the summer of 1598 approached. Some three months previously the Castor had disembarked her human cargo on the Isle of Sable. During this time the unfortunates encouraged themselves each day with the hope of seeing at the horizon the vessel which had brought them; but each day they were doomed to disappointment. Anxiety made them look haggard; discouragement enfeebled their arms, and anger excited their minds. Still, on the sea-shore, and on the brink of the lake, tents first, and then cabins, were constructed; the existence of the proscribed was systematized; they enjoyed a certain amount of comfort. Some killed game, others caught fish; all worked more or less; there was no lack of provisions. Besides a pretty large quantity of salt meat, but little damaged, which they had saved from the wreck of the Erable, they still found in the place of their exile a goodly number of sheep, deer, and other domestic animals, which had probably been left there by colonists who had previously inhabited the island. Yet, the causes of affliction abounded; for the majority, the absolute ignorance of the situation of the island which they occupied, the obligation of attending to labors to which they had not been accustomed, the severity of the discipline to which they were subjected by the viscount, the monotony of their relations were sufficient motives for corroding cares; for some, for the better natures, the sterility of the soil, isolation, and uncertainty, were sufficient reasons for disgust; and besides the prospect of a winter in these savage regions, excited terrible apprehensions.

Viscount de Ganay himself was a prey to doubt and fear. His faithful sailor, Philip Francœur, tried in vain to reassure him. The equerry triumphed with difficulty over his regrets; for a thousand anguishes lacerated his heart. The recollection of his dear Burgundy, of his family, of his friends, of the gay romances which youthful imagination had embroidered with flowers, often recurred to his mind. Nevertheless, he thought but seldom of Laura de Kerskoën, the object of his former love; and when her image did return, he hastened to dispel it as an illusion.

Wishing to be prepared against all attempts which the convicts were likely to make, the equerry proceeded with Maleficieux to the camp at the lake.

Some, he thought, are enemies of agriculture, who prefer to devote themselves exclusively to fishing and the chase, while others were willing to remain with him to cultivate the soil. By this means, as soon as there is a harvest, the two bands will exchange their products. But in reflecting on this plan, he thought that after all it might produce disastrous results.

After having promenaded for some minutes amongst the groups, the viscount approached a tent, at the door of which Maleficieux was engaged in making mats.

"Well?" said the equerry, with a mysterious air.

Francœur glanced around him before making any response.

"Is there any improvement?" pursued the viscount.

"Improvement? no master. Alas! the fever is rather on the increase; and nothing grieves me more than to think——"

"Hush!" said the equerry, putting his finger to his lips, at the sight of a convict who lounged about the cabin.

The sailor understood the gesture, and addressed the bandit:

"Oh, Porturin! go and draw the net I left this morning at the bottom of the lake; you know. It ought to be well freighted now."

"Yes, indeed, by the trident of Neptune!"

When the intruder was gone, Philip said in a loud voice to the viscount:

"However, there is still some hope—much hope—I know something about medical affairs, master——"

"Has the delirium ceased?"

"I believe so. See for yourself. I will watch while you are away."

The viscount put aside some platted osiers which served as a door for the hut, and entered. The interior was naked, but remarkably neat. Filtrating through an opening in the top, and passing through a linen screen placed before that opening, the sun shed a soft and rosy light through the cabin. Opposite to the window, on a bed of heather, lay a woman. She seemed in a sound sleep, although her respiration was somewhat difficult; a coarse, but neat cloth, was spread over her.

The viscount advanced slowly, holding his breath. He regarded the patient in silence for some minutes.

Need we say that it was Guyonne?

She had been transferred to the camp. Fever and delirium had seized her the very evening of her arrival, and had not since quitted her.

Philip Francœur, the first charged with taking care of her, had discovered the sex of the pretended Yvon. Informed of this discovery, John de Ganay enjoined the strictest secresy.

Suffering had committed cruel ravages on the features of the poor girl. A morbid paleness replaced the roses on her complexion, and her cheeks were hollow, her eyeballs inflamed, and her parched lips scaled with yellow pellicles. Still, her beauty had not disappeared; it had only altered its character. The languor had removed all that was masculine in her features, to replace it with that feminine expression, more characteristic of woman.

Thus, seen in this cabin by the feeble light of the setting sun, Guyonne presented an admirable incarnation of physical suffering.

In her sleep she murmured incoherent words, in the midst of which the first name of the viscount frequently occurred, accompanied with sighs.

John took her by the arm and examined her pulse; it beat quick, but the pulsations were not irregular. This examination seemed a good augury to the viscount, for a ray of joy crossed his eyes. Then, taking from his pocket the portrait which he had found in the coffer, he began to study its details, contemplating in turn the physiognomy of the great lady, and that of the exile.

"It is, indeed, she," thought he; "the resemblance is complete: nothing is wanting; not even that little red mole, under her right ear. What an enigma! Oh, I must question her, and tell her how——"

The young woman moved in her couch, and the viscount promptly put up the medallion.

"Do you still suffer from the fracture?" asked the viscount?

Guyonne did not reply at once; and observing that she tried to move her leg, in order, doubtless, to see whether it was healing, John added:

"No, no! don't stir. Moving may hurt it; remain still."

After these remarks, there was a silence of several minutes between the young people. They avoided looking at each other, and seemed as if they were afraid to communicate to each other their thoughts.

John de Ganay remained in the same position. Prostrated before Guyonne, he held the right hand of the patient in his left, and leaning on the bed with his elbow, concealed his face in his right hand. The beating of his heart beat in unison with that of the heart of the young woman; and burning sighs escaped from their surcharged breasts.

CHAPTER XIV.

THE INTRIGUE.

This movement having disarranged the cloth that covered Guyonne, her arms, shoulders, and neck, appeared so white as involuntarily to remind one of alabaster. John de Ganay lowered his eyes, his countenance assumed a purple hue, and an indescribable tremor pervaded his whole frame.

"I'm thirsty," murmured Guyonne, with a voice expressive of pain.

The viscount gave a hurried glance around.

"I'm thirsty," repeated the young woman, opening her eyes for the first time.

First she did not know the equerry, who, in a corner of the cabin, poured some water in a wooden mug; but remarking the disorder of her toilet, she hastily readjusted the cloth, which would betray her modesty.

The viscount returned to the bed, bringing the only drink he could give the poor patient.

While approaching, he trembled all over; a lively carnation suffused his cheeks, and the perspiration flowed from his face. He seemed as if about to commit a bad action.

Guyonne made an exclamation on seeing him; then bashful and confused, she closed her eyes without venturing to utter a word.

"Take a drink," said he, in a low tone, more timid, more frightened, perhaps, than his protégée.

And while she hesitated, or rather did not understand what he said, he added, kneeling before the bed, and putting the mug to her lips:

"Drink! This water will appease the thirst which devours you. Would that I could offer you something better."

"Thank you, monseigneur; your kindness to me is very great," stammered the pretended Yvon, with a voice deeply moved.

Was the malady of Guyonne contagious? had John contracted it? and were both now laboring under fever?

Suddenly the viscount seized the hand of Guyonne passionately, and bent forward as if going to kiss it, then as suddenly repressing the thought which prompted him, he stood up abruptly and commenced to walk up and down in the cabin.

Had the obscurity not prevented her, Guyonne might have remarked, that the features of the lover of Laura de Kerskoëu were discomposed, and that burning tears gushed from his eyes.

John de Ganay might also have perceived that the pretended Guyonne wept.

A quarter of an hour had passed before they exchanged a word. A world of thoughts struggled in the mind of the viscount; Guyonne awaited with feverish impatience the end of this scene. An involuntary sob escaped her; at this ebullition of grief, the equerry started. He paused, made a violent effort against his emotion, and then, with a tranquil and firm step, he went and sat down beside the patient

Silence was resumed, but it was of short duration. Soon John de Ganay, who seemed a prey to an internal struggle, triumphed over his hesitation; and with a voice almost solemn, he asked the young woman:

"Have you not said that you are the *son* of a fisherman, who was a vassal of the Marquis de la Roche?"

"Yes, sir," murmured Guyonne, in an unintelligible tone, intimidated by the tenor of the question.

"His *son*," repeated the viscount, without disguising the discontent which her reply caused him.

Guyonne made no reply. She was afraid; she saw that her position was no longer a secret to the viscount; and when the latter repeated the third time "his *son*," incapable of dissimulating any longer, she exclaimed, wringing her hands:

"Oh, messire, pardon, pardon, pardon a poor girl! I will tell you all—the whole truth."

Overwhelmed with this confession, she heaved a deep sigh, and was silent.

It was now night; the objects in the cabin could no longer be distinguished.

John de Ganay, astonished, and frightened at not hearing her voice any more, called:

"Yvon! Yvon!"

His call elicited no reply. Trembling, in turn, the young man laid his hand on the face of Guyonne; it was as cold as marble.

"Great God!" exclaimed he, "has my brutality hastened the death of the unfortunate girl!"

Then he added, running towards the door:

"Philip, Philip! a light—a torch!"

But at the same instant, Maleficieux entered abruptly, shouting:

"To arms, messire! to arms! Our men have revolted."

A discharge of musketry, accompanied with frightful vociferations, immediately confirmed the assertion of Philip Francœur.

Forgetting everything else, the viscount bounded rather than ran outside.

He had drawn his sword, and while his right hand brandished the glittering blade in the darkness, his left was armed with a pistol.

Behind him, but finding it difficult to keep up with him, so precipitate were his movements, ran Philip Francœur. The sailor, too, was, so to speak, armed to the teeth.

* * * * * *

A thousand strange cries broke the stilness of the night; and then occasional detonations, preceded by flashes, had added to the horror of the scene.

"Death! death! death to the tyrant! Death to Viscount John de Ganay," howled distant voices.

"Help! help! Saint Dennis! Montjoy! To arms! to arms!" exclaimed other voices, more convenient.

CHAPTER XV.

THE INSURRECTION.

BEFORE reporting the events of that night, so remarkable in the lives of the convicts abandoned on the Isle of Sable, by the Marquis de la Roche, let us mention in a few words what had passed the preceding days.

The reader will doubtless remember, that the viscount had deemed it advisable to divide his people into two bands; the one to remain in the camp, at the sea-shore, the other to establish itself beside the lake, and employ itself more particularly in works of agriculture and colonization. This second troop, composed of only twenty-nine men, since the death of Brise-tout, formed, so to speak, the staff. The place which it occupied was a sort of headquarters, whither the equerry had caused all munitions, and all other things not necessary for immediate and daily use, to be carried. Having left under the detatchment commanded by the sailor Pierre but a small number of arms, he thought himself safe against all attempts at revolt, on the part of those whom he rightly regarded as the most undisciplined of the troop. It has been observed in a preceding chapter, that at the time of the wreck of the Erable, the sailor Pierre had clandestinely conveyed away and concealed a chest of arms. All this time the sailor was engaged in getting up a conspiracy. Sullen and ambitious, he aspired to overthrow John de Ganay, no matter how, and place himself in command. If Pierre had not that vigor of mind and muscular force which overawe the masses, he possessed in a high degree the art of dissimulation, and of fostering around him the bad designs conceived by himself. The suspicions of John de Ganay, in reference to this miscreant, were therefore but too well founded.

* * * * * *

Although he lulled himself into no false sense of security, but suspected a part of the truth, he did not believe that a revolt was possible, much less so near. The day the events were accomplished, which we are about to note here, he had condemned one of the soldiers to corporal punishment, for having provoked, assaulted, and seriously wounded a colonist. The punishment was just, but not from the point of view of the soldiers. In the evening, as was their custom, they met together and threatened the colonists, whom they said the viscount was constantly favoring at their expense. This must not be, thought they; it must be put an end to; and if they were put to it, they would show that they had blood in their veins. The orator of the band, an Italian, named Ludovico Ruggi, but better known under the sobriquet of Long-croc, mounted an empty barrel and harangued the crowd. He recalled the sentence which had been passed in the morning, demonstrated, in animadverting on the incidents of the quarrel between the soldier and the colonist, that the punishment inflicted on the former should have been on the latter, passed in review several previous sentences passed by the viscount against his brave companions, for the benefit of the privileged, recapitulated a hundred imaginary wrongs, spoke of courage, valor, equality, and finally wound up with protesting, that in the name of justice they were all bound to demand, to exact, and to obtain reparation. Ludovico improvised warmly; his eloquence was well calculated to vibrate the susceptible chords of such an audience. Thunders of applause welcomed his peroration. The opportunity was good, and Pierre did not fail to avail himself of it.

"Yes," said he, when Ruggi had finished his speech, "yes, I begin to perceive that at last we are treated, as if we had the leprosy, and that we are but the serfs of the colonists. Hitherto I had closed my eyes against the light; but now I am forced to open them. * * * I tremble to think that my good faith has been basely imposed upon, * * and like our dear friend Long-croc, I am convinced that, in the name of justice, we are bound to demand, exact, and obtain, a prompt and decisive reparation for our grievances."

The speech of the sailor was received with cheers not less energetic or less enthusiastic than that of Ruggi. *Bis repetita placet.*

But if it be easy to make speeches, it is not so easy to act. Pierre was not ignorant of this. When one of the malcontents exclaimed, "How are we to have a reparation?" there was a profound silence in the assembly. The Italian twirled his mustache, interrogating Pierre by his looks. The latter pinched his nose with an embarrassed air, not that he was not prepared for that question. He had combined his tactics in advance; but he was a poltroon; he did not like to compromise himself; he preferred to wait until another would take the initiative; then he would direct every part of the programme; what he expected happened.

The ice was broken. Timid and uncertain at first, but soon violent and menacing imprecations were heard on all sides, against Viscount de Ganay.

CHAPTER XVI.

THE COMBAT.

The command of the rebels had been offered to the sailor Pierre, but the latter, too cunning to assume so heavy a responsibility, had refused it. His associate, Ruggi, then called to the chief command, readily accepted it. Braggart and bully, but nevertheless brave, and fond of dangers, the Italian had all the necessary qualities for the chief of an insurrection.

Taken by surprise, the convicts near the lake had not had time to make any preparations for defense.

Not knowing, besides, what kind of enemies they were to encounter, fearing that they were the Indian savages, of whose horrible expeditions they had heard, they first permitted themselves to get terribly frightened.

But John de Ganay knew the assailants. With a commanding voice he ordered his people to follow him, and defend themselves. Each person armed himself in haste; and in a few minutes the colonists were drawn up on the brink of the ditch which they had dug before their tents, ready to receive the aggressors. Nothing could be distinguished yet, more than figures moving in the shade. From time to time clamors resounded in the midst of a well-supported fusilade, which issued only from the wood.

The ex-lancer Grosbec, and Philip Francœur, were ranged on each side of the viscount, near the principal entrance. Access to the camp became, then, difficult; for it was protected by the ditch, which formed a semi-circle around it, of which the lake was the cord.

With less precipitation, more skill, and combined action, the conspirators might easily have overpowered their companions. For this purpose it was only necessary to come to the entrance without noise, and then precipitate themselves into the camp. But the first troop perceived a troop of men promenading. Caliban, the chief of this troop, believed that one of these men was John de Ganay. As the object of the rebel was, above all things, to rid himself of the viscount, he ordered his men to fire. Several shots were now fired in succession, but no harm was done. Whether it was that the darkness prevented them from taking aim, or that they were unaccustomed to handle fire-arms, the soldiers hit nobody.

John de Ganay had given orders to his faithful subordinates not to fire without his express command.

Remarking that the insurgents had slackened their fire, he regarded the moment as favorable to call on them to return to their duty, telling them, if they had grievances, to make them known to him, and that he would endeavor to redress them.

This speech was rendered inaudible by savage cries, and a triple discharge convinced the colonists that the soldiers were resolved to risk all, in order to give vent to their passions.

"Venison stomach!" said Grosbec, "I am struck."

John de Ganay turned about.

"The ruffians have shipped me for eternity.—Adieu, monseigneur!—Let there be another death for this—"

"One killed," murmured Malificieux between his teeth. "By the trident of Neptune! I will avenge him, yes, indeed ——"

A loud voice, followed by two discharges of musketry, the one from the north, the other from the south of the camp, cut short the soliloquy of the sailor.

"They have formed a plan," said the viscount coolly. "It is not difficult to resist them; but we must try to seize their chiefs. This Pierre ——"

"Pierre, yes, monseigneur, he alone has been able to excite them to an attack like this."

"Very well. Take five men with you; I will take an equal number, and we will go out. The others will keep guard."

"Let you remain in rather, master, you would expose ——"

"No reply! go, and do quick!"

Philip Francœur went in haste.

The viscount called. Immediately five of the most robust, and best armed of the convicts were by his side.

"You will follow me," said he, "and, let what may happen, make no use of your arms except in a case of absolute necessity. Remember that it is not enemies, but misguided brothers in misfortune we have to combat."

Philip Francœur, and five other men, having joined them, they marched out of the intrenchment in good order, and notwithstanding the incessant fire of the soldiers, proceeded towards the wood.

Soon the assailed and assailants were able to see each other.

Finding himself discovered, the chief of the insurgents resolved to sell his life at the dearest possible rate.

"Surrender, and you will be pardoned!" cried John de Ganay.

"Death to the favorites!" replied Pierre.

He covered the viscount with his musket, and fired; the ball whistled by the ear of the equerry, but without touching him.

This was the signal for the engagement.

The colonists, furious, fired in turn without waiting for orders. The soldiers responded, and several fell on both sides.

Pierre, fearing that his troop could not be strong enough, whistled, in order to rally the two detachments which he had ordered to attack the camp in flank. Philip Francœur comprehended of what importance it would be to prevent this movement. With his five men he threw himself in front of the Italian Ludovico Ruggi, and charged him vigorously. Having attained the brink of the wood, he seized him by the arm, and tried to make him a prisoner; but the Italian was as supple, as Malificieux was robust. For some minutes he defied all the efforts of the sailor to throw him.

"Surrender!" said he.

"I am choking," stammered Ludovico.

"Give me your word that you will obey me, and I will give you mercy."

"I swear by all the holy relics," replied the Italian.

Philip Francœur, not doubting the loyalty of this oath, withdrew his knee, but at the same moment Ruggi drew from his breast a long stilletto, leaped at the sailor, and was going to assassinate him, when a report was heard.

The Italian turned about two or three times, and fell.

The struggle continued fierce, where Philip had left the viscount. He now ran to him. The aurora borealis which had afforded abundant light for some time, was now extinguished, and darkness resumed its empire.

When Malificieux re-appeared in the melée, he perceived an individual stooped behind a pine, who, with a musket at his shoulder, and his finger on the trigger, was taking aim at John de Ganay. To precipitate himself on this individual, and to strike the weapon violently, was but the work of a second for the sailor; but the gun went off, and Philip Francœur received the ball in his thigh.

Exasperated at this, the colonists rushed on the sailors, who commenced to fly in all directions. A quarter of an hour after, they were entirely dispersed.

The revolt being suppressed, the viscount called for torches, and then proceeded to examine the losses. Happily they were not considerable. Two colonists and two soldiers remained on the field of battle. The former had besides four wounded, more or less seriously; the latter had carried away theirs. The victims were transferred to the camp, some to receive the care which their condition required, the others to a common sepulchre.

These duties accomplished, the viscount posted sentinels around the camp, and, before retiring, wished to re-assure his mysterious protegée.

The day was dawning.

John found Maleficieux extended across the door of the cabin.

"What are you doing here?" asked John.

"Master, I am on guard."

"But your wound?"

"It is nothing. Those who brought me here wanted to bring me to the hospital, but—"

Philip put his finger on his lip, and laughed.

"Generous friend!" exclaimed the viscount with sincere emotion; "oh, I will never forget the nobleness of your heart!"

"Do not think of me, master, but enter."

John de Ganay opened the wicker door, and immediately a tremulous exclamation darted from his lips.

Guyonne had disappeared!

FIVE YEARS AFTER.

CHAPTER XVII.

THE MUTE.

PHILIP FRANCOEUR was the first to awake. It was not yet day. Profound darkness, scarcely relieved by the flickering light of a few burning sticks, reigned in the cabin. The sailor listened an instant, leaning on his elbow. The regular cadence of a respiration told him that Guyonne was fast asleep. He then busied himself in lighting the fire. This being done, he placed on the hot cinders an earthen vase, the rude workmanship of which was such as to show that the manufacturers had but little knowledge of kneading fuller's earth; he put some peas into the vase, some grains of Indian corn, some water, covered all with a lid, and sitting on a billet of wood, superintended the cooking of the breakfast.

The flame lit up the cabin, and caused in its interior some combinations of light and shade, truly fantastic.

When the flame of the sticks began to grow pale before the light of day, the young woman opened her eyes.

Philip, who had been watching her, immediately approached her.

"I am well," said Guyonne, divining that he went to inform himself in regard to her health.

"And your limbs?"

"A little fatigued," said she, "but I can walk and—monseigneur—"

"Noble viscount; he is cruelly charged!" said Philip, with emotion.

"Ah! he is alive!" exclaimed Guyonne, with transport.

"He is alive. Yes; but sorrow and privations—Ah! sad events have passed since that night—and you?"

Guyonne made no reply; she prayed mentally.

The sailor, fearing to interrupt the pious hymn which the young girl offered from her heart to the throne of the Eternal, discreetly retired.

When he returned in a quarter of an hour, Guyonne was up.

"We are going to breakfast," said Philip, gayly, "and then, if you feel strong enough, we will set out for the camp. The viscount will be so happy ——"

Philip ended this phrase with a significant glance at Guyonne, who blushed.

The sailor was perfectly aware, as we have said, of the sex of the pretended Guyonne; but a sentiment of exquisite delicacy prevented him from showing the young girl, even under such circumstances, that he possessed that knowledge. Guyonne, on her part, understood very well that her secret was no longer such to Francœur, but her modesty prevented her from *feminizing* her person. It seemed that a tacit understanding guided these two beings, so noble, so pure, so worthy of being united by the ties of a filial and paternal tenderness.

* * * * *

At all events Malificieux had served the breakfast on a wooden bench.

It was a frugal meal: some maise soup, and some fish, broiled on the coals. But hunger seasoned it; and the guests did it honor.

When they had done, Philip remarked:

"Now, we are able to navigate towards the camp."

"Oh, yes, yes! let us start," replied she eagerly.

"One moment, one moment! Before sailing it is necessary to take in ballast, yes, indeed, by the trident of Neptune! Come, take a mouthful!"

Guyonne made a gesture of refusal.

"Drink, drink!" insisted the sailor. "We have twelve full knots to sail, and a drop of this liquor ——"

"No, I thank you."

"It will do you no harm; on the contrary, yes, indeed.—It is a distillation of our invention, you see, my boy! Just a small drop!"

Much more to avoid disobliging him, than on account of any taste she had for it, the young girl accepted. She contented herself with moistening her lips with the gourd which Philip handed her. Malificieux swallowed three or four mouthfulls, smacked his lips, and taking two clubs from the corner of the cabin:

"Let us weigh anchor," said he, presenting one of the sticks to Guyonne.

He opened the door, and a flood of dazzling light invaded the hut.

"Let you walk in front?" said Philip.

"What?"

"By the star-board! you don't know all the devilish tricks these damned soldiers have played on us. Ah! if they could prevent the colonists from fishing ——"

While making this remark, he heaped up the snow before the cabin, went on the roof, covered the chimney-hole with a plate of ice, and covered the ice, in turn, with snow, so that, at a distance, the hut had the appearance of a large heap of ice, massed by the wind.

After he had finished it, he rejoined the young girl, who looked mournfully at the sea.

"What is the matter with my child?" asked he, seeing that her eyes filled with tears.

"Oh, good Philip, I am grieved," replied she in broken accents.

"Come," said the sailor in a tone of sympathy which touched her to the heart, "you will tell me your troubles on the way, and this will console you."

She disengaged herself from her painful reverie, and followed him.

The sky was clear, and of a turquoise blue. In the mirror of the Atlantic the sun reflected his golden rays. A light breeze trembled across the branches of the trees. It was the opening of one of those fine April days, full of promises of balmy spring.

The two travellers walked on in silence, as absorbed in their own reflections.

The way they passed was very difficult, full of hills and hollows, formed by fragments of ice. But when they had removed a little from the sea-shore, the route became more practicable. Then Philip remarked, shaking his head:

"Five years ago!"

"Five years!" repeated she, like an echo.

"Ah! that cursed Chedotel!"

The young girl grew pale.

"If ever I lay my grapple upon him ——"

"Probably the Castor has been wrecked."

"Wrecked? no;" said Philip in a mournful tone; "there is something that tells me that."

"But enough. By the trident of Neptune, the carcass of Malificieux is still solid, yes, indeed!"

"My God, what an existence for monseigneur, the viscount!" murmured the young girl.

"An existence which has blanched and bent him like an old man," said Philip sadly. "Brave young man, he has borne all—hunger, thirst, cold, nakedness, and without a murmur. He has always encouraged us; he——, poor young man!"

The old sailor wiped away a tear with the cuff of his coat.

"And you?" said he abruptly, in order to put an end to these painful souvenirs.

"Me!" said she, with the tone of one interrupted in the middle of a profound pre-occupation.

"Did you not disappear in the middle of the night of the revolt of the soldiers?"

"The same night!"

"And how?"

"You remember," said Guyonne, "that I was sick?"

"Yes, very well; you had fever—in consequence of—"

"The fall I had received which broke my leg."

"True, I remember it as I do yesterday."

"Monseigneur had the kindness to come to visit me," continued Guyonne, lowering her eyes.

The sailor smiled with a knowing look.

"And then," pursued she, "you came in, crying 'To arms!' and I heard reports of muskets."

"The brigands! They wished to cut our throats!"

"While I listened, without being able to move, the Mute—"

"The Mute! Who is that?"

"The man who had previously saved my life."

"Ah, yes! that sort of monkey that killed Brise-tout."

"I don't know," said Guyonne, "but—"

"By the trident of Neptune! that devil of a Camus, as Nabot called him, stabbed him to the heart, and the convicts would have hanged him for it, but Monseigneur de Ganay ——. But you were saying?"

"The Mute entered the cabin where I was sleeping. On seeing me, the poor man threw himself on his knees, weeping and laughing in turn, like a fool, making signs to me, and ——"

"And?"

"Kissing my hands!"

"Ah, the scoundrel!" exclaimed Philip.

"And," continued she, "he became more sane, opened the door, looked outside, returned to me, rolled me in the bed-clothes, put me on his shoulder ——"

"Yes, truly!" said Malificieux.

"Put me on his shoulder, and began to run."

"So I had suspected," said Philip, beating his forehead.

"It was impossible for me to resist. An overwhelming torpor paralyzed all my movements; I had scarcely any consciousness of what had happened to me. The Mute proceeded on to the sea-shore. There he put me into a little skiff, and commenced to row, uttering a strange sort of cry, such as I had heard him make, when he was successful in hunting, or fishing."

"But who was this man?" inquired Philip.

"He was my father!" replied Guyonne with emotion.

"Your father!"

"Ah, I can not doubt it any longer! He had a mark on his breast which I happened to see one day—"

She burst into tears.

"What!" said Malificieux, when she was somewhat calmed.

Guyonne resumed in a voice, broken by sobs.

"Had been shipwrecked; he was supposed to be dead. My mother married again; but it seems, he succeeded in reaching the Isle of Sable, where the absence of all companions doubtless made him mute, and at length an idiot."

"It is very strange—very strange.—What has become of him?"

"He is dead!"

"Dead!"

"Yes, alas! but let me finish my narrative."

"Whether it was that my fever increased, or that my fatigue overcame my resolution to remain awake until I saw where he brought me, I fell asleep. When I awoke, he was at my side, seeming to wait until I opened my eyes, to give me a drink. I was stretched on the grass, a large bush serving to protect us from the heat of the sun. On reflection, I thought the poor lunatic had brought me to another part of the Isle of Sable. In order to be sure, I made signs to him, which he did not understand, or. if he did, he pretended not."

"He was insane?" said the sailor.

"Yes, alas! he had lost his reason. He promptly constructed a cabin of branches; it was in this cabin we spent five years!"

"But where were you?"

"I don't know. When my health returned, I availed myself of his absence one morning, to examine the place, and then I felt convinced that we must have left the Isle of Sable. The place we were in was an islet of at most a league in circumference. This discovery frightened me very much. I searched for the skiff that had brought us; but, without doubt, he had sunk it, for I could see no trace of it."

Guyonne was silent, and Philip regarded her with profound surprise.

In a moment she resumed:

"Oh, if you only knew, Philip, how kind and devoted he was always to me, although he knew nothing of me. I was his idol. When he saw me grieved, he threw himself at my feet, and wept; when, sometimes, I was gay, he was full of joy. * * Poor unfortunate, he perished for me! His life was sacrificed to save me.—During the five years I passed with him in that islet, he never manifested ill-humor. —He did not like to see me work. Scarcely would he permit me to accompany him hunting or fishing. Poor Mute, dear, beloved father! for he was my father, I am sure, that mark on his breast I remember well. May God have mercy on his soul! When I went to my devotions, he knelt near me, and seemed also to address an invocation to heaven."

"What a strange adventure!" said the sailor. "And your subsistence?" added he.

"Oh, he provided it in abundance. The islet is full of game. The Mute possessed extraordinary skill; he had made a bow, and rarely did his arrows miss their object."

"But the winter?"

"We lived on smoked fish. I made my clothing of seal skins. As to his, he made them himself, without wishing that I would put a hand on them."

"Did he refuse to take you back to the Isle of Sable?"

"Very often, you will understand, I made known to him that desire; but then he sobbed, and his tears went to my heart ——"

"What a horrible situation!" said the sailor with emotion.

"Oh, I have suffered a great deal; but however painful my sufferings were during these long days of mysery and misfortune, they were not equal to those which I felt when I saw him disappear beneath the waves."

"Then he drowned himself?"

"Yesterday morning we went to fish on the ice-bank, at the southern shore of the islet. While we were fishing, an enormous bear approached us. My father precipitated himself before the animal, who caught him between his paws, and was crushing him in his embrace, when I ran to his assistance. At this moment the ice broke under his foot, and the unfortunate was engulfed in the hole with the monster."

"But you?"

"By chance I found myself on the detached ice," replied Guyonne, with the tears in her eyes. The bear returned to the surface; he swam towards the piece of ice, and attempted to get up on it; I killed him with a pike, but I fell myself into the sea. It was with great difficulty that I succeeded in regaining the ice."

"Poor, dear child!" exclaimed Philip, pressing the young girl to his breast.

CHAPTER XVIII.

PHILIP AND GUYONNE.

FORGETTING her *role* for the moment, Guyonne threw herself on the neck of the sailor, and embraced him tenderly.

"Dear child," resumed Philip, "oh, I am as happy to have found you, as if you were my own daughter. But tell me, how it is that you happened to be included in the category of the transports?"

The young girl related her history.

"Oh, it is noble, too noble!" exclaimed Malificieux, in listening to the narrative of that admirable devotion!"

"But, holy Virgin, I only did my duty," replied Guyonne with charming candor. "You don't know how much my step-father loved his son. If he had been wrested from him, he would have died of grief. And besides that, poor Yvon was not capable of enduring the fatigues and and privations of colonial life. I, on the contrary, was naturally strong; my departure could only cause temporary affliction to old Perrin. You see then that my conduct has been simple. Had you been in my place, would you not have done as much, Philip?"

"I, I!" said Malificieux, covering her with caresses, "I am not quite sure about that. So —— at all events that does not prevent—I did not believe, to tell you the truth, that there was so much virtue under a petticoat. But does Monseigneur de Ganay know all this?"

"Oh," exclaimed the young girl with a supplicating gesture, "I beg of you, Philip, that he will remain ignorant of it for ever!"

"That he remain ignorant of it! Why, my child?"

"Why?" said she, fixing on Malificieux her beautiful eyes, moistened with tears.

"Is not the action you have accomplished, heroic, as our late friend Grosbec would say."

"But I have told a falsehood to monseigneur; it is a great sin!"

Philip smiled.

"Would that such sins were committed often, noble girl! There would be fewer miscreants under the canopy of heaven; yes, indeed.—Besides, Guyonne," added he in a serious air, "you are, perhaps, not what you believe yourself to be."

"What?" said the young girl with surprise.

"Well, well; I know what I say. Malificieux has a good eye, good nose, good ears."

The sister of Yvon gave a look at the sailor which was full of curiosity.

"Ah!" said he joyously, "I have put a flea in your ear, Demoiselle Guyonne. He! he! By the arrows of Cupid, how these large eyes do sparkle on me! If my good mother had only conceived, and brought me to the world some twenty-five years later; he, he!"

"You naughty man! then you would not have been here, and poor Guyonne had succumbed," replied she, participating in the gayety of her companion.

"By my faith, that's true," said Philip surprised at an observation which seemed to him very profound.

After these remarks, they walked along some time, without a word. Guyonne was a woman at heart, after all; and the half-confidence of Malificieux really put a flea in her ear, according to the phraseology of the latter. Re-calling her conversation with Viscount de Ganay, an instant before the revolt had given an opportunity for her abduction, she suspected a mystery. This is what the young woman wished to hear more about, but which she could not resolve. The sailor eyed her waggishly, but whether it was that he did not wish to speak, or that he was afraid, he had already said too much, he was silent.

Both proceeded along the sea-shore. A chain of ice-hills, formed on the beach, prevented them from seeing the Atlantic. Coming to a little bay, they had to make a sudden halt.

"*Diable!*" exclaimed Malificieux, examining with his eye the obstacle before which they had arrived. "*Diable!*

here is a citadel which it does not seem easy to storm. A good sign, however, a good sign! By the trident of Neptune, I much prefer these icy rocks to white frost. This, at least, indicates that Monsieur Winter makes a grimace at Monsieur Spring who responds with contempt. Come, Yvon, give me your hand, and to the assault!"

"Oh," said Guyonne, "thank you; I will get up alone."

"Forward! then."

They commenced to ascend, and aiding themselves with their pikes, their hands, and their knees. But the ascent was still more difficult than the sailor had supposed. The blocks of ice had been precipitated pellmell on each other. * * * Guyone had occasionally to have recourse to her companion, and the latter, although he did not like to ask the assistance of the young girl, was equally obliged to claim her services on more than one occasion. Finally, they reached a sort of aufractuosity, situated nearly at the top of the ice-berg Alps. There they halted to rest. In order to reach the top, they had only to scale an enormous iceberg, standing perpendicularly on its flank. But while Malificieux borrowed philosophically from his gourd a dose of vigor, the ice broke under the feet of our travellers, and they fell into a puddle.

Guyonne uttered a cry of fright. But Philip, although surprised by the suddenness of the movement, did not lose his presence of mind. In his fall he managed to cling to the brink of the excavation, and thanks to his hairy gloves, he was able to sustain himself to calculate the size of the orifice. Remarking that it was narrow, like the tunnel of a chimney, he bent himself to the opposite side, drew out his knife, fastened it between the two icebergs, set his foot on the handle, and jumped out of the well.

He scarcely occupied a minute in thus raising himself.

Guyonne remained.

Philip immediately stretched at full length on the ice, and looking down into the orifice, saw the young girl. She was more than ten feet below him. But she was standing, and spoke to him; this made him breathe easier.

"The two pikes are near you, are they not?" asked he.

"Here they are."

"Fasten one of them at the height of your waist, the other at the height of your head; you will stand on the one, using the other as a support for your hands. Then I will give you my belt to aid you in getting up on the second pike, so that I can give you my hand and draw you up."

Guyonne hastened to put this plan in execution.

It had all the desired success; the young girl was soon in the arms of her friend.

"Dear child, I hope you are not hurt?"

"No, no, my brave Philip."

"But this blood!" exclaimed the sailor, palpitating with uneasiness.

"Oh, it is nothing! A slight scratch I gave myself on the cheek."

Philip examined the wound, and found it was but slight.

"Holy Patroness! how are we to get out of this?" asked Guyonne.

The sailor reflected for a minute.

"There is but one means," said he. "I will put my back against the iceberg, and you will stand on my shoulder."

"But you, Philip?"

"Oh, never mind. Have'nt I the foot of a mariner? Could a cat pass where Malificieux could not?"

"It would puzzle even a cat," said Guyonne, smiling, "to make her way here."

* * * * * *

"Ouf!" cried Philip, in joining his companion. "If the way to Hell were as difficult as this, I should grieve sorely for my poor soul."

"Oh, don't blaspheme, my dear friend. It is bad to make a jest of sacred things," said Guyonne, in a tone of gentle reproach.

"You are right," replied Philip. "But what do you expect? We sea-wolves have always a little word to give as an excuse for a laugh. Now let us proceed."

The southern side of the ice-mountain had a declivity sufficiently easy; and so our heroes were soon at the base.

"A thousand port-holes!" exclaimed Philip, in a tone half angry, half sorry.

"What's the matter?"

"By the trident of Neptune, my gourd remains in the hole. There is no longer any hope of a vessel that has lost its rudder. A gourd full to the brim! I have a mind to go in search of it."

"In search of it!"

"It was quite full, repeated the sailor, piteously, looking anxiously at the ice-hill."

"But Philip, you will not be guilty of such folly."

"In fact," said he, recollecting himself, "it is but mislaid for the present. When the snow thaws, I can get it. Yes, indeed! Let us proceed. It was a famous gourd, nevertheless. I would not have changed it for ten ingots of silver."

"I believe you, indeed," retorted Guyonne, smiling. "What use would ten ingots even of gold, be to you here?"

"She has the wit of a demon," whispered Philip. Then he added in a loud tone:

"We are drawing near, Yvon. No one but Monseigneur de Ganay, you, and I, should know——You understand, my child?"

"Oh, yes," exclaimed Guyonne, thanking him with her looks.

"Before entering the camp, you will halt until I go and give word to the viscount."

"But," said the young girl, "are you all reunited?"

"No, alas! that miserable Pierre has been to us a firebrand of discord, and an instrument of evil. It was at his instigation that the sailors and the soldiers mutinied for the first time in five years. Since then, neither a community of miseries, nor the efforts of Viscount de Ganay have been able to bring them to better sentiments. I do believe that scoundrel Pierre has bewitched them. Twenty times we have been compelled to repel them by force of arms; twenty times they have endeavored to surprise us under cover of the night, and massacre us. Meantime, God knows if the viscount has not been indulgent to those bandits. Had it not been for him, all would have died of hunger. All has been useless. At present, all that remains of that clique, are disseminated through the island, and subsist by pillaging the fruits of our labors. But that Pierre, that Pierre! Ah, if ever I get my hand on his neck——"

A menacing gesture completed the phrase of Malificieux, whose contracted features indicated a determined and terrible anger.

"But I see the headquarters," resumed he, after some minutes. "Yvon, let you conceal yourself behind these pines, while I go to bear the news to Monseigneur de Ganay."

Having affectionately pressed the hand of Guyonne, Philip Francœur disappeared at a rapid pace.

CHAPTER XIX.

FRAGMENTS OF A JOURNAL.

We are in a little quadrangular chamber. This chamber has an appearance more than rustic. It was hung with speckled furs, in the middle of which sparkled the silvery mantle of the fox, the buckled fleece of the sheep, the short and lustrous hair of the seal, and the white robe of the ermine. A plain linen cloth, become yellow by use, covered the ceiling. On the floor, instead of a carpet there was a mosaic of skins. The furniture was scarce; some wooden stools, two valises, a trunk rudely constructed, and a coarse table, composed it. A large mantle-piece of pebbles, not of mortar, embraced all one side of the room. The opposite side was occupied by a bed, covered with fur skins, like the walls and the floor. In the middle of one of the other sides was a window, glazed with parchment, instead of glass; and a low door opposite.

Arms were suspended here and there, or grouped in bundles.

A man was seated near the table; his legs were crossed, one over the other; his left elbow supported on his thigh, and his head sustained on the palm of his hand. Before him were spread various papers, and a copy-book, which he turned over mechanically. This man was entirely clothed with furs. A sword, with the guard adorned with a faded ribbon, was at his waist. He wore long hair and long beard; hair and beard were brown, silken, and abundant. His physiognomy had a typical beauty. Visage, bronzed by the heat; features regular, fine, the features of a race; expression proud, but tinged with melancholy; eye lively, bold, and yet darkened by slow but continual grief; form slim, wiry, although a little bent, by a habit of concentration. Such is the portrait of the man whose age was estimated at from thirty-five to forty years.

"With what rapidity time flies!" murmured he, turning one by one the pages of the manuscript, covered with compact hurried writing. "Soon five years!—five years of affliction! Yet it seems to me as if it had been only yesterday we disembarked. Do we live more, then, on hope, than recollection? Good or bad, the past is always at the back of the future, and rarely is the present a bill which possesses any value for us. An inscrutable thing is human life. Awake we dream, asleep we have a reverie. How vast, then, is the distance which separates our littleness from divine grandeur! One cannot even control his own will!"

He stopped suddenly, and contemplated the flame of the lamp which burned on the table; for although it was clear day, the panes of parchment allowed too little of the light to pass to render it possible to read without the help of an artificial light.

After an instant of mute contemplation, his eyes rested on the manuscript.

"Isle of Sable, October 29, 1598.

"Lord, Lord! smite not thy humble servant! Behold! my body is bowed down; my soul is grieved; I am going to the abyss of despair.

"What emotions agitate me! I feel, and yet do not feel; the thoughts rise to my brain, as the bubbles rise to the surface of boiling water; everything strikes me—everything binds me; tears soothe me, but my eyes are dry and burning. I have not even the weakness of grief. Pains exhaust me, and I cannot tell the seat of my malady. How strange. Of my dear France, and my dear Laura, I think less. Privations of all kinds have made me indifferent; still I suffer. Mystery, will thou permit me to tear away thy veil. Whence this agitation? Whence come these troubles? I await with impatience the return of the Marquis de la Roche; and I know not why it is that I dread to see him arrive. This island pleases me, all sterile as it is. To live here with a tender and affectionate wife, surrounded by honest and laborious vassals, appears happiness to me. A wife did I say?—What has become of her who was among us? How, with what object did she place herself among that band of malefactors? She seemed good; her conduct was exemplary; her courage, her energy, surpassed imagination; and then, what a beautiful face. Oh, the life of that woman must veil a profound secret! Without doubt some sublime devotion has prompted her. * * *

"But am I not foolish? This woman had perhaps a lover among the convicts! Oh, no, no! banish that monstrous proposition! She a lover! She a depraved woman—'tis not the case; my heart tells me so; my reason proves it to me! Is it thus I honor the memory of her who, at the peril of her own, saved the life of Monseigneur de la Roche and mine? Will my gratitude be manifested by an insult?

"Ah, pardon, noble unknown! pardon, if you are dead; forgive, if you still breathe. God, how beautiful she was! What a queenly bearing! What dignity of deportment! What angelic sweetness in her countenance! No, that angel was not born in the cabin of a serf; I refuse to believe it. It was a manor she had for a cradle; it was great and powerful lords she had for relatives.

"Still that thought; it haunts me incessantly; I chase it under one form, it reappears under another. I close my eyes, it is reflected as in a mirror; I turn about, still it is before me; I promenade, it follows me; I work, it continues with my labors; I go to bed, it is at my pillow; I sleep, it hovers about my head.

"It is said that divine Providence often sends us warnings, in order to instruct us. Is this one? Yet, what is the use in my occupying myself with it? What is the use in searching for a thing henceforth useless? Have not more than two months passed sinco she disappeared? Have I not caused the island to be searched from one corner to another, in the hope of finding her? Has not the lake been sounded by Philip? * * *

"Poor, dear girl, she is dead! Perhaps of a horrible death! Who knows? Perhaps during the night of the revolt, one of those wretches ——Oh, I tremble at that single apprehension. What! has there been found a person with a human face, cowardly enough, ferocious enough, to take advantage of the sickness of the poor child. My God! men are wicked indeed, since they can even be supposed to be guilty of such crimes.

"Thick darkness surrounds me. These papers, picked up on board the Erable—this picture, of which the resemblance to her is so striking—this portrait; I have again examined it attentively. The more I compare it, the more my suspicions assume consistence. She is her daughter; something tells me at the bottom of my heart. Have I a right to deceive myself. And do I not remember the last words exchanged between her and me; when I asked her whether it was true that her name was Yvon, did she not stammer? Did she not avow her sex? What a labyrinth I am in? Am I never to see her again, or know the truth in regard to her? Lord, aid me in effacing those impressions which burn me like red irons. Re-establish peace in my mind, and enable me to renounce reprehensible worldliness, in order to be able to fulfil my duties towards you and these poor people, whom you have made it my mission to conform to the adoration of thy name, and obedience to your laws."

The viscount had not perused these lines without making frequent pauses to meditate.

"My God!" exclaimed he, on finishing, "how the hours, days, weeks, months, seasons, years have flown; and neither time that corrodes all; physical maladies which enfeeble the body, nor moral maladies which obliterate sensibility, have been able to eradicate those impressions left on my mind, and on my heart. The All-Powerful has not had pity on me."

He bowed his head sadly, and turned over some leaves of his journal.

"January 2, 1599.

"What a sweet emotion I felt yesterday. I was far from expecting that delicious surprise. Brave Philip! what a heart, beneath his rough sailor's garb! It is he, doubtless, who has induced the colonists to wish me a happy new year. Oh, I should indeed be happy if all would return. The certainty that I have enemies here, where all ought to be like brothers, has cast a cloud over that family re-union. Grant, Divine Redeemer, that the soldiers—those who strayed rather by lassitude than malignity—may not persist in their hardness of heart. How much more agreeable it would have been for us all to have thanked heaven together for having hitherto provided us with subsistence, and to have supplicated Him to continue his benefits.

"It was eight o'clock when my dear colonists arrived, dressed in their best clothes. Philip marched at their head; the honest sailor tried to pay me a compliment. But his eloquence did not equal his expectation, and he threw himself at my feet, kissed my hand, and, with tears in his eyes, exclaimed, 'Excuse me, monseigneur. I had wished—I had desired—in short, to tell you in a word, my comrades and I wish you every prosperity——'

"Well, well, Philip," replied I, seeing that he could not proceed, and addressing myself to the troop, who cried with their heads bare: 'Vive, vive! Monseigneur de Ganay!' I made a little speech, which touched these good people. Then we devoted our hearts to God.

"The dinner was pleasant, more bountiful than usual, and at the desert I caused to be distributed all that remained of our last barrel of brandy. How joyful, then, were my subjects! In an instant they forgot the precariousness of their situation, and the rigor of that horrible winter which subjected the sea itself to its dominion. Poor fellows, they forgot, that if fish failed to-morrow, we should die of hunger! Ah! I could not forget. Alas!"

"February 6th.

"It is horrible! two of our men have been frozen this morning, going to hunt. I am told that the soldiers are a prey to famine. I am going to send them some fish. My God! why do they refuse to take my advice."

"February 11th.

"We must fight to-day; we must defend ourselves against pillage and murder; we must shed the blood of our brethren! Has an evil genius taken possession of these unfortunates? They came thus armed to the teeth, and had it not been for the bravery of our colonists, we should have fallen under the fire of the bandits. The struggle lasted two hours. We were obliged to use our muskets. Six men were killed; two colonists, and four soldiers. Will this lesson teach the latter? I doubt it. At least, except Pierre, their chief, is killed, they will return, sooner or later, to the charge." * *

"March 1st.

"The divine wrath rests on us with all its weight. My God, may your will be done on earth as in heaven! But I beseech you to spare these poor unfortunates. The scurvy rages in the camp."

"March 2nd.

"A bandit, named Ludovico Bernard, has died of scurvy this morning at ten o'clock. Two others are affected with this horrible malady. A soldier has deserted, in order to join us. I have given orders that he be well received. Let us hope that his example will find imitators."

"The wretch!" said the reader, rising hurriedly, "he was sent by his accomplices to assassinate me. Had not the prudence of Philip discovered the plot, he would have done so."

He walked up and down the apartment, returned to his seat, and opened his journal at random.

"April 7th.

"The cold is still excessive, and we are hungry.—Ah! what a hideous thing hunger is! Sunken faces, irritable minds; men who sob, or blaspheme, with such am I surrounded. With the exception of Francœur whose firmness and self-abnegation are proof against all; I see only prostration and hatred. I feel myself that my energy is failing. I am suffering from hunger. Fishing having failed, we have had to eat boiled sheepskins; then we had to dig holes in the snow, in order to extract some roots, and at the moment I write, this last resource has failed.—Good God, I am informed that they are going to disinter the bodies of the two men, frozen to death in March. * * O Lord, O Lord, grant that this profanation may not take place."

"April 8th.

"I have fever; my head burns; a cold sweat bedews my body.—The hair stands on my head—the pen trembles in my hand. * * Unfortunates, they have realized their design. They have taken these dead, livid bodies from beneath the ice.—I dare not finish—"

"April 9th.

"All-powerful God, cause me to die—famine devours me—There is a fire in my stomach—Oh, if I could die—."

"Yes," said the young man, "I wished to die then, but it was less on account of the frightful tortures I endured, than in consequence of the sinister projects which hunger had excited in my brain. I trembled at these.—I was seized with the fury of a cannibal. Far from loathing human flesh, it attracted me irresistibly. I remember that I got up from my bed, seized a poignard, and if a man had been present that moment, I would have cut his throat, to suck his blood, to tear his limbs with my teeth.—Horror—."

He hid his face in his hands, and remained absorbed in thought, interrupted from time to time by spasmodic tremblings.

The noise outside diverted the dreamer from his bitter reflections. He ran to the window, and seeing that the noise had been occasioned by the fall of an avalanche of snow from the top of his cabin, he returned to his seat.

"May 1st.

"At last Spring has dissipated the frosts of winter; Nature is smiling. Ah! who can fail to recognize the goodness of God in the magnificent scenes around us! The sun, warm and vivifying, bathes its golden rays in the sea; the sky, without a cloud, which dazzles by the purity of its azure, and then that world which becomes animate at our feet, by our sides, over our heads. * * Listen! these are small birds; they tell the timidities, the impatiences, the jealousies, and the pleasures of love, and their language fill you with ecstacy. Sing, sing on, little birds! your romances sooth my cares as formerly the ballad of my nurse put my infancy to sleep. * * Wait! Will Providence guide a ship to these shores? Has the Castor been wrecked? These questions constantly recur in my mind. But now, I wish to dispel them, * * destinies are in the hands of the Most High. I commit myself humbly to his care. With the faith, the certainty, of being again in a better world, the human creature is never unfortunate."

"October 3d.

* * * * * *

"This morning, during a solitary promenade, I went as far as the hut, now in ruins, which *she* inhabited with the shipwrecked man. Seating myself on a beam, I had a long revery in regard to *her*. Who was *she?* Where can *she* have perished? Night casts its shades over that extinct life, and never will any light be shed upon it! My God, if so many presentiments had not deceived me!"

As he concluded this phrase, he heard a gentle tap at the door. He hastened to close the journal, and hide it at the bottom of the coffer.

"Come in!" said he.

CHAPTER XX.

THE SURPRISE.

THE door opened, and Philip Francœur appeared.

"Ah! it is you, my old friend," said the viscount, rising and shaking the sailor by the hand. "But what is the matter? you are quite excited—"

"Oh, monseigneur, monseigneur!" replied Philip in broken accents, "I know very well, I know very well——"

"What did you know?"

"Ah! old Francœur is more cunning than he seems."

"What do you mean?"

"That nearly chokes me, yes, indeed! ——"

"Sit down, and get over your emotion."

"My—excitement; you have said the word. I am devilishly excited. The means of not being so too!"

"Relate to me, what it is," said the viscount, tapping him encouragingly on the shoulder.

"But, at least, monseigneur, you will promise—"

"All you wish."

"It is, you see," said Philip whose eyes sparkled with joy, "that this news is so extraordinary—"

"Have you discovered a shoal of herrings?"

"Not at all."

"Lord! a ship—"

"No, no!" replied Philip, shaking his head; "the hour of our deliverance has not yet come."

The light that illuminated the countenance of De Ganay, was extinguished.

"Then speak, my devoted servant," said he.

"I fear this news—'

"Will it be bad?" exclaimed John, knitting his brows.

"On the contrary."

"Explain yourself then."

"If I were sure that—well I can't hold out any longer, yes, indeed, by the trident of Neptune! *She* is found again!"

The sailor spoke this last phrase with a vivacity, so great that one would think, the words burned his throat.

"Found again!"

"Who?" asked the viscount, growing pale.

"Oh!" exclaimed Philip, "pardon; I was too abrupt. I knew that if I let you know that suddenly ——. Excuse me, I don't know how to manage such things."

"But who is she?" repeated the viscount in an excited tone.

"Monseigneur, monseigneur! do not ask me to tell," replied Philip frightened at the agitation of his master.

"Who is she?—for the third time."

"Yvon," said the sailor, in a tone so low that John thought he had misunderstood.

"Yvon!—that young girl—found again!—"

"Yes, monseigneur."

"You have found her?"

"Yes, monseigneur."

"Ah! but you only deceive me, Philip—is not that it, my friend?" pressing feverishly in his fingers the sailor's hand.

"Deceive you? I to deceive you, monseigneur?"

"But where is she, Philip? quick! run!"

Then all of a sudden, the countenance of the viscount brightened up, his muscles quivered. He supported himself against the table, to avoid falling. He made a movement, he opened his mouth to speak, but the sounds died on his lips.

Philip was frightened at the change produced in the viscount.

"Give me some water!" stammered John with much difficulty.

He swallowed a few drops, and moistened his temples. By degrees he seemed to become calm; and although a volcano smouldered in his heart, he said quietly to the sailor:

"Where have you found her?"

"Fishing on the sea-shore."

"Drowned," stammered the viscount with a painful effort.

"Drowned, no, monseigneur, but on the point of dying with cold."

"Then she is alive! you say she is alive!" exclaimed John in a passionate tone.

"She is but a few steps from this."

"Oh! thank you, my God," said he, raising towards heaven his eyes, radiant with gratitude.

The sailor briefly related to the viscount the history of Guyonne, from her disappearance from the camp to the moment when he had so miraculously saved her. John listened to the recital with mute attention, suspended, so to speak, from the lips of the narrator.

"Come, come," said he, as soon as Philip was done. "Let us go for her; for you do not know who that young girl is.—You have no idea of what a noble family she belongs to. But let us hasten!"—

"Pardon, monseigneur," said the sailor without moving.

"Not go! I am burning with impatience, all trembling with that selfish impetuosity with which unforeseen happiness animates our blood."

"Monseigneur, listen to me, I beg of you," objected Philip, stopping the equerry with a look. "First of all, it is necessary for us to take precautions. Let us be circumspect. The return of Guyonne might prove disastrous to all, if her sex was known. Coolness, therefore."

"You are right, my dear Philip, I am insane," said he, extending his hand to Malificieux.

"Oh, I understand this haste," replied Philip with a smile, permitted him by his age, and the numerous services he had rendered the viscount. "You will remain here, your rank and dignity require it. I will return to Yvon, and bring her to you." * *

"All right, my good Philip, all is permitted to you."

"Now," said the sailor, rubbing his face, "now, monseigneur, you know what you have to do."

"Yes, yes, run, and bring her."

"It is Yvon, nothing but Yvon, No. 40; don't forget, monseigneur," said Philip starting.

* * * * *

Philip gave her his arm, fearing that her emotions might betray her in passing the colonists, whispering "be firm!"

She advanced timidly. The viscount congratulated her with sufficient calmness on her almost miraculous deliverance. She replied by an unintelligible stammer; and John de Ganay, in order to put an end to a scene that might be embarrassing, said:

"Yvon, go in, and warm yourself. The cold may injure your health which seems to have suffered so much already."

The sailor conducted his protégée into the sitting-room of the viscount, who was by her side, *tete-a-tete*, in a few minutes.

CHAPTER XXI.

QUESTIONS AND RESPONSES.

SEATED near the fire, Guyonne had her eyes down. What she experienced we can not describe. It was an indefinable combination of timidity, fear shame and love.

John de Ganay was not less agitated, nor less confused. Standing near the table, he affected to arrange some papers to keep himself in countenance. But the shaking of his hand, the indecisive looks he gave now at the young woman, then to the right, then to the left, betraying the perturbation to which he was a prey.

A quarter of an hour passed in this way. The silence of the two young people was interrupted only by the crackling of the wood in the fire. Ten times the viscount opened his mouth to speak, and as often did his strength fail him.

At last he sat near our heroine who, succumbing to the weight of her impressions, burst into tears, and hid her face in her hands. This incident served as a re-action to the equerry. He appeased the disordered palpitations of his heart, and questioned Guyonne gently:

"Mademoiselle ——"

"Oh, pardon, monseigneur! pardon, for having deceived you," sobbed the young girl, falling at his feet.

"Get up, get up," said he, turning his head aside to conceal the tears that moistened his eyes.

"No, monseigneur, it is the only posture that becomes a miserable sinner like me," replied she with emotion. "I have gravely offended our Father who is in heaven, and you, monseigneur. But believe my word: if my brother Yvon had gone, his father would have died with grief. As a penitence impose on me the hardest labors. * * Oh, I shall be too happy to be useful to you in any way ——"

"Noble girl!" exclaimed the viscount, forcing her to sit; "dry these tears. The deed you have accomplished, is worthy of the highest praise on earth, and of an eternal recompense in the next world. Do not bow your head, Guyonne, for you are the honor of your sex. What! I to blame such devotion, or dare to treat it as a fault! No, no! Much rather would I proclaim before the world that you are the most virtuous, and the most heroic of women."

"Then, monseigneur, you will not repel me! You absolve me?" said Guyonne, seizing the hand of the viscount, and kissing it in spite of herself.

"I admire you," murmured he in an enthusiastic tone.

It was not until then that she ventured to raise her tearful eyes towards John de Ganay, who, in turn, seized her hand, and pressed it to his lips.

By this act the viscount elevated to his own rank Guyonne, the fisher-girl. However, the latter was more charmed than surprised; for, with the penetration which women preserve in the most complicated positions, she knew that the young man loved her.

"Your name is Guyonne?" asked he, after a moment of silent reverie.

"Yes, monseigneur."

"Where are you from?"

"From the hamlet of De la Roche."

"From the hamlet of De la Roche! it is not that," said the equerry thoughtfully.

Guyonne did not understand, and the viscount added:

"What occupation had your father?"

"He was a fisherman, monseigneur."

"A fisherman! but did you not tell me formerly that he was a coaster?"

"It is true."

"Was he engaged in both professions?"

"No, monseigneur, my father—my own father—was a coaster; he was shipwrecked; he was supposed to be dead, and my mother married a fisherman of the manor of De la Roche for her second husband—that is old Perrin, who has thus become my step-father."

"Ah!" exclaimed the viscount with marked satisfaction. "But you have a brother?"

"Yvon, monseigneur. He is an issue of the second marriage, and he cost our mother her life."

"And your mother's name is—?"

"Margaret, monseigneur."

"Margaret!" exclaimed the viscount, running to the table, opening a letter, reading it with avidity, and returning.

"Was not your father's name Simeon?"

"Simeon, yes, monseigneur," replied she with profound astonishment.

"His surname was Leroux, was it not?"

"Yes, indeed."

"He was originally from Normandy—and had established himself in a little village near Nantes, at Chauteray, where he married your mother—"

"Yes, yes," replied Guyonne to these questions, asked with feverish rapidity. "But how is it that you know, monseigneur?"—

"He resided at this village at the time of your birth?"

"Yes, monseigneur; for I was born in 1573."

"Oh, what a flood of light!" said the viscount, reading aloud the following words from a letter which he held in his hand.

"It was the fifth of February, 1573, towards four o'clock in the morning, that I gave birth to the fruit of this unfortunate love, reproved by the justice of God and man. It was a child of the female sex. The chaplain of the chateau baptized it under the name of Guyonne, then, without regard to the prayers of the mother who asked to see her daughter, it was carried away ——"

The fisher-girl heard the reading of this passage with a stupefaction which extended almost to unconsciousness. Since the previous evening, she had experienced so many commotions that she asked herself whether she was not the prey of a frightful nightmare. Incidents which in former times had seemed to her to have no importance, forgotten souvenirs, presented themselves in multitudes to her memory, classed themselves, and formed the thread of a conductor.

Thus, when the viscount, interrupting himself, said:

"Does not your infancy bring anything to your memory, Guyonne?"

"My infancy reminds me of strange things."

John drew his stool near that of the young woman.

"I was very little," continued Guyonne, "when we lived at Chauteray near Nantes. However, I recollect that a beautiful lady, richly dressed, came to our house every Sunday after high mass."

"Of tall size?" said the viscount.

"Yes, monseigneur, her form was tall and majestic. When my father was in, she contented herself with giving me some candies, or ginger-bread; but if I was alone, or with my mother, she took me on her knee, and covered me with caresses. So I was very fond of her; she was so good to us."

Guyonne ceased to speak; briny tears gushed from under her long eye-lashes.

"Do you remember the name of that lady?" asked the viscount.

"Her name? no I can no longer recall it; but my mother always called her the Countess——"

"Is that all?"

"All? Oh, wait! One night, my father was at sea, an old woman came to our house. She spoke some words to my mother who uttered a loud cry. Then I was hastily dressed in my best clothes; the old woman, my mother, and myself entered a carriage which awaited us at the door. I soon fell asleep; on awaking, I found myself in a large room, lying on a bed. The beautiful lady I had seen at our house, was lying beside me. She was livid with sickness, and yet an infinite tenderness lit up her eye, when she looked at me. Knelt at the foot of the bed my mother, and the old woman sobbed and cried. The lady embraced me sighing, then she said to my mother:

"Margaret, you have promised to rear her as your own daughter."

"Oh, she is that; she is that!" exclaimed my poor mother.

"You will take good care of her, will you not, my good woman?" continued the lady in a voice, so feeble that one could scarcely hear her.

"She will be my daughter," said my mother, pressing me to her breast.

"Thank you, Margaret, I rely on your word. Adieu, I can now die in peace. Adieu, then, Margaret! Pray for me, when I am no more."

A priest entered the room, and my mother took me in her arms. The same carriage took us back home. I slept again on the way. When I asked my mother next day about the scene which I had witnessed, she told me I must have been dreaming. We left the country a few days after. My mother was sad, and dressed in black." * *

"Do you know this face?" asked John de Ganay, showing Guyonne the portrait of which we have already spoken.

Guyonne took it from the hand of the viscount, and went to examine it by the light of the lamp.

"My God!" she exclaimed, "it is she."

"That lady, is it not?"

"Yes, yes, I cannot be mistaken. This is certainly her physiognomy, at once gracious and grave; her magnificent curls, with which I played, the robe of brown taffeta, the fine lace, and the velvet boddice which she wore habitually. * * Oh, monseigneur, it is she; I would swear to it."—

The doubts of the viscount vanished. His radiant countenance reflected the joy that cheered his heart. Still he wished a complete assurance; hence it was that he asked this question:

"Did your mother not reveal you the secret?"—

"What secret, monseigneur?"

"She told you nothing?"

"Nothing."

"At the hour of her death?" insisted the viscount, whose looks more than his words questioned Guyonne.

"At the hour of her death the poor lady gave me a scapular from her neck, wishing me never to part with it, and adding in a tone that still rings in my ear: 'Remember, my child, that this is the only heritage which your unfortunâte mother has left you.'"

The young girl blushing, drew from her corset two little morsels of stuff, sewed together, and suspended from her neck by a leather cord.

"Could you confide it to me?" said John, examining the object.

"I swore to my mother, never to part with it," replied the young girl.

"For a few moments?"

"I would not like to refuse you, monseigneur, but I promised my mother—a dying woman—."

"If your future, your happiness, depended on that infraction!"

"I would not willingly commit it."

"And if I ordered it?" said the viscount, more suppliant, than commanding.

"My duty, monseigneur," replied she sadly, "is to obey you. I would obey!"

"Then," continued the viscount, not without some hesitation, "Guyonne, I order you to hand me that scapular, and I promise to return it to you this very day."

She handed the object to the viscount with mournful resignation. The latter put it under his coat, and remarked:

"One word more, Guyonne: have you not a little redness above the breast, in the form of a butterfly?"

"Yes, monseigneur," said she in a low tone, while a deep blush suffused her cheeks.

Immediately John de Ganay called:

"Philip!"

Malificieux entered, and approached the viscount.

"Yvon is fatigued," said John. "Show her her chamber."

Philip beckoned to Guyonne, who followed him, not a little excited by the scene which had passed between her and the equerry.

No sooner was the door closed, than John de Ganay cut the threads that united the two pieces of the scapular.

On one of them was found embroidered in red silk a "𝔊," on the other a "𝔓."

CHAPTER XXII.

GUYONNE AND JOHN.

Love presents two distinct traits; either it springs up voluntarily, spontaneously; or it grows slowly, involuntarily. In the former case, it results most frequently from a predisposition of the individual who has received the germ from a ray of the physiognomy, or of the *esprit* of the individual who has transmitted it. In the second case, love derives its origin from an acquaintance between the subjective and the objective; it is the fruit of a sort of study, always of a thoughtful appreciation. It is sufficient to say, that one resembles those ephemeral flowers, resplendent in colors, saturated with perfumes in the morning, but withered and dry in the evening; and that the other appears like a frail plant, almost imperceptible at the hour of its birth, but which days and months develop gently, until its expansion is complete. Then in turn it sparkles with a thousand colors; its perfumes are embalmed; and far from fading with a revolution of the sun, it preserves its freshness and its magnificence.

Oh, how good it is, how delightful that love which softly insinuates itself into our senses! How it teaches us to appreciate the pure and delicate! The principle of devotion, creator of self-denial, servant of harmony, torch of intelligence, source of ineffable felicities, it baptizes great actions, enlightens ignorance, polishes the manners, smoothes the inequalities of character, inspires the artist, civilizes the savage, disposes all nature to a holy embrace.

* * * * * *

Let us, then, bless the sentiment which attracts various beings towards a common pole, and while despising its vague caprices, inconstant as meteors, falsely decorated with the name of love, let us admire the great passions which have inflamed the hearts of geniuses of generations past and present. Yes, without love we could not have possessed those inimitable paintings of Raphael, those sublime poems of Tasso, those profound political dissertations of Machiaveli, and those sonnets of Petrarch, embroidered and pearled like the morning rose, and those thousands of other *chefs d'œuvre*, which are the glory and the happiness of us all. Yes, let us love well, and when we can love a being worthy of us by her qualities, when we are sure that we love her with all our power, with all our instincts, with all our will, uniting our destinies to hers, let us be attached to her as the stem is to the flower! But if she will not respond to our love without violating the divine laws——

Such were in substance the thoughts of Viscount de Ganay during the first days subsequent to his interview with Guyonne, the fisherwoman——

*   *   *   *   *   *

Guyonne loved the equerry, and knew that her love was returned. She was certain that there was a veil over her origin; and her uneasiness was all the more painful from the inflictions she had previously endured.

However, she did not dare to speak; she feared, as much as she desired, the presence of her lover. It was not, therefore, without inexpressible emotion that she heard herself addressed:

"Yvon, will you accompany me?"

Guyonne trembled from head to foot, and replied by following the viscount.

They followed a winding path, along the shores of the lake. John walked in front. Now, he strided on without raising his head, and anon turning himself suddenly to cast a long look at his companion. This strange conduct gave a faithful transcript of the uncertainties to which the equerry was a prey. Although the young woman kept her head down, constantly she imitated, as if by intuition, the movements of her guide. She hastened her step, when he hastened, and halted when he halted.

After a quarter of an hour spent in this way, the viscount spoke:

"Guyonne," said he, in a voice so timid, that the instinct of the young woman, rather than her ear, heard her name.

She approached him.

"I have," said the equerry, "important revelations to make to you."

He glanced at Guyonne, who bowed, without ceasing to walk.

"These revelations I ought perhaps to have made the day that good Philip brought you back to the camp; but it was of so much importance to initiate you into the secret which they embody, the certainty of being heard only by God and yourself, was necessary. I had to wait until time allowed me to conduct you to a discreet place. That place is some two leagues from here. Before introducing you there, permit me, mademoiselle, to ask pardon for the sad condition into which circumstances have forced me to keep you ever since I became aware——"

"Oh, monseigneur," exclaimed she, with emotion, "rather pardon me; let me bless the generous and noble master——"

"Stop!" interrupted he. "Between you and me, there is no other master than the Eternal."

Then, observing that the young woman regarded him as if interdicted, he added, rapidly;

"Come, Guyonne. Oh, come, quick."

They resumed their way without saying a word, and did not stop until they reached the sea-shore.

There, at the side of a cliff, nature had formed a grotto, which afforded an extensive view of the ocean, and of a part of the Isle of Sable. At the bottom of the grotto extended a bank, covered with moss.

"Come in," said the viscount, showing her the entrance.

She wished, from deference, to let him take the lead; but he said, in a solemn tone:

"Will Mademoiselle la Comtesse de Pentoëk do me the honor——"

His gesture concluded the invitation.

Guyonne entered the grotto, and at the request of the nobleman, sat on the grassy bank.

The Viscount de Ganay took off his hat, took from it a sealed paper, put his knee on the ground, and presented the paper with these words:

"Noble demoiselle, Maria Antonetti Guyonne, Comtesse of Pentoëk, suffer that the humblest of your servants offer you a copy of your baptismal certificate."

Still more astonished by the act of the viscount, than by the sight of the seals which adorned the paper, Guyonne did not move.

"Take it," said the equerry, in a gentle voice; this paper contains the proof of the illustrious origin from which you have descended."

* * * * * *

"Monseigneur," stammered Guyonne, "I don't understand——"

"Listen to me," said the viscount. "Hear me, noble girl; you no longer owe me the title of monseigneur. Before you, I am simply an equerry; and you, Demoiselle Guyonne, count among your ancestors, the most illustrious and the most valiant lords of Normandy and Brittany.

Demoiselle Guyonne, her whom you have been in the habit of calling your mother, was not such at all; him whom you have been in the habit of calling your father, was not such either. Your mother's name was Elizabeth Guyonne de la Roche; she was the sister of the Marquis William de la Roche-Gommard, and of Adelaide de la Roche, mother of Laura de Kerskoën. You belong, then, Demoiselle Guyonne, to the De la Roche's, by the mother's side, and Monseigneur William de la Roche is your maternal uncle."

"Holy Virgin! Can it be possible? Is it not a dream?"

"Your father, Demoiselle Guyonne, was a valiant captain. George Maximus de Pentoëk, Count of St. Lo."

"But how? It is a mistake. You deceive yourself, monseigneur."

"Read this parchment, and you will recognize the truth."

"No, no, my sweet Saviour! I could never dare——"

"Well, if you will authorize me, noble demoiselle," said John de Ganay, taking back the parchment which she held in her half-opened hand.

"Ah, quit that posture, monseigneur," murmured she.

This request was made with charming amiability, but it was equivalent to an order.

The young woman had recovered her feminine tact, and with that promptitude with which women adapt themselves to circumstances, she knew already how to be gracious and imperative, both in her manners and words.

The equerry rose, and remained standing, with his head uncovered.

In this position his face was towards her, and his person being placed at, the entrance of the grotto, prevented her from looking out.

"Deign to sit down," said she, inviting him with her hand to sit beside her.

John joyously proceeded to obey her, when an explosion was heard, only a few paces distant.

The viscount uttered a cry, and fell, bathed in blood.

CHAPTER XXIII.

LOVE.

To the cry of the young man two other cries responded, like a lugubrious echo. One heart-rending, full of anguish; the other terrible and menacing. Guyonne had uttered the first, Philip Francœur the second. Debouching from a clump of fir-trees, the latter precipitated himself towards a sand-hill, behind which a man was sitting. Malificieux was purple with rage; he brandished a long cutlas. He leaped at the man, and attacked him with fury. A struggle commenced; it was short and fatal. The sailor soon disarmed his adversary, who defended himself with the stock of a musket; then he threw him down, and plunged his knife into his heart.

This combat was as rapid as lightning. After having assured himself that his enemy was no more, Philip advanced towards tho grotto. He found Guyonne kneeling beside the viscount, who was wounded in the shoulder by a ball. The young woman had torn De Ganay's clothes, in her anxious efforts to stop the blood which flowed from the open wound.

During this operation he smiled on her kindly; he seemed pleased with an accident, which, more convincingly than an avowal, proved that Guyonne loved him.

"Oh, Philip," said she, on perceiving the sailor, "it is the Almighty that has sent you at this time. Come, come quick, monseigneur is dying. Aid me in assisting him."

"Monseigneur!" repeated Philip, in a mournful tone.

"Be not uneasy, my dear friends," said the viscount; "it is nothing; no vital part has been touched. Merely try to stop the flow of blood; for I am getting very weak."

"My God! my God! save his life and take mine!" sobbed poor Guyonne.

"Let me see," said Philip, stooping down. I know something of surgery myself. Yes, indeed——"

And turning towards Guyonne:

"Will you, my child, go to the nearest spring and fetch some water; in the mean time, I will examine the wound."

It was not necessary to repeat the suggestion to the young girl; and while Philip proceeded to examine the wound with all the skill of an accomplished practitioner, John de Ganay said:

"But how——"

"It was that miserable——"

"He has received his punishment, monseigneur; I have settled with him. Come, all's well; this wound is but a scratch. Eight days of rest will be sufficient to heal it. The shoulder-blade is bruised; but nothing has been broken.—Yes, indeed, I have done him the service of ridding the colony of him. I knew he was prowling about here; one of our people had seen him; so this morning, when I saw you going out, I took the liberty of following you at a distance. This was not exactly right, I know; I was prying after you. Punish me, monseigneur; I deserve it."

"Good Philip!" murmured the viscount, extending to him his hand.

"Then," resumed the pilot, "I arrived at the corner of a little grove, a few perches from this, and like a novice, instead of mounting guard, I amused myself by pulling grass."

"Here is some water," interrupted Guyonne, bringing a skin pitcher filled with cold water. "But how is monseigneur, tell me, Philip? It is not serious, is it? Oh, holy Virgin! how the blood flows."

"Fear nothing, my daughter," replied Malificieux. "Fortunately, the awkward fellow has missed his aim."

Assisted by the young girl, he washed the wound, applying cold water to it, in order to stop the blood, bandaged all tolerably well, while he continued his history; and when he had finished it, he presented a bottle to the viscount.

"Take a small drop, monseigneur; nothing is better to restore one's strength. This has been my *vade mecum*, as our late friend, Grosbec, used to say. Happily I have found it, for I had lost it in the snow. A famous gourd—Yes, indeed, by the trident of Neptune! I would not give it for ten ingots of gold. Good, my tonic has produced its effect. What did I tell you? Does not his color return, my child?"

Guyonne's only response was to put her arm about his neck and embrace him.

"A kiss like that always does good, although fifty winters may press on one's shoulders," said he, gayly.

Then he took the viscount in his arms, laid him on the mossy seat, and seemed to question himself. From time to time he looked up at the sky, and murmured incoherent words. One, enfeebled by the loss of much blood, remained in a sort of voluptuous torpor, the ordinary result of an hemorrhage; the other kneeled at his side, made a pillow for him of her arms, and contemplated him with that expression of divine love, which Raphael has imparted to the face of his Mary.

"A thousand hatches!" suddenly exclaimed the sailor, stamping with his foot; "nothing more was needed! Rain!"

This exclamation awoke Guyonne.

"It rains," she repeated.

"Yes, indeed, it rains. By the trident——But no matter. You, my child, will stay here, with the viscount; and I will go for some of our men to remove him to the camp."

"Oh no! not you, Philip, but I; it is preferable that you remain with monseigneur. If another attempt were made on his life, then remember I could not defend him as well as you."

"As to another attack, it is not to be feared. However, as you have a lighter foot than I——"

"Very well. Come and keep up the head of monseigneur, and before two hours I shall be back."

She stooped to withdraw her arms, and the viscount, profiting by the opportunity, put his left arm about her neck, gently pressed down her head, and kissed her forehead.

A burning blush protested for the modesty of the young girl; but a sensation of indefinable pleasure had gained the cause of the lover.

"All right, start!" said Philip, pretending not to have noticed this interesting little scene.

Guyonne started, but not without having multiplied her recommendations to the sailor, and left as an adieu to the idol of her heart a long look. Her absence was as brief as possible. She returned, followed by four colonists, who carried a litter covered with skins, for it rained in torrents. Towards evening, John de Ganay found himself reposing in his bed, at the castle of the camp; and Guyonne watching at his side. From this date, the relations between the two young persons changed completely. The illness of John de Ganay was the bond of union which wedded their noble souls. They mutually understood that they were kind, virtuous, and noble. Had not this accident happened to the viscount, many months, perhaps, would have passed before Guyonne would dare to familiarize herself with the idea of being loved by John de Ganay, and before the latter was aware of the suavity of sentiment which animated the young girl. But the hours which they passed *tete-a-tete*, without being disturbed by external influences, the little cares which the condition of the patient required, and the mutual effusions of mind, succeeded in uniting together two beings so well calculated for each other.

The young woman was so weary of her assumed character, that she invited a thousand little frivolities to recall her sex. A boarding-school girl could not be more chaste, a lover more tender, or a mother more affectionate. It might well be said that the three best qualities of the woman were united in her modesty, love, devotion. To the viscount she appeared an angel descended from heaven, to guide him to happiness; and he was so happy, that he almost feared to see himself fully recovered. What was he to do when his health was re-established? Would he discover to his companions the sex of the false Yvon? Would he wed her before God? Or would he continue to comport himself as he did when ignorant of all? The dilemma was frightful. He could not decide in favor of one or the other. The only chance of safety was the arrival of a vessel, which would deliver all. But was he to wait for that illusion? For five years, during which he had clung to it, he had not learned to regard it in its true light. Poor John, these anxieties poisoned the source from which he derived so much pleasure. Often, in contemplating Guyonne, overcome by fatigue, and sleeping on a stool at his bed-side, the young man groaned, and tears filled his eyes. Often, in the midst of mute consultations, the language of which lovers understand so well, he sighed mournfully. But Guyonne immediately divined the cause of this sigh, and in order to dispel painful reflections from the breast of her well-beloved, she smiled. As the sun dissipates the clouds, so did her smile dissipate the grief of the viscount. Their tenderness was as profound as the cause which had engendered it, pure as the dove's wing.

They loved each other like children, sipping the honey of that first love with ardor, and struggling to conceal their torments; for Guyonne did not feel less than John their equivocal position; and the future alarmed her. But it was at the hours of this doubt and bitterness, that she collected the treasures of her affection, to bestow them on the viscount; it was at these hours, especially, that she fondled him with chaste caresses, that she sang to him the divine melodies of love; and soothed his agitated spirit in the rosy arms of Hope.

It was on a fine day that John de Ganay left his bed. The eight colonists, who still remained, came to congratulate him, and bring him the best fruits of their hunting and fishing.

Disease, privations, and revolt, had reduced to four the number of the soldiers. However, they would not rejoin the colonists, but lived miserably in a corner of the island.

The viscount having gone into his chamber one evening, after having partaken of a repast, said to Guyonne, in a touching and sympathetic tone:

"Now, my friend, I am going to give you the heritage of your parents. Here," added he, opening the coffer, "is the portrait of your mother, the noble Elizabeth Guyonne de la Roche; and here is the correspondence of your unfortunate parents."

Guyonne kissed tenderly the *souvenir* which the viscount presented her, and the latter continued:

"You will pardon me, I hope, for having violated the secret of these letters, when you learn how they have fallen into my hands."

Having stated to her what had taken place on the wreck of the Erable, John continued:

"When I forced the casket, the portrait which it contained impressed me very deeply. I knew well I had its resemblance somewhere. But had it not been for Philip, who enlightened me, I should not have thought of my well-beloved as soon as I did."

Guyonne pressed his hand by way of thanking him.

"Then I had the indiscretion to read that correspondence of two unfortunate lovers here below who, without doubt, enjoy in another world that happiness which they never obtained in this. * * Oh, I weep while reading these eloquent papers, written with the tears of grief.—Your father had devoted himself to a military life at an early age. At the age of twenty he was considered one of the most distinguished officers in his profession. Coming on furlough to Nantes towards 1571, he there formed the acquaintance of your mother, Guyonne de la Roche; but an old feud separated the families of De la Roche and that of De Pentoëk. At the thought of a marriage with a Pentoëk, the old Marquis de la Roche knitted his brows, and your mother was convinced that she could never obtain the consent of her father. Obstacles only served to inflame the passions of the young people. They swore to each other eternal fidelity. A compassionate priest consented to unite them in secret. The marriage took place in the cabin of a peasant. Only one person was intrusted with the secret. This person, my Guyonne, was Margaret, your foster-mother. She aided his mistress in concealing her being in the family-way, which, however, soon became known. Then, at your birth, she nursed and reared you like her own child. During this time your father was absent at Brest. It was there he learned that his adored wife had given him a daughter. Oh, if you will only read the letter he sent your mother then, Guyonne! How he loved her—how he knew how to alleviate her sorrows. *Mon Dieu!* I wish I could love you in that way—."

"Good friend, proceed, I beg of you," said the young girl with the tear in her eye.

"Alas! what I have to relate you now, is very painful. The *Navarre*, in which Maximus de Pentoëk served, received orders to go to the Indies. Four years had passed before anything was heard of her. Then the news came that she had been wrecked; this was the death-blow to your mother—."

John de Ganay made a pause, in order to avoid disturbing the grief of the young woman who sobbed aloud; and when she had somewhat calmed, he terminated as follows that melancholy history:

"Your father had not perished, however. The vessel which bore him, having been cast on the shores of the East Indias, he remained there until he could return to France, where he hoped to find his cherished wife, and a little angel to console him for his past misfortunes. Judge of his despair when he arrived at Nantes!—He inquired for Catharine; no one knew what had become of her—."

"My friend," murmured Guyonne in broken accents, falling on her knees, "let us pray to God for those who are no more."

CHAPTER XXIV.

RETURN OF THE CASTOR.

In a week after, Viscount de Ganay was completely re-established. On a beautiful afternoon he proposed to go fishing. The young woman eagerly accepted. Being duly provided with lines, they embarked in a large skiff which had been constructed from the *debris* of the Erable, they started, accompanied by Malificieux, who was to perform the duty of rowing. The young couple sat at the poop of the vessel, and Philip, not doubting that they would occupy themselves more in speaking of love affairs than in making war on the inhabitants of the water, so placed himself that his back was towards them. In order to inconvenience them as little as possible by his presence, the brave sailor began to hum an old war song.

Thus pre-occupied with their future as they were themselves by their mutual tenderness, Francœur took no notice either of time which flew with the rapidity of an eagle, nor of the circle of small clouds which surrounded the setting sun.

Overcome by the effluvia of that magnetic fluid which love communicates and receives at the same time by the presence of lovers, Guyonne and John reflected much more than they conversed. But this reverie was the harmonious language of their hearts. They read each other's thoughts much more easily than if they had been written; they understood better than they could have spoken.

True love is so immaterial that every effort, every physical movement it makes to express itself, is repugnant. It is a delicate flower which can be known only by its perfume and natural colors; an evening melody which one enjoys silently, but of which the charm is destroyed by any effort to annalize it. One may also compare that exquisite sensibility of our whole being, when loving sincerely, we are beside the object we love, to the disposition, in which we find ourselves, when on an evening in autumn at the commencement of twilight, plunged in an arm-chair, before a good fire, we evoke the gracious images of the imagination. They run; we see them; we feel them; we respire their breath; we devise with them, and we no longer belong to this world. Bathed in a flood of delight, we desire to swim there, and we are afraid to stir our head, afraid to move, so much do we dread to dispel the phantoms of our reverie.

*　　*　　*　　*　　*　　*

Suddenly Philip Francœur suspended his song, and stood up in his skiff.

Guyonne and John started.

"What is the matter?" asked the latter.

The sailor, having his eyes fixed on the Atlantic, made no reply.

At this moment a black cloud, fringed with red, concealed the sun.

"The cape at the north-east, monseigneur, the cape at the north-east!" exclaimed Philip, without attempting to disguise his emotion.

John de Ganay gave such a push to the rudder fixed behind him, that he broke the plank which held it. At the same instant a dull roaring noise was heard in the distance.

The sailor betook himself to his oars.

Two successive squalls whistled in the air.

"My God," said Guyonne, supporting herself against the viscount who put his arms about her by that instinct with which we all struggle against danger, even when the struggle is fruitless.

"Is it necessary to assist you, Philip?" said the equerry.

Malificieux did not hear him, a new squall having precipitated against the skiff mountains of water.

"Cling fast to the seat!" exclaimed Francœur.

Fortunately the waves passed by their side.

Disengaged from its veil, the sun cast a parting glance at the angry sea.

"A ship! I see a ship!" exclaimed Guyonne.

In point of fact, a vessel was in sight.

"Ah, we are saved! she is steering towards the Isle of Sable," said the viscount, who had already forgotten the danger to which he was exposed.

Philip remained silent; all his efforts were necessary to maintain the equilibrium of the skiff.

The night fell rapidly. The Atlantic howled like a wild beast, and mingled its formidable voice with the whistling of the wind.

One dared not open his mouth, or move a limb in the boat.

Suddenly as the skiff mounted on the top of a wave, a dark mass appeared before it.

"Help, help!" cried John de Ganay, recognizing the ship which he had distinguished two hours previously.

Guyonne rose her head, and uttered a cry of horror.

A ray of the moon had shown her the sardonic face of the pilot Alexis Chedotel, standing at the wing-transoms on the starboard side of the ship.

* * * * *

Next morning there was great joy at the Isle of Sable. A bark of a hundred tons balanced herself coquettishly half a mile from the shore.

Chedotel commanded her.

Five years previously after he had disposed forty individuals on the Isle of Sable, pretending that storms drove him to the coast of Europe, the pilot had brought back William de la Roche to France. The latter had hardly set his foot on shore, than he found himself enveloped in a multitude of difficulties, in the midst of which the Duke de Mercœur, who commanded in Brittany, retained him a prisoner for some time. It was not until the end of five years that he was able to relate to the king what had happened to him during his voyage. The monarch, touched with the fate of the unfortunates, abandoned on the Isle of

Sable, ordered the pilot who had taken them there, to go for them. The latter found no more than twelve.—

On their return Henry IV. wished to see them dressed as they had been found. Their hair and beard, which they had allowed to grow, hung in disorder on their breast, and on their shoulders. Their features had already assumed a savage appearance, which made them resemble Indians rather then civilized men. The king caused fifty crowns to be distributed to each, and permitted them to return to their families, without being liable to be brought to justice for their old offenses."

Thus finished the drama of the Isle of Sable.

CHAPTER XXV.

CONCLUSION.

"And John de Ganay! John de Ganay! the brave John de Ganay!" exclaims my fair reader, shaking this book with disappointment.

"And Guyonne, the divine, the incomparable Guyonne?" asks the masculine reader, with indignant impatience.

"What has become of the good Malificieux? my God, I would like to know!" demands an infantine voice.

Not being able to resist this charming trinity, which presses him, ought the narrator to commit an indiscretion to satisfy his auditory? Let us respond.

Philip Francœur, Guyonne de Kerskoën, and John de Ganay, after having confronted a thousand deaths, landed on the shores of Acadia. They were received by some families who had settled there. The two lovers married each other. For a year they enjoyed unalloyed happiness, but at the end of this time, Guyonne died in giving birth to a male child.

"Pardon me, my friend," said she to her husband before expiring, "I had concealed from you the vow I had made the day I was going to die with cold on the ice, to consecrate to the worship of Jesus the remainder of my days, if he spared them. You know that I have failed in this vow; the Lord has not blessed our union; but let his holy will be done! Could the example of its mother recall unceasingly to the poor infant who has just been born, that she should religiously observe her vows, if she wishes to be happy in this world, and in the next!"

Overwhelmed with grief, John de Ganay responded only with an explosion of sobs.

"P.S. But Laura de Kerskoën?"

The chronicle reports that she was abducted, and married by Bertrand de Mercœur.

Were they happy?

—?

FINIS.

CPSIA information can be obtained
at www.ICGtesting.com
Printed in the USA
LVHW040338110522
718423LV00001B/306

9 783375 007782